Wind in the Web

A Cherokee warrior's epic journey of rebirth

A novel
Frederick E. Bryson

Order this book online at www.trafford.com/08-0512
or email orders@trafford.com

Most Trafford titles are also available at major online book retailers.

Note for Librarians: A cataloguing record for this book is available from Library
and Archives Canada at www.collectionscanada.ca/amicus/index-e.html

Printed in Victoria, BC, Canada.

ISBN: 978-1-4251-7655-6

*We at Trafford believe that it is the responsibility of us all, as both individuals
and corporations, to make choices that are environmentally and socially sound.
You, in turn, are supporting this responsible conduct each time you purchase a
Trafford book, or make use of our publishing services. To find out how you are
helping, please visit www.trafford.com/responsiblepublishing.html*

*Our mission is to efficiently provide the world's finest, most comprehensive
book publishing service, enabling every author to experience success.
To find out how to publish your book, your way, and have it available
worldwide, visit us online at www.trafford.com/10510*

www.trafford.com

North America & international
toll-free: 1 888 232 4444 (USA & Canada)
phone: 250 383 6864 ♦ fax: 250 383 6804
email: info@trafford.com

The United Kingdom & Europe
phone: +44 (0)1865 722 113 ♦ local rate: 0845 230 9601
facsimile: +44 (0)1865 722 868 ♦ email: info.uk@trafford.com

10 9 8 7 6 5 4 3 2

Dedication
This work is dedicated to Ann Bryson Martin who lived to challenge her own boundaries and, by example, demonstrated how to do so with grace and passion. It was good when she agreed with you . . . even better when she disagreed.

Ann provided the cover art for this book as well as that for the preceding book, *Scent of the River*.

Acknowledgments
Wind in the Web is the second book in a planned trilogy about the removal of the Cherokee Indians from Southern Appalachia, and the aftermath of their removal. Those who read the first book, *Scent of the River*, may be surprised to find that this sequel differs in both structure and purpose from the first. *Scent of the River* began as a timeline of the execution of the legendary Cherokee, Tsali, and as such is steeped in historical details of the era.

Wind in the Web examines the inevitable destruction of the Cherokee culture caused by uprooting the tribe from where they had lived for 10,000 years, then traces a path of identity recovery for them. My thanks to those who read the manuscript and encouraged this approach, one that is more intuitive than historical. Special thanks to David and Anita Smith for showing me where the principal character, Euchella, is buried, and sharing the spiritual experience of that place.

This book is fiction and the characters herein described are the products of the author's imagination.

Conventions
Cherokee words and names that are not in common usage today appear italicized.

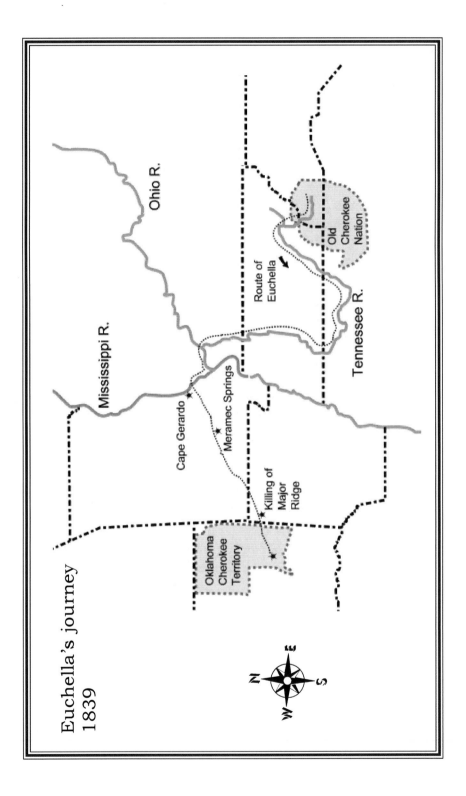

Euchella's journey
1839

Mississippi R.

Ohio R.

Cape Gerardo

Meramec Springs

Route of
Euchella

Tennessee R.

Old
Cherokee
Nation

Killing of
Major
Ridge

Oklahoma
Cherokee
Territory

Preface
1839

The history of the Cherokee Indians—or *Ani'-Yun'wiya'* (Principal People) as they called themselves—tends to be recorded from the time of first contact with Whites, assumed to be the Spanish explorer Hernando Desoto. Archaeological diggings in Southern Appalachia, however, reveal them to be much older. Whatever the age of their society, these facts would have had no relevance for the ancient Cherokees, themselves, because history as we perceive it had no meaning for them. For the Cherokee, writing their history would be as pointless as writing the history of a mountain range or river. They simply *were*, and theirs was a timeless life, the most important moments being the season at hand and the season to come, and remembering this endlessly repeated order. What passed for history were myths, legends, and parables to explain natural phenomena from a storyteller's point of view.

By the time of first contact, the Cherokees had occupied the Southern Highlands for at least 500 years and perhaps much longer than that, and had developed an elaborate system of laws, domestic customs, religion, agriculture, and medical practices that were founded on, and in harmony with, their surroundings. Their tribe was knit together from seven interdependent clans, each with its own lore, but bound by intermarriage, as marriage within a clan was so strictly forbidden as to be punishable by death. In this matrilineal society, a Cherokee husband would leave his own clan to join that of the wife to become part of her family. Rituals for marriage, naming children, games, funerals, and celebrating harvests were well established and purposeful. For instance, like the ancient Hebrew Day of Atonement, the

Cherokee celebrated an annual Green Corn Festival in which all transgressions from the year past, save murder, were forgiven. Even their superstitions were evolved and complex. They believed that they were shadowed by a race known as the Little People, described as an impish bunch that delighted in making mischief with their full-sized counterparts. And when a Cherokee died, the family burned fires to drive away witches that might steal the multiple souls of the deceased. As a people, they were loving, clever, indulgent of children, taciturn, mystical, protective of territory and villages, and somewhat arrogant toward neighboring tribes.

This complex social apparatus ended in May, 1838, when the U.S. Army came to Southern Appalachia and moved almost all of the Cherokees 1200 miles west to their Diaspora in the Oklahoma Territory. Into the geographic vacuum left behind rushed White settlers, eager for free land, to occupy vacant homesteads, fields, and villages.

What was left of the formidable nation, whose territory had once stretched from Ohio to Alabama, and its centuries of tradition? Protected by treaties with the State of North Carolina, a small fragment— probably less than 800 members of the original tribe— was spared removal. This small splinter group held fast to land around the village of Quallatown, at the confluence of Soco Creek and the Oconaluftee River, not far from a place called *Kituwah*, the Mother Town of the ancient Cherokees. This region is well suited to the hunter-gatherer culture of the Cherokees, with mountains reaching heights well above 5,000 feet, and to their advantage it is unsuited to agrarian or commercial development. Slopes are steep, often impassible for horses, difficult to plow, and the terrain resists modern incursions such as road building. Some peaks are covered near the top by thickets of laurel and rhododendron that, from a distance, resemble shrouds of dense, green fleece. Down in the valleys, narrow plots of corn, beans, and squash lay along rivers that tumble too fast for navigation.

In 1839, the status of this remnant of the Cherokees was uncertain. The prevailing question for them was: Were they, too, to be taken west or allowed to remain in their homeland?

On this question, things finally broke right for the Cherokees. There was no immediate threat of removal as the army had left the mountains by December of the previous year, and the White militia that assisted the army was disbanded. However, the opinion in much of the government, particularly the War Department and in the surrounding community of White settlers, was that this fragment of the tribe should go west as well.

That this never came about is the result of a string of unrelated circumstances. Foremost of these was the fact that the government had no stomach for spending more money to transport Indians west. Creeks, Choctaws, Chickasaws, and some Seminoles had already been removed. As the Panic of 1837 lingered with its negative effect on the national economy, the burden of the $5 million that the government already owed the Cherokees as part of the removal treaty loomed formidable. And then there was the lost political capital. The administration of Martin Van Buren was tarnished by the news of massive loss of life in the brutal manner by which the Cherokees were moved to Oklahoma. Finally, the army that had enforced the Removal Act was occupied far up north, protecting the border with Eastern Canada which was in a turmoil that threatened to spill over into the United States. To take the remaining Cherokees west, the War Department would have to order a portion of the army back south.

As the saga unfolded, resistance to further removal solidified, coalescing around one man, a White, whose name was William Holland Thomas. In Thomas, the Cherokees found both spine and voice to not only halt further removal, but to also recover a semblance of what they had lost.

Thomas was destined for the task. As an adult, he operated a string of five trading posts throughout Western North Carolina, gaining a measure of wealth in a region where most people of the time lived hand-to-mouth. But Thomas was an unusual man, the sort that comes along only once in a generation, bright, resourceful, creative, stubborn—and, later, mercurial. How he came to champion the cause of the Cherokees is, once again, part of the chain of circumstances.

Thomas was brought by his widowed mother to live near the Cherokees of Quallatown at the age of twelve, working there at a trading post that was owned by his uncle. Ironically, this was the same year when the first of two treaties between the State of North Carolina and the breakaway faction of Cherokees was signed, beginning an "experiment in citizenship" for those Indians in the Quallatown region. These treaties would become the cornerstone of his efforts to preserve the territory of the remaining Cherokees.

Thomas' attachment to the Cherokees took root early. As an adolescent, he was adopted by the presiding village chief, a man known as Yonaguska, or Drowning Bear. In time, he learned the native language, an Iroquois-based dialect that confounds most Whites even today. Thus began what modern pundits might call his enmeshment with the Cherokees that would prove to be emotional, political, and lifelong. As he grew to manhood, he formed a relationship with a young Cherokee woman who bore him at least one and possibly five children. Upon the death of Yonaguska, a year after removal, he would be named chief of the tribe, the only completely White man to do so.

Thomas cannot be described simply. That he contributed greatly to what came to be known as the Eastern Band of Cherokee Indians is indisputable. Yet even today when his name comes up, acknowledgement of his contribution is given grudgingly and without fanfare because, in the end, Thomas made a mess of what he tried to create and alienated most of those who benefited from his efforts.

How much his Cherokee/White duality aided or confused him is open to speculation. What is clear, however, is that throughout his life, Thomas pursued parallel paths, alternately living as an Indian and as a White. As a Cherokee, he protected the tribe and celebrated the ceremonies. As a White, he amassed wealth and became an imposing political force, traveling to Washington and Raleigh for tribal and commercial purposes. Sometimes, one side of his personality acted in a way that was inimical to the other, such as when he became instrumental in bringing in a rail line, opening the region to trade and travel. This two-path lifestyle affected his relationships, as well. The first child by his Cherokee mate was brought into the house that Thomas built for himself and his mother, to be raised as a White; however, the child's mother was not included.

The story of how Thomas came to the role he assumed began at the age of fourteen when his uncle's trading post failed. Ordinarily, this would seem a misfortune, but once again, circumstance interceded. Owing him back wages that he could not pay, the uncle gave Thomas a set of law books in lieu of wages. In those days, reading law was how most lawyers came to their profession, including the man who was to be Thomas' future nemesis, Andrew Jackson. But unlike Jackson, Will became so accomplished with it that he

9

understood both the letter and nuance of law. Some men see the practice of law as a way of life or as a business. To others it is a stepping stone into politics. To Thomas, law became a weapon that uniquely fit his mental gifts, the obsidian point on the arrow of his ambition. The tribe at Quallatown became one of his first clients, and in his struggle to keep them in North Carolina, he would use the law to obscure the obvious, confuse opponents, and make the outrageous seem reasonable. In other words, Thomas' genius lay in what is today known as *spin doctoring.*

The extent of his genius remains evident more than a century and a half later. Having only a homeland reservation of a tribe in Upstate New York as a model, he conceived the Qualla Reservation of the Eastern Band of Cherokee Indians.

Conceiving, however, is one thing; doing is another, and, in this case, the doing may have been Thomas' undoing. As both tribal Chief and the government's agent for the Cherokees, he found himself in the position of having almost total control over the future of the tribe. And here sprouted the seeds of his excess. In a process of financial chicanery that eventually bewildered even himself, Thomas acquired land in his own name, with his own funds, and some with funds paid later by the federal government as part of the treaty agreement. Altogether, well over 50,000 acres were accumulated for the reservation.

Unanimously, those Cherokees who were left behind wanted to remain in their eastern homeland. Word of massive death on the trail west and the strangeness of the countryside beyond the Mississippi filtered back to them. After all, their legends, spirituality, and very way of life were founded and matured in the mountains and valleys where they had always lived.

As benevolent as his intentions appear today, Thomas' methods to secure the right of the remaining Cherokees to stay in the East was resisted by a faction of the Cherokees themselves. Perhaps some mistrusted his verbal trickery. He was, after all, a White man, one who was no stranger to the process of say-one-thing-and-mean-another. One member particularly had first-hand experience with his manipulations. This man was named Euchella, and he was the leader of an independent group of about two-dozen Cherokees that occupied locations on or around the Oconaluftee and Nantahala Rivers. They were known simply as the Lufty Band. Euchella fell into one of Thomas' most complex machinations, and spent the remainder of his life living with the consequences. During the removal, after the revolt by the captive Cherokee Tsali who had been involved in the killing of two soldiers, Thomas convinced Euchella that it was in the best interest of the remaining Cherokees that Euchella and the Luftys recapture and execute Tsali. Thomas argued that doing so would make the Luftys, and hence the other remaining Cherokees, appear to be civilly responsive to the murders of the soldiers.

To this, Euchella agreed, and the execution was accomplished on November 25, 1838, at a place called Big Bear Springs, a marsh just off the north shore of the Tuckasegee River.

That this act served Thomas' purpose of advancing the image of the Quallatown Cherokees as responsible citizens proved to be true. However, if Euchella felt used by Thomas, this idea is nowhere recorded, but it was likely his conclusion. Already his mind was fertile ground for resentment of Whites. In the uncertain years leading up to removal, his wife and child starved during the winter of 1837-38 while Euchella conducted a one-man protest of the pending removal. And later, he and the Lufty Band were pursued by the army and militia during the active phase of the removal, but were never caught. So, even after the roundup ended, they had reason to be wary of what was being planned for them.

Another point of contention with Thomas' stewardship of the Eastern Band lay in its direction. Thomas' choice was to make the Cherokees less threatening to the surrounding settlers by making them less *different.* This meant taking the Cherokees farther from their aboriginal way of life. For the first time, Quallatown was touched with "progress." Progress was made in convincing authorities of the State of North Carolina of the civility of the Cherokees. Progress was made in reducing public drunkenness and the abuse of women that sometimes followed. Progress was made in converting the Indians into a patrilineal society. Progress was made in Christianizing the tribe.

This progress took the Cherokees in a direction that they had resisted since Whites were first encountered almost 300 years before. Perhaps things would have gone smoother had Thomas consulted members of the tribe about their preferences, but that was not his style. With the death of Yonaguska, he lost his emotional counterweight, and seemed gripped by his own messianic vision of their future, a future that he would make for them. He was autocratic and did not easily accommodate contrary opinions. There is little evidence that, in his zeal to ensure that these Cherokees remain in their homeland, he consulted any tribal members on his methods—or even asked what they wanted their future to be.

As Thomas led the Eastern Cherokees toward assimilation with the settlers, resentment of his stewardship stiffened among some members of the tribe, particularly the Lufty Band. Few that they were, these Cherokees viewed themselves as an ancient people with well-developed traditions, language, and spirituality—and as the seed for potential regeneration of the tribe. How was a man like Euchella and the other Luftys to accept assimilation? How could they give up their naturalistic religion and reverence for a way of life that had evolved for thousands of years to take on another that was punitive and patriarchal? Like learning a second language and discovering that the new words are not one-for-one substitutions for familiar ones, these Cherokees came to realize that the future laid out for them by Thomas required not only new words, but a new way of thinking as well, one that they neither understood nor relished.

As the years rolled on past removal, the struggle between two dissimilar cultures represented by Thomas and Euchella went on unceasing. That the dominant culture would remain dominant was not in doubt; Thomas would leave his mark and not be forgotten. What remained in doubt, however, was whether or not this splinter group of the Cherokee Nation could rekindle the sacred fire of their ancestors, or would it be extinguished?

For the Luftys and those who agreed with them, this was perhaps, the only option. The stamp that a region leaves on the culture of a tribal people is indelible, and this is as true for the Cherokees as it is the Berbers of the Sahara or the Celts of Ireland. In the ancient mountains and foothills where their culture matured to full flower, they lived in relative harmony with natural events. The hills were the anvil that shaped their lore and spirituality. The larger segment of the tribe that was moved west was able to hold onto its Appalachian-based roots, and spent considerable energy doing so. But Oklahoma not being Appalachia, the first generation born in Oklahoma grew up as Westerners. Thus, to Thomas' dissenters in the East fell the responsibility to recapture and continue their timeless Appalachian-based culture.

What irony that the resolution of this lay in the hands of the one who had shot the old warrior Tsali, the man who might rightfully have thought of himself as the last of the *Ani'-Yun'wiya'*.

Chapter 1
Balsam Gap
Late April, 1839

eyond the glow of the fire, a cricket chirped its mating call from the broom sage in a clearing that lay below a stand of trees where Euchella and the others of the Lufty Band hid out. The chirp reminded him that it was spring. Far down the mountain, where trees already sprouted leaves and grass was standing high, it was nearing time to plant. Morning frosts still brushed the high ridges of the Smoky Mountains with white crystals, but were long gone down there. In the valleys, the little *du'stu'* frogs were bearing clusters of eggs in puddles and the eddy currents of rivers, under the watchful eyes of curious damselflies. It was the wet season there, when the earth brings forth things that sprout from its digestive brew of soil and water.

Euchella had forgotten spring. His instinct for the seasons, developed in childhood, had long gone quiet. So much had happened to make him forget, and much had happened that he would like to forget, but could not, and these were such overpowering memories that they had blotted out the coming of spring. He had survived a disaster that had no equal in the legends of the *Ani'-Yun'wiya'*. The first of it was the worst, the death of his wife and child. Then afterward he failed to avenge them, leaving their spirits in a perpetual state of disquiet. But that, bad as it was, was only the beginning of a rip in the fabric of his Cherokee soul that could never be mended.

When he closed his eyes, it all came back to him, and the first thing that he could see was the face of Tsali. Was what Tsali had done so wrong that it deserved killing? Had he gone too far? Had he not done what any warrior should have done? But that was past. Tsali and his sons had been dead for six months. By the time of his execution, almost all the other Cherokees had been taken from the mountains and foothills of the Southeast to the place in the West, even the chief, John Ross, and Junaluska, too. But when they were gone, was the nightmare really over? Although the soldiers had ridden out of the mountains last November, the Luftys remained uneasy, fearful of returning to the villages in the valleys below. They did not trust that they would not somehow be taken west too, or robbed by the Whites who now mingled and settled freely on land that had once been the land of the Principal People.

Almost a year ago the roundup had begun. Hundreds of men in dark blue uniforms rode in long lines along the rivers. Euchella and his brother, Wachacha, and the others had escaped to high passes, knowing that the soldiers would not follow them here. It was too much trouble. Soldiers liked to stay on their horses or else walk where horses could walk, and the high ridges were not horse country. But if they had chosen to come up to the high passes out of whatever stubbornness drove White men, then the Luftys would simply have vanished and reformed elsewhere, perhaps in the Snowbirds that Euchella knew so well . . . or perhaps in the dense tangle above Deep Creek where they finally caught Tsali.

Euchella was tired and the war that raged within him showed on his face. He and his men had been eating rabbits and squirrels for a year because, moving frequently as they did, there had been no time and no place to grow corn or beans or squash. They ate rabbits still; three were cooking over the fire now and that was all they had to share. Perhaps soon it would be safe to go back down. As the days grew warmer, people down below would turn their attention to pulling wild morning glories and ragweed from their gardens and feeding their animals. Then, surely, the Luftys could find better food there. What he would give now for a mouthful of watercress that would be sprouting in tight clumps in the small streams below.

Euchella wondered if their apprehension was a waste of time. The army colonel with the fine uniform and weary expression had said that the Luftys did not have to go west, that he would write a paper allowing them to stay, that they did not have to hide. There was much talk of this paper. Even Will Thomas told them that it meant that they could stay. It was what he called their "deal" for shooting Tsali. Thomas had said that if they shot Tsali then they could stay. So they shot him, along with his sons and son-in-law. Only the women and his grandson were spared. But how could they trust what they were told? Thomas was, after all, a White man, in spite of the fact that Drowning Bear had made him his son. And since the colonel was gone, who would believe his paper? These people, whom Euchella believed to be true of heart, had a way of saying one thing then doing another, and in the end their words proved to be untrue. Many times he had seen this happen, as though they placed more importance on what they said than what they did. It was one of the things that made them different from the Cherokee; they talked all the time.

Wachacha nudged him from behind. "My brother, I can tell when you are thinking. You think too much."

Euchella stretched and sat up. In the year that they had wandered the high reaches of the mountains, the ground had grown no softer. Both he and his thirty men looked like they had been living outside for a long time. Their bodies were lean with skin stretched tightly across their faces so that cheekbones protruded, and they smelled of many fires and of wintering beneath shelters built quickly to protect

them from wind and snow and frost. They learned to
live like the rabbits that they ate, sleeping in nests of
sage and leaves and grass, and while they did not
freeze, they never were entirely warm. Euchella's
lanky body was even more angular, and his hands
ached now. He was too young to have the pain of old
men. It must be the cold, he supposed.

Wachacha was wrong about his mood, however.
Euchella was not thinking. He was trying to avoid
thinking and the effort made him restless. It was
Tsali's dream—the one with the weeping soldier—that
preoccupied him and dogged his sleep. Also, he could
not blot out the memory of Tsali as he lay dead on the
ground beside the trickle of water that seeped from the
place they called Big Bear Springs. It was a good place
to have one's soul slip from one's body, if it had to be
that way. It was springtime there all the time. Water
and soft ooze and the land all mixed in degrees of each
other, so that you could not be sure on which you
stood, wet or dry or something in between. Tsali's
blood would become part of the ooze; his body was
buried on the hill there to become part of the land,
then as it decayed, part of the water again. It was the
way that the Principal People would see it, Euchella
told himself. Life becomes the land, then land feeds
life, becoming life again.

So why could he not stop seeing Tsali's face?
And why did this soldier trouble his sleep? The men
gathered around him needed meat more than rabbit,
cabins in which to sleep without being robbed, farms
to raise the three sisters—corn, beans, and squash.
They did not have time for dreams. The hundreds of
the Principal People who evaded the soldiers' roundup
and were scattered throughout the mountains were
like bees returning to their hive, only to find the bee
tree cut down and burned. If spring were the season
of rebirth, then this year could be a stillbirth as it had

18

been the year before. The tribe and all that goes with it were snatched from them. The stories, the celebrations, the births, the meals, the farming, the singing, the gossip—but mostly the dreams—were gone. Only Tsali's sad dream was left behind.

Euchella tried to make a picture in his mind of the place where the rest of the people were taken last year, but he could not. Will Thomas had described it as a place where the mountains were only small hills. Euchella could not imagine a place where there were no towering mountains, nowhere to climb and to see and to hunt. Will also said that much of the land was covered in deep grass, something like the broom sage in which they now lay. Grass, not trees. Where would squirrels and owls and hawks and crows live? He had explained that perhaps there were not squirrels, but an animal like them that lived in the ground. Squirrels that lived in the ground—what a strange place. For the first time, Euchella was glad that his wife and daughter were dead. A place such as Thomas described was no place for children.

The cricket chirped in the deepening night. Across the campfire, someone chucked a stone in the direction of the sound and it ceased for a moment, then began chirping again. Euchella put his head back and listened to the rhythmic call. In the long walk down the valley of Deep Creek before they shot him last November, Tsali told Euchella that he had sought the truth of what he should do—to fight those that hunted him or not to fight them. Tsali said that he had asked this question of the spirits of the mountain, of the mist that blew in from the west, of the creatures that lived on the mountain itself. He said that he had waited patiently for a reply, but never received one. In the end, he was left alone to decide what to do, but this was less certain than being given a sign.

Euchella remembered something else about Tsali. Tsali had approached his death the same methodical way he took fish from the basket in his trap in the water of the Nantahala River, simply, as though it was just the beginning of some task of no great consequence. For Tsali, death became a conclusion to which he had arrived after much contemplation. It neither frightened him nor lured him, but was just an instant of passage for which its time had come.

Euchella felt less than a man to remember how he, himself, had approached death. There was the moment of his own last year when Euchella had stared at it. Tsali was still alive then and had come to him when he was hiding in the Snowbirds, bringing news of the deaths of his wife and child. The loss was beyond imagining. No one could understand what it was like to lose someone who had the power to make you see things in a different way. His wife had given order to his life; when he was hunting with the other men, he did not regret the end of the hunt because it brought him back to her. Later, after she had died and he returned to their cabin in Soco Valley, he felt ashamed for continuing to live and eat and feel the warmth of a fire and know the coming of dawn. Then there was the pivotal moment when he meant to avenge their deaths, by killing his White friend Jonas Jenkins, but he could not let the arrow go. Weakness was in him. But Tsali had showed no weakness. How had he avoided that weakness so that he could go to death without the clinching that Euchella felt in his belly?

Was there some message in the cricket's persistent chirping that would direct him to what he should do next? He waited, as he had been taught, as they all had been taught in the old traditions, to sense a sign that would direct him. But sleep overtook him before he could find a sign in the rhythm. The only thing that was different was the certainty that tomorrow he would have to go down the mountain to find out what was left for him and the other Cherokees.

Tsali had been right. It was harder to decide for one's self what to do than to receive a sign that would point the way. Perhaps, the soldiers had taken the sacred spirits of the Cherokees west, too.

Chapter 2
Soco Creek
Late April, 1839

illiam Holland Thomas should have anticipated tough times. In the coldest mercantile terms, the loss of nearly 17,000 customers could not be replaced overnight, and the removal of almost all of the Cherokees last year was devastating to his business. By the time of the first roundup in last spring, he had built a string of five trading posts throughout the high country of the Cherokees, selling flour, traps, nails, cloth—whatever people needed to stay alive here. Within the bounds of this hardscrabble place, he was prosperous. This was, in part, due to the fact that he was resourceful and could do many things. New business would come with the influx of new, White settlers. They would need a broker for what they grew or made . . . burley tobacco for the markets in Maryland or whiskey made from the corn that they grew. And, if a settler needed legal advice or a deed drawn up, he could provide that, too. As a boy, he had read the law, and people looked to him for advice. He did not charge for advice—unless a paper was written. How could one charge for words unless they were written down?

Perhaps Andrew Jackson could. Jackson had a better way of making money than he, Will Thomas, did. Jackson could do anything it seemed—even make money by talking—and that was not necessarily a good thing. God, how he hated Jackson. The ex-president had been back in his Tennessee home now for two years, and even though Martin Van Buren sat in the White House during removal, it was Jackson who was responsible for the disaster to the Cherokees.

And to Thomas. It was a personal thing to him,

as though Jackson had intended to strip him of a people whom he admired and who accepted him, a White man, far more than he ever imagined that they could. Particularly Drowning Bear. The old man had made him his son and had given him a Cherokee name, *Wil-Usdi*. Now, all that remained of the tribe was the knot of people huddled nearby at Quallatown, plus a few others scattered, some in hiding like Euchella and the other Luftys, not knowing what to do, where to live, or what—if anything—of their former life still belonged to them. How long would these continue to hide, he wondered?

Will was responsible for the Quallatown Cherokees being here at all. Since the Removal Act passed Congress in 1830, the Cherokees faced a disaster that was beyond comprehension. To counteract this, Will had pressed the cause of "citizen Cherokees" with the State of North Carolina and the federal government, quietly blurring realities and smudging lines of authority where he could. That the Quallatown Cherokees were considered to be citizens of the state was partly true and partly fiction, depending on whose argument one believed. Well over half of the thousand or so Indians that remained in North Carolina qualified for this status under the provisions of the treaties made in 1817 and 1819. These agreements ceded a large chunk of land on the eastern boundary of the Cherokee Nation to the state. By renouncing their membership in the overall nation, each of this remnant of the tribe was given a 640-acre tract of land within the ceded tract in North Carolina.

In treaty terms, this was described as an *experiment in citizenship*. Lawyer that he was, Thomas pounced on the inexactness of this expression, giving substance to the *citizenship* fraction in Raleigh and Washington. As an additional protection, there was a technicality in the hated Treaty of New Euchota—the document that finally sent the others west—that abetted his fight for the remaining Cherokees. For the life of him, Thomas could not understand why John Ross and the others who had gone west had overlooked this. It was Article 12, and it stated, *"Those individuals and families of the Cherokee Nation that are averse to removal to the Cherokee country west of the Mississippi and are desirous to become citizens of the States where they reside and such as are qualified to take care of themselves and their property shall be entitled to receive their due portion of all the personal benefits accruing under this treaty . . . "* Could this have been the legal justification for staying? Had they simply failed to comprehend the possibilities of it? Following this line, as Thomas chose to interpret the words, the Cherokees were entitled to stay on their land—and still receive the compensation that was due them if they had moved. In any case, that was the argument that he advanced on numerous trips to the federal capital.

Thomas adjusted his chair and leaned it back against a nail keg that sat behind him on the porch of the trading post. The overhanging roof protected him from a brief rain. He was tired and his ankle still throbbed from that fateful day last fall when his horse slipped and rolled on him. It had been the luckiest accident that he ever had, and it probably saved his life. The accident happened shortly before the old Indian, Tsali, and his family revolted during the last days of the roundup, killing two of the soldiers who guarded them. What a stink that caused! Like sheep turning to bite herd dogs, it was not supposed to happen. The army's idea was that these people were too dispirited to resist eviction, no matter how crude the means. It made sense. The bulk of the tribe— about 16,000—had already been removed and not one of them had resisted. Only Tsali and his sons and son-in-law. So, in the late afternoon of November 1, on the banks of the Tuckasegee, two soldiers lay dead and a third mutilated. Their officer—a Lieutenant Smith—had run like a rabbit from the fight, then later did all he could to cover up his inept leadership. Shortly before this took place, Thomas had been riding with them; had he not been put back on his horse after the mishap and sent upriver, he, too, probably would have been killed. Any White man would have been killed at that moment, even one adopted by the tribe.

Now, almost a year after removal, confusion hung in the air over the mountains. There was a stunned reaction that the Cherokees were actually gone. Although it was a thing for which the expanding White nation had campaigned for two generations, they seemed not to know what to do with their gains. Tsali's revolt had helped by giving some momentary justification to mask the greed of the wholesale eviction. But as the horror stories about the trek west made their way back to the mountains—almost 4,000 of those who were marched away, including Quatie, the wife of Principal Chief John Ross, died—the feeling of guilt returned. Those Whites who did not want the Indians to leave in the first place, such as Thomas and some of the local farmers who had long dealings with Cherokees, felt as though they had not done enough to prevent removal. Those who advocated eviction were uncomfortable in their victory. Will needed to grasp this ambiguity. There was something here to exploit if he could figure out how to do it.

Staring vacantly at the splashing water of Soco Creek, his thoughts drifted back to Andrew Jackson. There was a measure of satisfaction in what Will was planning now. If Jackson knew of it, he would probably have one of his famous fits of apoplexy and call Thomas a scoundrel, maybe even challenge him to a duel. Jackson was known to favor the all-or-nothing passion of duels. Rumor had it that this uncompromising quality was the reason his only term in the senate had been cut short years ago. He had a way of allowing himself to be drawn too far into arguments, exposing his own weaknesses. A couple of sharp-tongued debaters had made him appear foolish, and rather than be a continuing embarrassment, he left the senate. It was probably this quality that was at the root of his hatred for the Cherokees. The land deal. John Ross and the other Cherokee leaders had outfoxed him on a land deal down in Alabama, and Jackson could never forgive them. Funny, Will mused, if Jackson had gotten the 1.9 million acres of Alabama land instead of the Cherokees, he might have been too busy to run for the presidency, and if he were not President, the Removal Act would never have been introduced in Congress. The Cherokees would still be here. And . . . Thomas would have no need of his plan.

The plan. No one must know about the plan yet—save the one person with whom Thomas could confide, Jonas Jenkins. Jonas was safe because no one else wanted to talk to him. People said that he was "touched." He had a way of starting a sentence in the middle of a thought, with no preamble, as though he had lived too long in the woods by himself and had forgotten how to talk to people. That was not true, of course; the man was married and had children, but this did not change the fact that he came across as peculiar. Whenever he showed up at the trading post on Soco Creek, others who were there tended to drift away quietly as though they remembered some place where they needed to be. Thomas was about the only one who did not mind that Jonas was strange and readily accepted his company and conversation. It had been Drowning Bear who had taught Will to be patient with people like Jonas, to look beyond their peculiarities. It may have been the most useful thing that he had ever learned.

As close as they were, Thomas had not told Jonas everything about his plan. It was not because Jonas could not understand it or be trusted. He was a little slow and his thought patterns sometimes proceeded like a switchback road, but he was not stupid. Thomas did not tell him much about his plan because there was risk in knowing too much. Some people—like Jackson and those who were compelled now to defend their position on removal—were not going to like what Thomas was up to. And in the case of Jackson, he hoped the old president would die before he found out.

For now, most of his plan would stay safely in his head. Things had a way of working themselves out if one did that. (That was a lesson that he had taught himself.) In any undertaking, there were times to advance and times to be still. Thomas could afford to wait, but not forever. There was money to be collected and land to be bought—in his own name for the moment. Later . . . who knew about later? Somehow, it would be transferred to the Cherokees. But when and in what form? Even his lawyerly head could not see that far into the future. Perhaps, if he used some of Drowning Bear's patience, it would come to him.

In his weariness, Thomas drifted back to the week before when he was in Washington. The satisfaction of what he had learned there almost made up for the fatigue of the ride to and from the capital. No matter how much he rode—and he had been to Washington so often that he no longer had to ask for directions—his body was not suited to a saddle. Now, even his favorite chair, the one with the seat that was woven from straps of leather and had over the years become contoured to his round backside, hurt. He

27

had gone to the capital to present testimonials from local White farmers, supporting the citizenship contention of the Qualla Cherokees, to the Commissioner of Indian Affairs and to the War Department. But the commissioner had surprised him by going farther that he had hoped, suggesting an unofficial arrangement between Thomas and the agency. It was an arrangement that would have far-reaching consequences.

Now Thomas tried to get his mind around the events and emotions that swirled about him. Depending on his choice, he could be either euphoric and self congratulatory, or despondent.

The Commissioner of Indian Affairs suggested that he begin to position himself as the agent responsible for the management of the reparations due the Cherokees who remained in the eastern mountains. This made sense; the government would not trust an Indian to do it. This also meant that he could begin to buy more land for the tribe, using his own money, and be assured of reimbursement when the tap of reparations began to flow. No one specified what was to be done with the money. And now was the time to buy before the mountains were overrun with settlers who came and found a way to stay. Many recent squatters discovered that the land was not to their liking—it was too vertical or too hard to clear—and could be persuaded to sell their claims. A few even gave up because in the end they found it distasteful to farm land that clearly belonged to someone else—even if that person were an Indian. In the past six months, Thomas spent more time dickering over land transactions than he did running his business. But this was more important than making money. This was for his dream and for the old man.

And that brought him back, full circle, to the

sadness within him. Drowning Bear—Yonaguska—
was dying. He knew it for sure now. He had put off
admitting the truth for months. But the towering,
strong body that seemed to shrivel before his eyes told
a truth that could no longer be ignored. Permanence
was a thing that Will took for granted, like rocks and
rivers. Death never failed to surprise and disorient the
part of him that clung to what was familiar. It was
capricious and made no sense, arriving without
warning, making abrupt subtractions, then
disappearing until, at a moment of it own choosing, it
showed up again. What was left was like a spot in a
forest where a tree had been cut, leaving an unnatural
scar on the hillside.

Drowning Bear would be gone in a week, or a
month, or two months at the most. Subtle proof lay in
the fact that women of the Qualla village kept the fires
in his cabin burning to ward off spiritual witches so
that they could not make mischief with one of the old
man's four souls. Will could not imagine life without
Yonaguska. The only memories that he had without
the old man came from early childhood, before his
mother, Temperance, had moved them to his uncle's
trading post on the Tuckasegee. After that, the old
Indian had always been there, showing him how to set
a fish trap, where to find the wild garlic that grew in
the spring, how—in the absence of an arrowhead—to
harden the tip of a wooden arrow shaft in a fire, and
how the sounds of the Cherokee language were
formed. They stalked bear together, told of dreams,
sat in counsel of the Qualla Clan. Half of who he was
came from Drowning Bear.

Will closed his eyes and his breathing became
shallow as he fought to control his emotions. If there
were words for that sort of thing, he could describe
how the old man smelled and the calming touch of his
hand. Will passed in and out of Drowning Bear's door

as if it were his own. The permanent image in his mind was of the old man seated upright in a chair, beneath a large walnut tree that grew down the cove from his cabin. His skin had the look of worn leather, more so now that he was near death. Sometimes Will would walk to Drowning Bear's cabin and find a chore that needed doing and quietly go about doing it. As the old Cherokee grew older, these chores became more common. The garden needed hoeing, a plank on the porch needed a nail, water needed to be drawn for cooking. Nothing was ever asked of him, he just did these things as he saw the need of them. When he had done something, nothing was ever said of it in the house. To Will, this was not ingratitude, quite the opposite. Silence from Drowning Bear was the implied acceptance of him as a son because this was just what a good Cherokee son would do for his father.

No single thought gave him more pleasure than this, but it was a pleasure tainted with guilt. The guilt stemmed from Temperance, and it ran through his head, sometimes in rivulets and sometimes in torrents. Because Will had been born fatherless, he had always described himself as an orphan, even though his mother was very much alive. Perhaps for this reason, she viewed his adopted Cherokee life stiffly, as though the comfort that he took from these people stood in contrast to the comfort that he did not get from her. Temperance was born in England and came to America steeped in Calvinist tradition that, as far as children were concerned, preferred the discipline of a starched collar to the comfort of flannel. To Will, his introduction to the Oconaluftee Cherokees broke some floodgate of expression and understanding within him. When he could get away from the trading post where he was employed by his uncle, he spent all his time at or around Quallatown, with boys his age or, often as not, with Drowning Bear. It was Drowning

Bear who taught him how to twist and dry a bear gut for a bowstring, and then later to shoot an arrow from the bow. He taught him how to chip a spear point and to track a rabbit, and how to listen to what the small creatures in the woodland could tell him about predators that were passing by. How he came to know the Indian language he could not say exactly, except that he remembered asking Drowning Bear or his wives, *Gowhistiski* and *Leester*, to repeat words, which they did indulgently. By the time he was fifteen, Will's roots were nearly as much Cherokee as they were English.

Although this did not sit well with Temperance, she was wise enough to know that she could do little about it. It was Kanaka who was the hardest for her to accept, however. Kanaka was a girl from the village who was a few years younger than Will. By a traveling preacher, she had been given the Christian name of Catherine Hyde, but just the cloak of a Christian name was not enough to make her acceptable to Temperance. Nature proved stronger than her quiet reproach, however. By the time that Will was twenty, the village accepted Will and Kanaka as a couple, and Kanaka moved into her own cabin, not far from the river. Will was there as much as he was at the home of his mother. Temperance's method of dealing with the situation was to pretend that it simply did not exist. In this way, Will came to live two lives, one White, one Cherokee. The bridge between them lay with a child, and this was something that Temperance could not ignore. Her sole recognition of this union was to insist that the child—a daughter named Demarius Angeline—be brought to her house to be raised Christian.

What it was like to be Cherokee and White at the same time was typified by what happened to Demarius Angeline. In the Cherokee village, a child was a

31

community experience. Even with the changing of the old way from living in a communal lodge to individual cabins, the children of a village remained a shared joy. So, when Temperance insisted that Will's child be brought into her home to be raised in a Christian environment, the Cherokee mother, lacking the White sense of possession, gradually acquiesced. Around the time that the Qualla village named Will to be their spokesman and agent, Demarius Angeline was brought into the home of her grandmother to be raised as though she were White.

Will chose not to fight his mother on this. The English half of him thought it was the right thing to do; the Cherokee half could go along with it.

The time for the pleasure drawn from thinking about Drowning Bear was running out, however. Will looked up to see Kanaka approaching the trading post. Except for the second baby that she now carried, she was a slender woman, and he thought of her body as a strung bow, lean and taut. To complete the impression, she wore her black hair pulled back into a cascade that draped down between her shoulder blades. Her face had the high cheek bones that were common to the Cherokees. Below a nose that was soft and small was a mouth that protruded appealingly from the bottom. Most days she was expressionless. However, he could read her temper in her eyes which varied from tranquil to stormy. He had not seen her since he arrived from Washington the evening before, but it was a warm distraction to watch her walk toward him now.

Kanaka was steady and Will needed that from her. Perhaps, he was unsettled because his real father had died before he was born, and he grew to the age of twelve before the gentle hand of Drowning Bear provided masculine direction. But it had never been enough. Swings of emotion came suddenly and full of fright. There were days when he did not know how he would do what he needed to do, the dark paralysis gripped him so. The "black dog" as he called these moods had been more present than ever since it became certain that the Cherokees were going to be forced to leave the mountains. To hide these mood swings, Will became something of an actor. Nobody could know how much he doubted himself or his ability to do what he was trying to do with his plans for the reservation. He was, after all, just a boy impersonating a man who consorted with governors and generals and cabinet secretaries. If they knew who he really was inside, no one would take him seriously. So he played the part of the middle-aged merchant whose business had been good to him over the years—a merchant with familial ties to his aboriginal neighbors. The role had the advantage of being true, but Thomas knew that it left out a lot, a lot. Even Kanaka did not know how much. But she knew him well enough to know that at the moment he was musing about Drowning Bear. "Much has happened while you were away, *Wil Usdi*."

Will was instantly on alert. "What has happened?"

She touched her slender brown hand to his. "Drowning Bear has gone," she said in a whisper.

Never had he experienced such a violent wrench between his English self and his Cherokee self, but his English self won as he gasped and recoiled from her. For a time, they just stared at each other. Death had come while he was not here. The bare spot on the hillside would be large and barren. But it was not just the old man's absence that was wrong, it was a terrible time to die and miss all that was going on. The spring had come in an explosion of dogwood, redbud, and apple blooms. Buttercups erupted in great yellow clumps along the banks of the creek, and orange azaleas unfolded their blossoms in the coves of the hills. Over on the Nantahala, the trilliums were abundant along the shady slopes. The earth was restoring itself. Somehow, the Cherokees would, too. They were going to rise again, using their memories as seeds with which they would regenerate the Cherokee Nation. They would be Cherokee again. Will would see to it. He would lead them with everything that Drowning Bear had taught him. Only, Drowning Bear would miss it, and that made it awful.

From behind him, he could hear Kanaka take a deep breath. He knew her well, after twenty years. That was her signal that she was preparing herself for something else, something to come. Will had never pointed out this habit to her, and wondered if she were even aware of it. "While you were away, something else has been settled," she said in her voice that tried to be both kindly and controlled.

The actor in him took over and he became hard again. He turned and eyed her. "What?"

Chapter 3
Quallatown
Late April, 1839

uchella squatted on his haunches and watched the early morning stirrings across the river in the village of Quallatown. Although the sun was not yet up, there was light enough to see everything that moved there. From the deep pine thicket, he could see out, but could not be seen. For the moment, that was how he wanted it. Women emerged from their cabins to dip a bucket of water from the fast running Oconaluftee, then returned inside again. Dogs stood and walked stiffly, and smoke from morning fires rose and mixed with the light rain that fell, stretching in a blue trail down the valley. In the air, there was the faint smell of corn meal baking.

Had he not known better, Euchella would have said that nothing had happened to this place, that the whirlwind that was the army that swept away the Cherokee Nation last year had somehow skirted this village, leaving these few hundred people untouched. It was early, but by the look of the garden plots near the cabins, the people were planting again, and the dark earth showed the first sprouts of vegetables. Perhaps, there would even be a Green Corn Festival at the end of the summer. No one had done any of this last year, and near starvation had visited them over the winter as it had the year before when Euchella's wife and daughter died on Soco Creek. But now the village looked as though the nightmare never happened. This was a good sign. It meant that the people had found reason to go on again. What brought this change, he wondered?

The thicket was quiet and smelled strongly of pine rosin that bulged from small fissures in the bark of the trees that closed in around him. A man could use the rosin to start a fire, and the strong smell of it kept away mosquitoes and the nearly invisible gnats. The misting rain helped with them, too. He had never learned to sit unmoving as these pests dug at his skin, but in here, he would not be bothered.

Across the river, near a cabin, a brown dog stared in his direction, testing the air with its nose, but there was little wind and it could hear nothing above the sound of the river, so when no scent came to it, it turned away.

For a moment, Euchella wondered what had he expected to find in the village. Starvation? People waiting to die? Soldiers lying in wait for the return of stragglers? White people occupying the cabins? He shifted his weight from one foot to another, feeling an uncertainty that seemed to have no cause. But there was something strange about the village now— something missing—that would have been there even last year when things were so bad for all the people. Euchella hated to overlook the obvious. It offended his pride as a warrior, but he could not tell what was missing.

Part of it was that the village looked untouched. But then he remembered that these people were protected—as much as a Cherokee could have been last year—by Will Thomas. Thomas had a paper that called the people of this village "citizen Cherokees." Even though they lived, married, sang, counseled, and hunted with the rest of the people, somehow that paper made them not part of the larger Cherokee Nation. And it was the nation that the soldiers were determined to drive out, so said another paper.

This was a thing that Euchella could not understand. How could a man be Cherokee and not be Cherokee? How could a paper allow a few to stay and force thousands to go? It was all White man's talk. They could see things as they are and then say that they are something else. Even Junaluska, the old chief of the Snowbird village, had said that they talked so much that it made him dizzy. But perhaps it was worse when they stopped talking because that was when the soldiers came.

He looked at the village again. Now he understood what bothered him. The idea about talking made it clear. None of the people who moved about were talking to each other. There were no greetings. Something was wrong. And there were too many men in the village. More should have been out hunting, even in the rain. There were no shouts, no waving to one another. And when they walked past each other, they kept their heads down . . . as if . . . in mourning. Someone has died, he realized, and that thought hit him like a thunderclap. It had to be Drowning Bear. He was known to be old and sick, and that his time to go was near. So Drowning Bear was dead.

Euchella was stunned. Drowning Bear was the founding stone for this village, as much as Junaluska had been in his own village. Drowning Bear *was* these people. Everything they did began with him. Euchella looked toward his cabin, sitting back in a cove above the river, by a towering walnut tree. Smoke from his chimney was twice as great as that from any of the other cabins. The witches fire—it burned to keep them away.

Euchella sat still. Something slipped into the pine thicket with him, moving with stealth, easing around the trees without disturbing a needle. He did not look around or even blink as he felt its presence wrap around him like the smoke from Drowning Bear's chimney, but he sensed no danger. Whatever it was had found him in the deepest woods as though it knew were to look, as though there was no place throughout all the mountains where he would not have been found. He breathed rhythmically, seeming to drift outside his own body the way one might in a dream. From a place above himself, he watched as his arms and legs took strength from this presence. The time of hiding on the mountain and the ravages of winter began to disappear. The fatigue that occupied his body slid away, and the ache in his hands subsided. Was this the magic of visitation? The old ones spoke of it when he was a boy. On rare occasions, when one of the Principal People dies, one of his souls visits the body of another, bringing a gift. It can be a gift of vision or a gift of wisdom or a gift of comfort to one consumed in grief. On those rarest of occasions, it brought a healing touch, and Euchella's heart felt light in a way that it had not since before there was talk of soldiers coming to the Nation. As rain seeped into the thicket and mixed with the smoke of the cook fires across the river, he felt whole again.

Euchella rose. It was time to return to the mountains and bring his men back down. They could live here again. It was not too late to plow and plant. They could sleep under a roof for the first time in a year and sit around a communal fire with the other men in the village. They could live like Cherokees, not like foxes, always on the run. In time, they might even dream again.

As he was about to leave the thicket, something out of place across the river caught his eye . . . a man on horseback. The horse plodded slowly through the village, in no hurry. Even from across the river, Euchella knew that the round shape of the rider was that of Will Thomas. There was a sadness in the way he rode, slightly slumped at the shoulders. But the presence of Will Thomas at the death of Drowning Bear—his adopted father—was something that Euchella had to witness. The men on the mountain could wait a little longer for him to return.

Slinging his rifle over his shoulder, Euchella waded into the river. Spring storms had washed away the line of rocks that the people in the village used to cross, and although he prepared himself for the shock, the water was colder than he remembered. A strong current pulled at his leggings and nearly caused him to trip. Placing one foot in front of the other, he could smell the river with its hint of fish and green moss that covered the rocks. His old White friend, Jonas Jenkins, had once told him that he could smell the difference between the rivers, but Jonas was strange, even for a White man. He was not sure that he believed him. As he climbed the bank on the village side, Euchella half expected to see Jonas standing above him. He would be here, soon enough. It was only a few miles down river to his farm, and as soon as he heard about Drowning Bear, he would come.

The people of the village who watched Euchella walk up the bank stood back and stared at him as if he were a stranger. For a moment, he did not understand. Then it came to him. He was marked as the man who shot Tsali. And even though the tribe's opinion of Tsali was that he had become hated like the she-witch of the old legend, Spear-Finger, Euchella had been the one to do the shooting. Besides, he had been in the mountains for months and he had the look of a wolf about him. People stood aside as he approached, as though they half expected him to attack. For the moment, he let that serve him. Fear in the hearts of others is not always a bad thing for a warrior. He stood taller than everyone here, and now they feared him, too. Perhaps he would not tell anyone that he, too, was haunted by his own vision of Tasli.

As he approached the cabin of Drowning Bear, Will Thomas emerged, hat in hand. He was dressed as

White men of their religion dressed, in all black except for a white shirt with a stiff collar that clutched uncomfortably at his neck. It was the same way he had dressed when Tsali's sons and son-in-law were sentenced to death in the military trial last fall. Euchella recognized it as a ceremonial costume of White men, but it seemed an odd choice to wear to visit one's dead father who was Cherokee.

Elders of the village stood around the cabin in the light rain, expecting a word from Thomas. He looked sad, but composed. After a moment, he laid a hand on the shoulder of one of the older men. "As you know, I was away in Washington when Yonaguska—my father—went on," he said in a low voice that was remarkably under control. "He was the greatest man that I ever knew, and he taught me the things that I needed to become a man on my own. He even gave me one of the things that I prize most, my Cherokee name. It is time for us to sing songs in his praise and remember how he guided us with wisdom." He paused to scan the faces of the crowd, but not pausing on any particular one. "Before he went on, I am told that he asked you to have me serve as your chief. I did not hear him say these words, but many of you did. Now I tell you, if that is what you want, then that is what I will do, but it is for you to decide." Within the crowd, there was a pause, which was followed by nods of many heads.

Euchella stood near others at the back, but not a part of the crowd. In his mind, Thomas was speaking to the rest of them, not to him. He heard the words but did not feel them the way that the others did. He knew Thomas to use words the way other men used a knife or plow, and when he was done speaking, something was changed, perhaps not by much, but at least to some small degree, and always in the direction that Thomas wanted it to change. Now, Euchella could see where this was going. Just as Tsali, the fisherman, had laid stones in a narrowing pattern to funnel fish toward his trap, Thomas was directing the will of this village. Words instead of stones. Words instead of guns. Then he remembered the day last fall when Thomas had come to find him and his men, in the Balsam Mountains, to speak to him about hunting down and shooting Tsali and his sons. Euchella had sent an arrow near him as a warning, but Thomas was not deterred. He laid out a story of how Euchella could change the future of the Cherokees that remained after removal. His words had appealed to something in Euchella, making him want to do the thing that Thomas said needed to be done. It had sounded reasonable: Euchella would be ridding the tribe of one who was possessed by the she-witch—and gaining favor with the army at the same time. And for that, the army would then let them stay in the mountains to which they were born.

Words. Perhaps it was a good thing, shooting Tsali. But it had not been Euchella's idea. He had come under the spell of Will Thomas' words. Now, the people of Quallatown were caught in the same spell. Euchella snorted and some in the crowd looked around at him for a moment, then turned their attention back to Thomas.

Euchella backed away from the others. Will Thomas was about to make the people of Quallatown name him as their new chief, in effect, making him chief of all the Cherokees who were left in the East. That was a step in their transformation from Cherokee to White, and eventually they would become just like all the White settlers who had moved into the lands of the Nation. Men would become like women and scratch in the earth. They would raise the foul animals in pens that stank of their droppings. They would forget how to make arrowheads and forget the

41

purification of the hunt. Worst of all, what remained of their Cherokee-ness would be seen by their neighbors as quaint or peculiar. Maybe some day people would come and stare at them because, long ago, they had been a separate nation with different ways.

Euchella would have no part of it. If he were the only one, then somehow he would find a way to remain Cherokee and find a place where this was possible.

Chapter 4
Kituwah
May, 1839

uchella sat alone beside the burial mound at the site of the ancient village of *Kituwah* and waited for the sun to rise. Where the village had once sat was now nothing more than a flat field that lay beside a long bend in the river, the people having long ago abandoned it for the more secure site of Quallatown a few miles upstream. One thing they could not take with them, however, was their dead who now rested in the mound that rose from the field, higher than his head. How many old ones were buried here Euchella did not know. But sitting in the tall grass beside the pile of earth and stone, he felt them all around him, like hummingbirds before they are seen. The river that periodically grew sullen and flooded the field had washed away the lodges, but it could not wash away the spirits that occupied this holy ground. It belonged to them and always would.

Euchella had come to this spot to listen to them. From hunts during his early boyhood, he knew daybreak to be the most spiritual time of day, the time when the old ones were most animated—after the owls had gone to roost and before crows took wing. In light that was almost too soft to see, they could pass undeterred from stream to tree to rock to cave. So Euchella had walked here from his new camp north of Quallatown in the deepest part of the night to catch their passage. On the way along the path beside the river, his hands touched familiar places on rocks and logs, and in the darkness it seemed that nothing had changed. But it had. Everything had changed. Tsali was right when he said, just before they shot him, that there would be no more Cherokee Nation. Physically, nothing was changed, but it did not feel like home as it used to, as though some bad smell now permanently fouled the air. Euchella wondered if the spirits of this place knew about Tsali. Surely they would. This morning, their voices were stirring as though they were glad that, at last, someone wanted to hear what they had to say. No one came here much anymore. There was little time in Quallatown now for the old ones. The people there were building something that Will Thomas called a "reservation."

Euchella hoped for word from the old ones to quiet his restiveness. He had lost his sense of belonging, lost the certainty of the seasons, lost the very rhythms of what it was to be Cherokee. Whatever Will Thomas was doing with the Quallatown people was not for him. His reason was simple. He did not trust Thomas. Thomas had a way of convincing people to do things that they would not do on their own. After all, he had convinced Euchella that he should shoot Tsali and the others. Perhaps the reason Euchella sat here now, surrounded by the old ones, was that they might carry his message of regret to Tsali—wherever he was. Yes, that was why he was here, he decided. Tsali and his family had gone to their deaths like warriors. During the removal, they were the only ones. All the others—the thousands taken to the West and the hundreds left behind—could not call themselves warriors.

What had become of the *Keetoowahs*—those keepers of the ancient traditions? The change from the old ways of the Principal People had begun long before the soldiers arrived three summers ago and began building the log forts where they would eventually herd the people before moving them west. The change had come subtly, like a shift of the seasons. Had it started when the nation, as a whole, had begun to act White at the urging of their leader,

John Ross, who was mostly White? After generations of sporadic fighting with Whites, then pauses for treaties that were soon ignored, then more sporadic fighting, the nation had let in the missionaries with their teachings of a White god, and then a few White settlers, like his friend Jonas Jenkins. These people—good or bad—brought something with them that had slowly depleted the will of the Principal People to act like warriors. It was said that a few Cherokees, including Ross and the traitorous Major Ridge, had become as rich as any White man, with slaves and big houses. It was all too seductive. Without realizing it, they found themselves wanting to mimic a race with which they had nothing in common, one that did not understand the harmony of the old ways. Yes, even in the dim light, Euchella knew that everything had changed. The discipline of the *Keetoowahs* had vanished just as Tsali had foretold. Now, men scratched in the ground to grow things to eat. When they hunted, they did so more out of habit than need, as though the serious purpose of hunting was forgotten and it had become nothing more than a game. Sacred celebrations and rituals were ignored, then lost altogether. Children heard stories from the White man's bible in place of tribal lore, and went to a school to learn a language that was not theirs. He had seen no one dance in years.

As the sun began to give color to the mountaintops, he waited for a sign. As his mind drifted, he thought about why he had come to dislike Thomas. Perhaps, it was just because he was White. Given all that had happened, that was reason enough. The Indian people traded things at his trading post, and doing so made their lives easier—iron pots being stronger than clay and steel knives being stronger than bone—but each time they did, they took one more step away from the ways that they used to know. It was said that Thomas protected them from the army and the Whites who wanted all their land, but why did the Principal People need protecting? Why could they not just be warriors? Somewhere in the storm of words that had lasted over a decade, they had forgotten how.

The only good thing about these last few weeks was that Euchella had begun to dream his own dreams again, the first since the death of his wife a year and a half before. Tsali's dream of the dog and the soldier had faded in his head, replaced by other fitful images, not all of which were frightening. And there were other signs. He now spent part of each day making arrowheads, methodically chipping them from the hard flint rocks that lay in the shallows of Soco Creek. His hands were sore from the constant pounding, and bled where chips of flint tore his skin. But that did not matter. One did not make arrowheads without bleeding a little. The other Luftys at their camp by the creek watched as he worked, but did not need to ask him why he worked. They knew. Sometimes one or more of them would join him. Logs of locust and hickory were split on hillsides, then carved and shaved until they took on the delicately tapered shape of a bow. Dried gut from a bear was twisted into strands for the bowstring. Finally, each was strung backwards and left to dry in the air. Straight shafts of cane were cut for arrows and their joints shaved smooth. So that they would fly true, feathers were attached to the nock end with glue made from the boiled hoofs of deer. When the bows were hard, the men practiced by shooting arrows at a rotten stump.

Now, as he sat unmoving beside the mound, Euchella could feel his mind speaking of these things to the old ones, and it seemed that they answered with pleased murmurs. He needed direction, for himself and for the men who steadfastly followed him, and he needed to calm the anger that still burned inside his chest. From far away came the sound of the river. Like the old ones, the river was everlasting. It could rise in spring and fall in summer and rise again when the leaves changed, but it went on, unceasing. This was the river that now bore the blood of Tsali and his sons, the river of the Principal People.

Katydids and crickets awoke to the morning light, and the web of a small spider hung, covered with dew, between two tall stalks of grass. He watched the spider mend damage done by wind and by the beetles and grasshoppers that were too large to be trapped. As it crawled crab-like from one point to another, it trailed new treads to anchor the net. The work went steadily, and although the strands were too small for Euchella to see what needed to be repaired, the spider could. It was in no rush, having all day to do its chore.

A thought occurred to him: How did the spider know to do this? There was no chief or shaman to give it direction. A light breeze buffeted the web and the spider grew still and hung on until the wind died. If the wind or wandering animal tore the web down, the spider would build it back again. It had to because it had no choice. It was born to do this simple thing.

Euchella rose. Where his face had reflected doubt before, it now showed peace that he had not felt in years. As his legs swished through the damp grass, carrying him away from the mound, he silently thanked the old ones. Perhaps, a little of the *Keetoowahs* lived on still. He would have to tell the other men of the Lufty Band.

Chapter 5
Oconaluftee River
May, 1839

s it slowly burned down, the cook fire crackled beside the Oconaluftee River, sending sparks into the darkness as glowing sticks collapsed. Beside him, Euchella's brother patiently worked a knife over a flat stone. He wore an absent look as the firelight flickered across his face. Euchella has always been able to read him, and what he read now—given their year of hiding and dodging the army—was astonishing. Wachacha was content. All the men of the Lufty Band were. Once again, they could be the hunters, not the hunted. Proof of this lay in the remains of a side of venison that sizzled over the fire. They had killed the deer in the afternoon and ate it with the coming of darkness. Maybe it was not so strange now that there were so many fewer people in the mountains, deer were more plentiful. Never found in great numbers here because the Southern Blue Ridge are softwood forests, deer seemed to come out of hiding now that most of the people were gone. This one had not been lucky. A yearling doe, she had passed up a draw where Wachacha and two other braves sat in a triangular shooting pattern. Their arrows struck her almost simultaneously, with one piercing her heart. She managed a single leap, then fell dead. It was a good kill. The men knelt beside the doe and asked the ritual forgiveness for killing her. Exchanging a haunch of meat for some salt from a family in Quallatown, they had enjoyed a particularly good feast tonight.

Euchella knew that the men hoped that the kill was a sign. When he returned to the camp that morning from his meditation at the mound in the old

village of *Kituwah*, he found that they had gone
hunting, and this deer was a special reward, perhaps a
portent of things to come. As they tore meat from the
bones, he told them the story of the spider and its
methodical repair of its web. They nodded at the
mention of the old ways. The deer was killed with
bows and arrows and arrowheads, all made the old
ways. It was something that he did not have to
explain. Signs were appearing. There was the simple
fact that they now camped beside the Oconaluftee
safely, and the only eyes that watched them belonged
to a fox that waited beyond the firelight for a chance to
steal a scrap of meat. Yes, the signs were good. Those
that chose to would make more than a camp here,
building lodges, planting gardens. The valley was not
as broad as Soco, but the ground was good and sandy
and easy to turn. With a fish planted in each hill of
corn, the corn would grow tall. Anyone who wanted to
go down river to Quallatown was welcome to do so, but
so far none had. Without saying so, they wanted to
keep the old ways.

"Build me a lodge," Euchella said to his brother
suddenly, breaking the silence around the fire.

Wachacha looked up from the knife that he was
sharpening, puzzled.

"Build me a lodge," he repeated.

"Why should I build you a lodge?"

"Because I will need it when I return. It will be
winter."

"Where are you going?" another asked.

"I am going to the West . . . to see what has
become of the others."

The men were silent again, but not for long.
"What if they make you stay?" came a voice from
across the fire.

"They will not even know that I am there."

"You have no horse. The journey is said to be

49

long."

"I will walk. The others did."

"You will get back too late to plant a garden."

"You will plant one for me."

Collectively, they considered this announcement. It had caught them off guard. Finally, one of the men across the fire spoke. "When did you plan this?"

"It came to me now. Maybe it began this morning as I watched the spider. Who can say?"

"Why do you need to go?"

"I am not sure, but perhaps it is because we find benefit in the old ways. Perhaps someone needs to tell them that, to remind them of the *Keetoowahs*."

No one could think of a reason why he should not go, except that if he were caught he would probably be forced to stay. Finally, one of the younger ones, named Swimmer, had an idea. "How will you find the way? None of us have been there before and there is no one to tell you."

Euchella considered the question. Then the answer came to him. "They say that many died along the way. I will follow the graves."

Wachacha nodded. It was a Cherokee answer. There would be many graves. "When you get there, find Junaluska. Tell him that we are well."

In the days that followed, Euchella assembled the things that he would need: A blanket, a good flint to sharpen his knife, and a second bowstring. Working steadily, he also made a second pair of moccasins and cut spare shafts for arrows from a dense stand of river bamboo. Although the preparations went well, doubt lingered like the vague discomfort of a tooth going bad. What troubled him was what he did not know. How long was the journey? He had heard of big rivers; was there one too deep or wide to wade across? How many Whites would he meet along the way and how would they treat him when he encountered them? Would he be seen as an outlaw or renegade, and shot at? Should he travel mostly at night? He was a good tracker, renown for following a bear around its entire range before killing it, but would the trail that the 16,000 people took be obvious to him a year later? Many had set off on boats; could he find where they had disembarked?

Euchella sighed. He would have to do the thing that he was most reluctant to do, and that was to ask the advice of a White man. Only a White man would know something of the country to the west of the old Cherokee Nation. But the problem with that was that the only White man whose advice he trusted was one that he had thought to kill. Euchella had known Jonas Jenkins since boyhood, when the older man had moved to Soco Valley with his wife, from some place they called Virginia. Euchella and his family had accepted them, sometimes exchanging small gifts of seed corn, buttons, or cloth. Sometimes, they even exchanged planting advice. In all the years that he had known Jonas, there had never been conflict between them. The killing point came after Euchella's wife and child were found dead. In the last year of the Cherokee Nation, Euchella had left Soco Valley and hid out in the high Snowbird Mountains, subsisting on what he could catch. It was the way of a warrior, an example that the Cherokees need not just passively accept removal. He ate rabbits. He slept in a cave that he filled with leaves. He chipped arrowheads from obsidian. He nearly froze in the brutally cold air. He was a Cherokee warrior. But no one followed his example. And, paralyzed by the dread of removal, no one took care of his wife and child back in the Soco Valley. The moment that he had seen the old man, Tsali, trudging through the spring snow in search of him, Euchella knew that something terrible had happened back in Soco. Later, in an attempt to restore balance in the Cherokee way, he had thought to kill two White people because Whites had brought the malaise to the tribe. Jonas and his wife were obvious targets. But when the moment came, he could not kill them. He had stood on a hill above the Jenkins farm and had been unable to let the arrow go that would have struck down Jonas. Now, he needed advice from Jonas. Perhaps that is the way things work out; mysteries are revealed in their own time. Perhaps, this was another lesson from the old ways.

On a morning when a heavy fog lay over the river and flooded into the adjacent coves, Euchella set out to find Jonas. The air smelled wet and leaves dripped from trees overhead. When the sun rose high, it would burn off the fog, but for now everything was cloaked in a cotton-like mist. Jonas lived about two miles below Quallatown, so the walk there would take only a small part of the morning. The thing was, he did not want to be seen in Quallatown and have to explain where he was going and why—particularly if Will Thomas were there. Certainly, Thomas would try to dissuade him from going west. Using the fog as a cloak, Euchella skirted the village. As he passed close to a lodge, a dog barked an alert, but he was gone before anyone could come to investigate.

Jonas would be awake early. He always was. Euchella remembered him from years ago, perched on a rock that overlooked Soco Creek, drinking from a cup. From his manner, one might have mistaken Jonas for an Indian. He was quiet, respectful, only offering his opinions when it was clear that his opinions were wanted. Also, he no longer chewed tobacco as most White men did. Except for his habit of keeping animals, Jonas acted as though he had been raised by Cherokees.

As he approached the farm, Euchella called out

in a series of whoops, announcing his arrival. He found Jonas stooped over in a shed, feeding his cows. The place smelled strongly of them. It offended Euchella's nature, but he made sure that this did not show on his face. When Jonas stood up, the two men stared at each other for some time, not sure of what to say. They had not seen each other since that day last fall when Jonas had gone with Euchella to bring in Tsali from Deep Creek and shoot him. After they buried Tsali's body on the hillside above the spring where they executed him, they had gone their separate ways. But the shame of Tsali's death united them, and it lay between them like a smell that was as bad as these animals.

"I am glad to find you well, old friend," Euchella said to break the awkwardness.

"And I you," Jonas replied. "I am glad to see you down from the mountain."

"It was time. The signs are changing."

"Yes," the White man agreed. "The signs are improving."

Euchella hesitated, not sure how to ask Jonas what he wanted to know. White people had a puzzling, indirect way of asking questions, as though one did not want the other to know the true reason for the question. Will Thomas did that. He kept his reasons cloaked. But Jonas was more Indian-like. He said what was on his mind, a habit that made other Whites think him strange. Euchella would risk the truth. "I want to travel to the West, but do not know the way. Can you tell me how to go?"

Jonas dropped the bundle of hay that he was holding and took off his hat. Uncovered, his face gave the impression of having been squeezed at the sides. "That could be dangerous," he said, slapping his hat against his knee. "But I assume that you have thought of that and still feel that you need to go."

53

Euchella nodded once.

"If . . . if you left here and walked in a straight line with the setting sun always at your left hand, you would get to where you want to go. But no one goes that way because it is too hard. They use the rivers . . . at least for much of the way. Then they walk the rest of the way." Jonas thought some more. "Can you build a canoe?"

"It is possible. My brother knows these things."

"It will go much easier if you can. Let me show you." He took a stick and began to scratch lines in the dirt of the corral. For some time he worked without speaking, examining the lines, then continuing to make more. Finally, when he was halfway across the corral, he dug a deeper, broader furrow and then straightened up. "This is a thing called a map. You must memorize it."

Euchella looked at the marks in the dirt. They meant nothing to him.

Jonas walked back to where he had started and pointed to the first line that lay on the ground like a lazy snake. "This is the Hiwassee River. You know of that?"

Euchella nodded. It ran to the west of the Snowbird Mountains. He had been to its edge several times on hunts. Suddenly, he understood that Jonas was showing him a picture of the land.

"Go there. Build your canoe there. It will carry you to the Tennessee," he said, pointing to a long westerly scratch. "This will take many days to cover, perhaps two weeks, perhaps a month, depending on how well it goes. Eventually, the Tennessee will turn north; the setting sun will be off your left shoulder. After many more days—I cannot tell you how many—you will come to a bigger river. It is called the Ohio. You will know it because it is always muddy. Follow the way it flows. But you will not be on this river long because it joins with the biggest river of all, the Mississippi." He paused to make sure that Euchella was following him. "This is as much as I know. I am told that the others who were taken west were put off here," he pointed to a kink in the big furrow in the dirt. "It is called Cape Gerardo. If I were you, I would get off there and follow the signs."

Euchella stared at the marks and tried to imagine them as rivers. "How do you know this?" he asked, spreading his hands across the image.

"Will Thomas has a real map. He showed me how the others would go last year. This is what I remember of it."

At the mention of Will Thomas, Euchella fell noticeably silent. It was said among Whites that Indians could sometimes look into a man and read what was in his heart. Jonas knew no such power, and he wondered what this particular Indian, whom he had known longer than any other, had against his friend Will.

Chapter 6
Tennessee River
End of May, 1839

he water here was much smoother and slower than it was back on the Hiwassee, but it was not clear and it smelled faintly of the brown silt on the bank. Euchella could not bring himself to drink it. In spite of his distaste, he decided that Jonas' advice to travel this way was good. The river, though it meandered back and forth, would eventually carry him to where the others had set off on foot last year. But he would have a hard time describing it if he ever returned home again. One day it flowed through hills that were dotted with sharp, gray outcroppings of rocks; the next it spread wider than he could have imagined, pushing itself deep into the surrounding fields. In the broad areas, the current slowed so as to be almost imperceptible. Long narrow islands growing thick with maple and willow lay parallel to the shore. In shallow stretches, the edge was often choked with beds of a floating round-leafed plant that held great, spreading blooms of white. These plants were unknown to Euchella, and he guessed that they could not grow in the faster moving rivers in the mountains.

Without a sound, the canoe cut around a fallen sycamore that reached out into the river like a giant dead claw. Near the edge, a fish rose to the surface and took a grasshopper that, in a desperate attempt to avoid a pursuing bird, had jumped the wrong way and swam for shore. Euchella smiled to himself. Everything had to eat something. The previous evening, he killed a turkey as it wandered out of a thicket and into range of his bow. The meat that he did not eat that night he had smoked, and now it lay wrapped in the bottom of the boat. Again, he would not sleep hungry. Somewhere on the far bank, a crow sounded a warning. Good, he had been spotted. That meant that he was probably the only thing moving this early on the river. Dipping the paddle into the water, he pushed on. The paddle would not last long. The poplar wood was too soft and porous for this kind of work, and his shoulders ached from the unaccustomed motion of paddling. When he stopped next to let the skins of the canoe dry out and repair the seams, he would rest his shoulders and carve another paddle, from hickory if he could find it.

The little canoe worked well. He was pleased. It was not a Cherokee canoe, rather the kind made by tribes up north as well as some of the Creeks in Georgia. A Cherokee canoe was cut from a whole log, hollowed out slowly with fire and axe, but Euchella had no time to do that. Besides, it would have been too heavy and took too much effort to paddle as far as he had to go. He needed something lighter, something that he could handle by himself. Wachacha had suggested this type: deer skins—because the birch that was favored by the northern tribes was scarce here—pulled over a bent hickory frame that was broad in the middle and pinched at the ends. The seams were overlapped and sown together with a double row of stitches, then coated with rosin that oozed from a fresh gash in a spruce that grew by the river. Almost four times the length of his body, it was light, simple, fast. How had Wachacha known how to make one of these? And where had Wachacha come up with the wide-brimmed hat that now shaded Euchella's eyes? He said that he had taken it from a drunk militiamen last year, and that Euchella should wear it on this journey because, from a distance, it would make him look like a White man. A White man. Euchella shrugged. It made sense. Thus far, no one had troubled him, but he had taken care not to be seen.

That had been easy on the Hiwassee where there was only an occasional cabin to avoid. At night when he stopped to sleep, he climbed the tallest tree to see if there were camps or cabins nearby. Now, stroking close to shore, he glided in the morning shadows of overhanging willows, swamp maples, and elms knotted together by an endless tangle of honeysuckle. Orange butterflies flitted between flowers. It was summer here, and he felt no urge to hurry. Under the canopy, travel was silent, and silence had its own benefit. He could hear the passage of creatures moving through the thick brush. So far, he had surprised deer, ground hogs, raccoons, and muskrats that had not expected to see anyone on the river and had not heard his approach.

The journey had not been all pleasure, however, nor had it been entirely safe. He learned to watch for the ugly gray-black water moccasins—*kanegwa'ti*—that sunned themselves along the riverbank. Unlike those in the mountains, these snakes did not always retreat to safety as he passed. Once, when floating close by a half-submerged stump, one surprised him by wriggling toward him. Euchella struck it hard with the paddle, cracking the blade—another reason to replace it.

What kept him on edge most, though, were the almost constant smells of smoke and farm animals that drifted across the river. A generation ago, this had been Creek—*Muskogee*—land. But all sign of the Creeks had vanished as though they had never lived or hunted here. Not even a trace of their spirit remained . . . no burial mound, not even a pile of stones to mark a cleared field. What had become of the masks, the belts, the drums, the songs, the trails through the woods that would mark the place as their territory? It had all been erased like footprints in sand after a heavy rain. Now, the low hills and widening plains were dotted with the farms of White men. Many ran to the edge of the river where domestic animals pushed through the tangle of growth to drink. These farms were not like those in the mountains, where a few animals and a small field fed a family. Here, many animals grazed across vast fields that took many strokes of his paddle to pass on the river. Occasionally, the edge of a field was bounded by a white fence. That they would spend the time to paint such a thing explained how strongly these people were prepared to defend their notion of ownership of the land—even from each other if necessary. How strange to limit where an animal could go, Euchella thought. Perhaps, that was why they smelled so badly. Fields that were not used for grazing were covered with thigh-high plants with ragged leaves that grew up the rising hills in the valley as far as he could see. Beneath the leaves grew tufts of something white. If they were good to eat, then these people could feed several villages on the output of one field alone. And it was not just the land that was different here, but the places where people lived were different, too—large frame buildings that sat well back from the river, away from the danger of flooding. Most were surrounded by trees, to cool them on days that could be sweltering. Some were even larger than the one Will Thomas had built on the Tuckasegee, or the one that old Major Ridge had left behind down in Georgia when he had gone west in '35 with the other Cherokee traitors. They were like cabins on top of cabins, with rooms above and rooms below. Euchella had no idea how many people could live in one or where they would build a sleeping fire. If he found the old chief Junaluska in the west, he would ask him if he knew of these things. Junaluska had, after all, been to the place where the greatest of the White chiefs lived, and spoke with wonder of a huge cabin where he and many other men slept.

The more that he saw, the more inclined Euchella was to travel quietly. In spite of the disguise afforded by the hat, he still looked like an Indian, with his long hair and dark features. Only at a distance would the hat hide that fact. If he surprised a White farmer up close, the man might react like the snake and shoot at him.

Approaching the trickle of a small stream that emptied into the river, Euchella steered the canoe in close. The water looked clean. He shook an overhead limb to make sure that there were no snakes hiding above, then beached the canoe. The morning air was warm with the promise of becoming hot later. Yesterday, by late afternoon, the air had become suffocating. Today would probably be the same. Already, his head was damp where the hat band rested. If he did not drink now, he would be thirsty later, and who knew when he would find good water. By cupping his hands into a shallow pool, he drank as crayfish and salamanders scurried to the safety of hiding places along the bottom. The water was good, but not as cool as he would have liked.

Beside the stream, he rested on a rock and wet his shirt to stay cool and to chase away the gnats that swarmed him now that he was still. Euchella sat for a long time assessing this place and trying to guess how far he had come. There was no way to tell exactly, except by counting days. He reckoned that he could cover thirty, maybe forty miles a day if he paddled steadily. Today marked the fourth day since he had passed Chattanooga and the gray rocky flanks of the mountain ridges there. He had drifted by Chattanooga on a moonless night, hiding in the bottom of the canoe and, just to be safe, not once lifting the paddle, letting the canoe turn and drift with the current. Recalling Jonas' map, he estimated that he was still on the upper part of the Tennessee River. The setting sun still faced his right shoulder. If the map were correct, the sun would set head-on in a few days. That meant that he was probably in Alabama. Much later, Jonas told him, the sun would be on his left shoulder. After that, there would be two more rivers to follow, then somewhere he would have to find the place where the people left the boats and set off on foot last year.

A moth flew by, pulling his vision toward the edge of the bramble that bordered the river. Beyond, in the field, something moved. Euchella became still, his breathing stopped. Drawing closer to the edge, he peered through the leaves. Above the trickle of the stream, he could now hear low voices. Some way off, about the longest distance that his bow could send an arrow, a man sat on horseback with a rifle lying across his lap. He did not look toward the river as his attention was fixed on something in the field. Euchella watched for a while until he determined that the man was guarding other people in the field who were bent over among the rows of plants. They seemed to be hoeing. Euchella was puzzled. Why would the man be standing guard? Was he protecting them from some threat, a bear or wildcat? Then, one with a hoe straightened up and took off his hat. From his hiding place, Euchella gasped. The man's skin was the color of the dark brown earth of the riverbank, and his hair stood almost straight out from his head. Sweat glistened on his broad face. Whatever he was doing with the hoe was hard work to make him sweat that much. Words were exchanged between the man and the White overseer, but it was obvious from the exchange that whatever the hatless man requested was denied.

Slowly, Euchella remembered something that Junaluska had explained a long time ago. These were slaves, but not like the slaves who were spoils of war that the Cherokee and other tribes kept. These were brought from a far-off land where everyone had dark skin. Negroes, that was what they were called. Euchella had never seen one, although Junaluska had said once that rich Cherokees like Major Ridge owned them down in Georgia. The name sounded mysterious and made him wonder if their darkness made them magical. They had the look of magic about them. But if they were magic, he reasoned, they would cast a spell on the White guard, and it was clear now that the guard was there to prevent the dark men from escaping.

The sight reminded him of the militia and the army herding Cherokees west last year. Several times he had sat in a laurel thicket and watched people whom he knew being marched down the Tuckaseegee, Little Tennessee, or Nantahala Rivers to one of the stockades. There was a strong will at work here if it compelled one man to stand over others with a gun, to make them work. Instinctively, Euchella knew that he must avoid this place and others like it. If one man was that determined to force another to work, then the sudden appearance of a stranger would be threatening. A part of him would like to put an arrow into the overseer, but this was not his fight. He did not even understand it. When a dog beside the guard barked in the direction of the river, the man turned slowly to gaze that way. His face had a slack look. Euchella eased back from where he hid at the edge of the bramble and quietly launched the canoe. With a few strokes of the paddle, he moved down river and out of sight of the little stream.

By afternoon, the heat made the air difficult to breathe again. Occasionally, horseflies swarmed after him, but they could not land on his head because he kept the hat pulled down low. Later, the sky turned dark suddenly and a storm rolled across the river from the south. For a few moments, rain fell in sheets so hard that he could not see the opposite shore, lashing the surface of the river into a dancing spray of droplets. Hanging on to an overhanging trunk of a willow, Euchella kept some of the rain out of the canoe. But as the storm saturated the canopy, he could not keep it all out, and feared that his remaining stash of meat would get wet. So he beached the canoe again, dragging it all the way onto the shore, and turned it over. Crawling underneath, he was able to stretch out. The storm came in hard. Lightning cracked over and over, with a noise like splitting timbers. Everywhere, the trees and bushes seemed to crouch down to wait for the outburst to pass. Beneath the canoe, Euchella stayed mostly dry. Rain dripped loudly on the upturned skins. A groundhog ran by, looking for shelter and was surprised to find Euchella under the canoe. After a frozen moment, it shuffled into the dense weeds.

When the storm finally passed, Euchella continued down the river. For a time the air was cooler and a low fog lay over the water so that he felt safe enough to paddle outside the cover of the protective canopy and avoid the leaves that dripped from the rain.

By twilight, he had reached a section of the river where low hills pinched in close to the water. He looked for signs of life and found only a muskrat along the bank and a kingfisher perched overhead in an oak. There was no smell of smoke or pungent odor of animals in the air. Finding a spot where the bank was nearly flat, he got out and lifted the canoe over his head, leaving no sign of dragging it in the sand. The weeds were thick and he walked carefully so as not to disturb them. At a point some forty yards from the river, a hill rose up sharply, and he put down the canoe. This was far enough away from the water so that snakes would likely not pass. Also, there was a thick stand of broom sage to soften the ground while he slept. As he set to cutting the stalks, he noticed a small path through the growth, probably made by rabbits. A snare fashioned from his spare bowstring might produce dinner for tomorrow.

By the time his preparations for the night were over, it was dark. He was too tired to climb to a high point and look around. A fire would have been nice to keep away the bugs that swarmed unseen, but that was more than he was willing to risk. Inside his nest within the thicket, Euchella settled back on the bedding and ate the last of the turkey, rubbing the grease on his face so that the trace of smoke would repel the gnats. Then he buried the bones to hide any evidence that he was there. He was tired and his legs were stiff from sitting in the canoe. As he lay back, he thought again of the dark man whom he had seen working in the field. A slave. What he had witnessed did not fit the meaning as he knew it. Cherokees made their slaves work, but often adopted them as members of the tribe after they had become as familiar as family. The man in the field was being worked to the edge of death. And what was the crop over which they labored so hard? It was nothing that he recognized and, as he thought about it, he could not see where any part of it was fit to eat. Why would people work so hard for something that they could not eat? This was a strange, bitter way to live he concluded as he drifted off the sleep.

How long he slept he had no idea, but he was awakened by a rustling not far off. Lying still, Euchella realized that the snare had worked and some animal was trapped. Rising deliberately, he had to kill the animal or it would flop around all night and there would be no sleep. Picking his way through the underbrush, he found a heavy stick of driftwood that was lodged against a tree from the last flood. As he approached the animal, it darted back and forth, unable to free itself from the snare. In the dim moonlight, Euchella could not see clearly and guessed where it was and swung the stick down powerfully. He missed and the rabbit, terrified, let loose a death shriek that split the night. Startled, he hesitated a moment, then took a step forward and swung again. This time there was a crunch of bone and the rabbit twitched for a moment, then was still.

From behind him now came other sounds, voices. Euchella turned and froze. With his back to the river, he had not noticed a light that he could now clearly see. More voices. Louder now. The light moved closer, outlining a boat of some type, much larger than his canoe, flat and wide and carrying a small shed. The men on board moved the boat toward shore with poles. Euchella watched as they neared the bank, then stopped to scan the darkness. He could make them out clearly, two White men. One was a giant with a full red beard; the other was half his size, wiry and slightly stooped.

"I swear . . . it sounded like a woman dyin'."

The big man spat. "Warn't no woman. Probably a panther."

"Panther don't make a noise like that. I'm tellin' you, it coulda been a woman. Sounded like she didn't like what was bein' done to her."

The big man continued to stare at the bank. "If it was a woman, I want to find out about it," he said, leaning on his pole until the boat moved into shore.

"You goin' ashore?"

"Reckon."

"What if there's a bunch of 'em?"

"I'm equal to a bunch," he said, stepping onto the bank and securing the boat to a tree root. "You comin'?"

The smaller man hesitated, then reached inside

the boat for a rifle. "What are you going to do with that?"

"This makes me equal, too."

"You can't shoot nothin' in all that brush."

"I'm bringing it all the same."

"Then bring one of those lanterns while you are at it."

The small man held the lantern high as it cast its yellow light out in front of them; the gun was tucked under his other arm. They edged slowly into the weeds, stamping a trail of flattened brush. Euchella slipped behind a thick sycamore that grew a few feet from where he had been sleeping. The men moved in the direction of the sound that they had heard and their instincts were good. In a few moments, they stood at the edge of the broom sage patch.

"Lookee here," the big man growled.

The smaller one came up beside him and swung the lantern out so that the light swept over the bed of grass and canoe. Euchella's bow and provisions were clearly visible inside.

"It's Injun," whispered the small man.

The big one moved cautiously around the canoe and looked toward the edge of the light. "Here's your woman," he grunted, pointing to the dead rabbit. "They make a noise sometimes when they're being killed. It's important that you get to know the difference between a woman and a rabbit."

"You're so smart, what will you do when that Injun—wherever he is—puts an arrow in your back."

"How's he gonna do that when his bow is still in his canoe? Just keep your gun handy, but don't shoot me."

The two searched the area as far as they could see, trying to decide what to do. "I'm takin' the canoe," the big one said finally. "Grab the back end and let's haul it to the boat."

"I can't carry nothin' with the gun."

"Put the gun in the canoe, stupid."

Euchella had no time to think about what he was doing. As the two White men passed the tree where he was hiding, he slipped around behind and swung the stick at the head of the small man. His body crumpled and the lantern fell to the ground.

"What the . . ." In the darkness, the big man did not see the stick coming as it broke over the side of his head. He sagged to his knees and pitched forward, unmoving.

Euchella did not know if they were dead or alive, but he knew that he could not stay here any longer. He needed to put a lot of distance between himself and these men, whether they came to or were found dead. Picking up the lantern, he searched the brush until he found the dead rabbit and snare. He would leave no obvious sign that he had been there. Dragging the canoe through the path that the other two had flattened, he came to the edge of the river. The large boat remained where it was tied. He would have to sink it or cut it loose. If he sunk it and it did not settle out of sight, it would attract attention. He would be better off to cut it loose and let it drift with the current. But first, he would see if there was anything useful aboard, maybe powder to go with the flintlock that now lay in his canoe.

Leaping onto the deck, he held the lantern up to inspect the thing. What had looked like a shed earlier was nothing more than a pole frame that was covered with canvas. When he swept the canvas aside, something inside moved. For the second time that day, Euchella received a profound shock. There, tied to one of the frame poles, was a man as dark as the one that he had seen back upriver in the field. Only this one was young and slightly built. He sat shirtless, his hands bound behind his back, to the pole. He was terrified and when Euchella came closer and touched his skin, the man screamed out something in a language that he did not understand.

Euchella backed up, then squatted so that he was at eye level with the other. He did not know what to make of the situation or why this man was tied here, but if the two on shore were thieves and this one was their prisoner, then it made sense that this one was not evil. Holding up one hand to indicate that he meant no harm, Euchella took out his knife and cut the ropes that bound the man. The dark stranger sprang to his feet and rubbed his wrists. Euchella motioned for him to follow him out of the shelter. Finding one of the poles that they others used to propel the boat, Euchella handed it to the stranger and pointed down river. Then he placed the lantern back on the hook where it had hung, and jumped to shore. With another swipe of his knife, he cut the rope that held it and the big boat drifted free.

He watched for a moment. The dark man did not know what to do, so Euchella made a motion with his hands that he should leave. Like an animal set free from a trap, the other hesitated, then found the pole and dug it into the bottom of the river.

Euchella slid the canoe into the water and climbed in. It would be a long night and a longer day tomorrow, but this was no time to give into weariness, so he stroked with a sense of urgency. Passing the flatboat, he caught the eye of the dark man poling determinedly, and wondered what would become of him.

Chapter 7
Oconaluftee River
End of May, 1839

When Will Thomas swung down from his horse, a dozen men of the Lufty Band circled around him, curious. Work was well underway on their lodges and the ground was littered with trimmed logs notched and waiting to be raised into position. Smaller roof poles lay to one side in a pile and a spread of newly split shingles were drying in the sun. In a month, at least four lodges would be standing on a knoll that overlooked the river. But for the moment, work was suspended to see what brought Thomas.

Will preferred that this construction take place down river in Quallatown or in one of the other five villages that he had laid out two years ago. Doing so it would strengthen the position of the tribe as acting in unison, but he kept his objections to himself. The Luftys had made it clear that he may be chief in Quallatown, but he was not chief here. No one was openly hostile toward him, but then no one was openly friendly either. He did not know how to handle people who disliked him, but there was no way to know if the Luftys really disliked him because their faces betrayed nothing. However, they had chosen to hold themselves separate from the primary remnant of the tribe. There were others like the Luftys who were now emerging from hiding—Will heard of one in the Snowbird Mountains—but none so close to Quallatown.

He could only take this building spree as defiance of his authority as chief. However, there was nothing that he could—or should—do about it and he knew it. If he objected, he would be resented and it probably would not do any good anyhow. The Cherokee nature included a strong streak of obstinacy.

In the past few years, the Luftys had been pushed as much as they could tolerate. Will resolved to live with their independence. At some point, they would need the benefits of a community and maybe then they would rethink this living arrangement. Until then, the best that he could do would be to appear helpful.

Wachacha rounded the corner of a new lodge and worked his way through the others. He was shorter than his brother, Euchella, thicker and less athletic looking. But looks were deceptive. Will knew him to be single-minded to the point of being dangerous. Once he made up his mind to do something, he was without fear or conscience in the execution of it. Wachacha was not a man that one wanted as an enemy.

As he approached, Will looked around for the older brother but did not see him. It was an undeclared fact that Euchella was the leader of these men. That had been clear even before the Tsali shooting. The others looked to Euchella because he seemed to have a sense of where he was going. And when they had been on the run from the soldiers and militia last year, he knew how to keep them alive through the winter. Wachacha never seemed troubled by his brother's leadership, but rather seemed content with it. If Euchella were a bow, Wachacha was an arrow.

Where was Euchella? Will expected him to appear, but as Wachacha came closer, it was obvious that he was in charge for the moment. Speaking before he considered what he was saying, Will blurted out, "Where is Euchella?"

Wachacha paused, acknowledging the impoliteness of the greeting. "He is not here."

Will reddened. He was being foolish. Resolving to get this impatience under control, he waited for an explanation, but none was offered. Wachacha simply stood before him expressionless. To break the tension, Will reached into his saddle bag and pulled out a bag of dried beans. "It is too late to plant corn, but you may have some luck with these."

Wachacha accepted the gift and peered into the bag. Custom called for an equivalent gift in return, but they had little. It was an uncomfortable moment as he took his time deciding what to do. Presently, he pointed to the last leg of venison that hung curing above a fire and signaled to one of the younger men, a boy named Swimmer, that it be brought to him. Handing it to Thomas, he knew that the men would go mostly hungry that night. But they could hunt the following day, and besides, the beans in the bag would one day grow into something that would last forever.

As a parting gift, Wachacha decided to tell Thomas what he wanted to know. "My brother has gone to find the people in the west."

The white man grew very pale as though most of the blood had been drawn suddenly from him. "When?" was all he could say.

"Some days ago. I do not remember how many."

"Will he stay?"

"He said that he will return. We build him a lodge," Wachacha said, pointing to the half-finished construction.

Will climbed back onto his horse. He made the short ride back down river to Quallatown, feeling little more than the steady bump of the leg of smoked meat that hung from his saddle horn. As he arrived, Kanaka—with whom he had one child and would, in a few weeks, have a second—watched him from her garden. As he rounded the last bend in the river and came into view, she knew instinctively that something was very wrong. His face was whiter than ever and he had the displaced look of one whose lodge had just burned down.

Her instinct was to put down her hoe and rush to him, to share whatever it was that troubled him so much. But she checked that impulse and just gripped the hoe handle tighter. That she did nothing troubled her, but she had reason for it. Several years before, they had crossed a watershed between them and had slowly drifted in different directions. At first, it was like a shift in the wind that went almost unnoticed. Then it became larger and a strangeness gradually settled in. She was not his wife and knew that she never would be, at least as long as his mother was alive. For the two of them, no one would purify the wedding ground for seven days, and they would not exchange the ham and corn as symbols of marital duties. The villagers would not cover them with the ceremonial blanket. So, she was what to him? His stopover in Quallatown? His cook? His bedmate? The one who kept the fire burning in the lodge that they shared when he was not sleeping at his mother's house or riding off to one of those great cities that he described? Yes, she was all these things, and the mother of his only daughter and also of the child to be. But she was not his wife—a wife would have run to her mate who was in trouble—so she stood where she was.

Years before, Kanaka and Will had come of age together and sung the Cherokee songs around the community fire as he slowly learned them from Drowning Bear. Maybe she was a little older than him, maybe younger; she was not sure. From across the fire, they made secret eye contact. She had watched with pride as he changed from a boy of little strength to a man who spoke his mind, a man who read the books that White men wrote. He became a man who could adapt his White-ness so that he could do most of the things that the other men of the village could do. He could hunt and, after some years of practice, was passably good with a bow. He could tell

his own stories. He could track the wild bees and find their honey. He could look at the evening clouds and know the weather the next day. And he was around so much that the people of the village forgot that he was White. But most of all, he could listen. Will was especially good at listening, as though he could soak up the feelings of whomever spoke to him. On those nights around the fire, he listened to the tales spun by Drowning Bear, of hunts and winters and games and wounds and battles. He learned of the old wars with the British. When one was done talking to Will Thomas, you were left with the sense that he knew your heart as well as you did yourself.

Perhaps, this was the reason for the extraordinary bond between Will and Drowning Bear. The old man, whose broad face sagged with age, took the boy in, recognizing that something was misplaced inside him. When Will had first come to the village, the people looked at him as though he were a stray puppy of some unknown breed, but one that needed feeding. And so they fed him, especially Drowning Bear. And like any other hungry puppy, he stayed and grew. But the union between the two was far from one sided. Drowning Bear benefited greatly from Will's presence, particularly in those moments when he was foolish and gambled with the respect that his people accorded him. The problem was, Drowning Bear liked whiskey. When he got his hands on it, he drank until it was gone or he was in a stupor. In those times, both of his wives and all of his children avoided him. The man they knew to be thoughtful became angry, profane, then morose. On afternoons when he staggered home, tripping over rocks and roots, his family quietly drifted out of the lodge to those of his neighbors, or else escaped into the forest. People were known to be hurt when Drowning Bear was drunk.

In these times, Drowning Bear would have been alone except for Will Thomas. Will sensed his sadness. There was trouble coming for the Principal People, trouble of a magnitude that they had never experienced and for which they had no remedy. Drowning Bear sensed that they were being pushed into a corner from which there might be no escape. The feeling left him angry and impotent. It is one thing to be big and imposing and fleet of foot and to be able to pull back a bow that no other man in the village could bend. But it is quite another thing, when asked by people who hungered for answers about their future, to be able to give them nothing. So, Will would build a fire and listen as frustration and fear tumbled out of the big man. What Drowning Bear knew was that the village, and in a greater sense the whole Cherokee Nation, was adrift in an angry sea. What he did not know was how and where the tribe would find shelter. On one hand, there was hope in the form of the young leadership in New Echota that was making great strides toward making the tribe appear to be good neighbors with the surrounding White nation. On the other hand, there was the growing pressure from the Whites, and in Drowning Bear's memory, the Whites always won a contest between themselves and the Cherokees.

Not all the episodes with Drowning Bear and whiskey were fearful. By the time Will was grown, Kanaka would come to the door of Drowning Bear's lodge and peer in at the two of them. Even drunk, Drowning Bear would invariably be seated in a stiff chair by the fire; Will would be sitting on the dirt floor, not far away. On his lap would be sheets of paper, and he read them aloud to Drowning Bear who would alternately grunt or spit into the fire. The papers were filled with strange words that even White men did not ordinarily use, and beside Will lay another book that he looked into when he came to a word that he did not know. He read deliberately. By instinct, she knew that the words were important to the Principal People, particularly to her own clan in Quallatown. The paper was a thing called a "treaty;" a few years before, it changed the lives of the people here, separating them from the six other clans that were still part of the nation to the west of them, down the Tuckasegee and Nantahala and beyond. Here in Quallatown, people could own their own land, as White people did, and even a few Whites, such as Will's mother and Jonas Jenkins, lived among them as land was sold off for a horse or a plow team.

Kanaka sat still in the doorway as Will read. Secrets lay in the talking leaves. At that time, the people of the nation were worried. It was said that they might have to move to some place in the West, some place that was nothing like it was in the mountains. Gold had been discovered on Cherokee land in Georgia, and stories made their way to Quallatown of raids by renegade Whites who wanted the land of the nation. A few of the Principal People were ambushed, stock was stolen. The great general who had beaten the Creeks a generation before was said to be plotting against them. He was the President now, and he did not like the Cherokee. He had written a law that would make them all go west—including the Choctaws, Creeks, Seminoles, and other tribes. Then the Whites who were left could have the land.

The Will Thomas who sat reading methodically to Drowning Bear was not the adopted Cherokee who Kanaka knew. As his fingers ran over the pages, he was a White man—not an excitable boy. This person was strange, distant, calculating. His voice was calm, although she believed that inside he was in turmoil. The calm was intended as a potion for Drowning Bear. Will read the pages over and over. Many nights she found him there, seated on the dirt floor or on a piece of firewood. But she would never forget the words that came from him one night: ". . . it means that we don't have to go," he whispered. Although he said *we*, the words were those of a White man to an Indian.

Drowning Bear had breathed deeply. "We may not be part of the nation anymore, but when they come for them, they will come for us." This was spoken Cherokee to Cherokee.

So clear it was, her memory. Will pointed to a spot on the paper. "Not if we emphasize the 'citizen' part of the treaty. That is the key. If we are citizens of North Carolina, they cannot make us go to Oklahoma any more than they could make other citizens, White or Cherokee. The others in the nation are not citizens. This treaty gives us a way out. We just have to remind the State of North Carolina of its own treaty with the Cherokees."

The old man thought for a long time, but it was impossible to tell what was on his mind because his face remained expressionless. Will did not interrupt. At last the old man sighed. "Then we must become more like *them.*"

As Kanaka reflected on it, this had been a pivotal moment for the village. Many things changed, great and small. Most startlingly, Drowning Bear stopped drinking the whiskey that fouled his wisdom, and his wives stopped being afraid of him. For the first time, White missionaries were welcomed into the village, to preach and convert the people to the White religion. Some of the people began to follow it, and there was much less drinking and the bad behavior that went with it. Although nothing was said of Drowning Bear's two wives, men now followed the Christian way and no longer married more than one woman. Community farms were abandoned for individual gardens. Less and less, the men wore the skins of animals that they killed. And although the old stories continued to be told and the people held all the old superstitions, there was a separateness about them. In private, they still burned fires to chase away the witches that would make mischief with the dead; in public they spoke of the Bible and of being saved and of baptism.

Kanaka, herself, did not hold to these changes, even though it was her man, Will Thomas, who was mostly responsible for bringing them to the village. It became part of a growing distance between them. Will had come to the village as a lost White boy and the village had taken him in and made him Cherokee. Now it seemed that he was making the village White. It was too strange for Kanaka. She could not make the conversion and did not want to anyway. Not that all of it was bad. The idea that the men could help out with the field work was not a bad thing. And she liked the sobriety. In the past, women and children had been hurt by husbands in a drunken rage. But most of what the Christian preachers had to say made no sense to her. Who was the White God to whom they prayed and how could a god forgive sins when it was the person who had been wronged who had to do the forgiving? If a man lay with a woman who was not his wife or he stole a thing from another man, was this not something that must be atoned for within the village? Was that not why they had the Green Corn Festival? To her, sin was a thing that spilled out of the mouths of the ministers and spread a plague of discontent among the people. She knew people to be, at their core, not bad. Envy, hatred, greed, and lust were things that one stumbled over like roots across a path. They were not part of birth. A person could be caught up by an evil spirit and driven to act like the dogs that went crazy in the summer. But the dog was not born with the craziness. The preachers taught that darkness was born in the people, that it was like water held in the palm of one's hand and could seep out at any time and make them do bad things.

Kanaka did not believe this. To do so would mean that there was no end to the evil that could find its way out and harm the village. How could people forgive a thing that had no end, and flowed from each of them like the trickle from a poisoned spring? It made no sense.

The child inside her stirred and she was overcome with a sense of protectiveness. The first of Will's children spent more and more time in the house of her White grandmother. She had even been given a Christian name—Demarius Angeline—and that was what people were calling her. It was a great loss to Kanaka, but one that she had allowed to happen. She vowed that it would not happen with the second child. The one that moved within her now would be Cherokee.

T he only sound in the darkness was that of Euchella's paddle making swirls through the water. The moon that had risen earlier was now obscured, and the canoe seemed to be floating, not on the surface of the water, but lifted above it in the humid black air. He stroked steadily for hours, guided only by the edge of the canopy of trees that hung over the river. Where they arched over the water, limbs brushed the side of the canoe, and although traveling blind in the darkness, Euchella used this to follow the turns of the river. It was possible that he could hit an unseen snag, but he was not moving so fast as to tip over.

Far behind, the two men whom he had ambushed were either stirring awake or they would never awaken. Their condition mattered little to him one way or another. Clubbing them gave him no satisfaction; they were simply thieves who had to be stopped. But judging by the sound that came from the smaller man's head, Euchella doubted that he would rise again. That would leave only the big man to come looking for their boat. Perhaps it would have been better to have slit his throat while he lay unconscious.

Far off in the distance, a light winked faintly above the river. Euchella lifted the paddle and drifted. He could hear nothing. As he moved downstream, the light flickered, gradually growing brighter. Occasional low noises could be heard now, voices of men, several men. Reflexively, Euchella edged the canoe under the canopy even though the light was not bright enough to give him away. The slow current eased the canoe forward and in time the light revealed a primitive camp, not much better than what the Luftys had built in the Balsam Mountains when they were on the run. It rested on a flat stretch of bottomland, about 30 feet above the water. There was a lean-to, covered by canvas, surrounded on two sides by a tumble of crates. Down on the river, three of the large flat boats were tied to a snag. Some number of men sat inside the shelter, voices loud now. From the sound of them, they had obviously been drinking whiskey for a long time. Closer now, Euchella could make out three or four different voices.

"Don't . . . much like the cards you're dealin'."

"You playin' or complainin'?"

The argument went on with no purpose. They variously cursed, grunted, whistled, and clapped at times that meant nothing to him. But it was clear that they were very drunk.

The simple thing to do at this point was to paddle on down the river, out of sight. By daylight, these men would be sleeping for a long time and he would be miles away, unnoticed. But Euchella was drawn to find out what they were about and why they were here. Drunk as they were, that might not be too risky.

What breeze there was drifted from the southwest, so he paddled quietly to a point upstream of where the flatboats were tied. This put him downwind of the men, and if they had dogs in the camp, the dogs would not get his scent. Pulling himself up on a tree trunk, he beached the canoe in the darkness and left his hat in the bottom of it. The voices were very loud now, alternately angry and victorious. Lying flat against the bank, Euchella dug his fingers into the soft silt and inched his way upward without a sound. At the top of the bank, he stopped and looked into the lean-to. Four White men were seated around a crate that served as a table, playing cards. Two were young, probably no more than twenty. The other two were older, judging by the gray in their beards. One was very fat and seemed to be in charge because he dealt the cards and directed the conversation. The others clearly did not like the results. On one side, two other men lay on the ground, asleep.

As the quarreling went on, Euchella scanned the rest of the camp. The crates were printed with words that he could not read, but he took it to mean that these men were traders, supplying other traders like Will Thomas with cloth, whiskey, black powder, and nails. This place was an intermediate stop for them, between river settlements. Now he understood the purpose of the flatboats; one could carry many crates on them.

Satisfied, he was about to slide back down the bank when movement to one side of the lean-to caught his attention. From where he lay, the light was too dim to make out what moved, so he backed down below the edge of the bank and slid carefully to his right. When he had shifted about twenty feet, he rose back up to peer over the edge. There, lying on the ground, were a man and a woman. Their faces were the color of the boy whom he had freed earlier. Ropes around their wrists told him that they were tied to something. More slaves. Not only did the men in the lean-to deal in cloth and metal, they dealt in people, too. Perhaps, they were waiting for the two up river.

These two on the ground must have seen his head rise above the bank, and now their eyes met. They were frightened the way the boy on the boat had been frightened. In their place, Euchella figured that he would be, too; he must look like some devil in the dark.

He weighed his options. He could wait until the men in the tent fell into a stupor as they surely would, then set these two free, maybe put them on a flatboat as he had the boy. Or he could leave now. This was not his struggle and he had other business to attend in the West. Why risk it for people whose circumstance he did not understand? In the end, he could not say why, but he decided to wait, so he slid back down the bank a little and dug his fingers into the dirt.

The quarreling voices above ebbed and flowed as money changed hands. But as the night passed, they became more slurred. Once, one of the younger men staggered over to the edge of the bank, not twenty feet from where Euchella was dug in, and vomited loudly. That seemed to put an end to the game. In another half-hour, the camp was filled with a chorus of snoring.

Euchella lifted himself back up to the edge of the bank. The lantern hanging inside the shelter had been left lit and the yellow light revealed the men lying in no order, sleeping. He thanked the whiskey for that. Slowly he raised himself and walked in a crouch to where the two slaves lay tied. Terrified, they whimpered and retreated as far as their rope would allow. Euchella raised a hand to still them, but their breathing came in gasps and he was afraid that one of the boatmen would awaken. The woman, particularly, was panicky and trembled as Euchella came near. He waited a moment for her to calm, then took the rope that held them and cut it free. But instead of being reassured, they backed up farther. Euchella squatted near and held his wrists together as if they were tied. Then with his right hand, he made a cutting motion along the left wrist. The man seemed to catch on and offered his tied hands to be freed which Euchella did as quietly as possible. With a little urging, the woman allowed hers to be cut, too.

Deliberately putting his knife away and rising to a crouch, he motioned for them to follow him. The three reached the bank and slowly slid down toward the water. Light from the lantern was just bright enough to illuminate the outline of the flatboats. Euchella indicated that they should get aboard the boat that was farthermost downstream, and when they did, he cut it loose. As it drifted silently away from the bank, they waited for him to come aboard. Only when he remained behind did they realize that they were free. The man found a pole and began to push into the darkness.

Euchella did not wait long. He cut the other boats loose and pushed them from shore with his foot. In the morning, the men up on the bank would want to find the one lost boat; setting the others adrift would slow them down some, how much depended on how far they drifted. For a moment, he almost laughed at the thought of these hungover men stumbling to the edge of the bank and finding their boats gone. He wished that he could stay around for that. But it was time to go. The last thing that he wanted was to have one of these men come awake and spot him. The canoe was where he left it, and he slid it into the river with barely a splash.

As they drifted away from the camp and what little light there was faded behind them, Euchella wondered if he had helped these people—or the young one who was still behind them. Now they were runaways. Would they survive in a strange land that wanted only to work them like mules? Worse, if they were caught on the stolen flatboats, they would be held responsible for the theft, and punishment at the hands of the men in the camp would be grim. He had seen faces like theirs before, on the militiamen who served with the army last year.

What Euchella could not answer was why he helped them escape. They were not his people—they were not even Creeks or Choctaws. They were strange in a way that even a shaman could not have envisioned, with hair that stood out from their heads and skin the color of river bottom. How they came to this land and where they came from he could not imagine. There was nothing in Cherokee lore that described them or foretold their coming. Perhaps it was their fear that had touched him, particularly that of the woman. Had she reminded him of his wife? Did he want to give her one more chance?

All in all, it had been a foolish risk. He vowed not to do it again.

The next morning when dawn broke over his shoulder, Euchella saw an extraordinary sight. A gently rolling plain lay on his left, occupied with the huge farms and fields that had become common along the river. On the other shore rose a line of low mountains that faced the river with rocky flanks and stark cliffs, similar to the mountains that he had seen south of Chattanooga. What was strange was that, instead of taking the easy course along the plane, the river made a right turn through a deep gorge in the mountains. As he drew closer, the current picked up and for the first time in days there were riffles around rocks and snags along the bank.

This was the turn north for the river that Jonas Jenkins had described. In a day or two, he would be back in the land that the Whites had named for the river, Tennessee. Beyond that would be the great muddy river that flowed west, the Ohio. Then he would find the biggest river of all, going south. So said Jonas Jenkins. And it was somewhere on the westerly shore of that great river that the Cherokee Nation had set off walking for Oklahoma last year.

All that was ahead of him. Now Euchella needed to rest, to eat, to sleep, to let the skins of the little canoe dry out and tighten in the sun. This was a good place to do it. On the sunny side of the river grew head-high thickets of river cane where he could hide the canoe and still have it exposed to the sun. In the rocky bluffs above, there were dark places where water seeped through the rock strata and fell far down to the river's edge. This place was a little like the gorge on the Nantahala River where Tsali had lived, only wider and more open; there might be a cave up there where he could sleep and—with a little luck—even have a fire.

The morning air was thick. As the sun rose, it would become hard to breathe again. Driving the canoe onto the bank, Euchella got out and removed the rifle, his bedroll, and the rabbit that he had caught the night before. Lifting the canoe overhead, he could feel the added weight of the soaked skins. He would stay here for a couple of days and let it dry, if there was no rain. That would give him time to find or build a shelter, to hunt, to sleep, to restore his spirit. Edging through the dense cane, he reached the middle of the thicket and put the canoe down, bottom side up. Shrouded by the thick growth, it was visible only from above, on the high ridge at the top of the gorge. Satisfied, Euchella retreated the way he had come in, pushing the stalks of the thicket upright to hide his trail. A good tracker could find it, but only if he were standing nearby. From a distance, it was not noticeable.

At the base of the bluff grew a stand of stubby pines. He notched the trunks of six of them so that they would seep the sticky sap that would seal the seams of the canoe. In a day or two when the skins were dry, there would be enough.

Leaving his provisions behind, he slung his bow over his shoulder and began to scale the bluff. The climb was steep but not difficult as he pulled himself up on tenacious saplings that grew out of the rocks. The branches hid him from the river and the plane beyond. Half way to the top, he halted on a ledge of rock and scanned the area. Off to the south, fields under cultivation ran as far as he could see. At the edge of the horizon, three plumes of smoke rose from morning cook fires. Seeing them reminded him to set his snare for another rabbit. The opposite side of the gorge was as steep as the one he was climbing, perhaps even steeper. His eye followed the ledge to his right, to a steady trickle of water that left a sulfurous stain on the face of the bluff. That stream would be worth looking into later, after he scaled the top.

Euchella continued to pull himself upward and the higher he climbed the more he could see to the south. Several of the large homes of White farmers came into view and were the source of the cook fires. Except for three crows passing overhead, there was no sign of any other life, nor was there movement of anything on the river.

When he finally reached the top and looked over, another low mountain ridge ran parallel to the one he was on, like a hogs back. A shadowed valley lay in between. Wind scented with the smell of summer stroked his face. For a long time, he sat still, long enough for the woodland creatures to ignore him. Below, there was no one, no village, no cabin, no muddy road. It made sense. With the river at hand, there would be no reason to live where it was hard to farm, and everyone passing here would pass through the gorge to some place that was easier to work.

Without disturbing anything, Euchella eased back down the bluff until he reached the ledge. Shuttling his feet and holding onto saplings, he inched his way toward the little stream. Where water ran over it, the stone slab was slippery with algae. To secure his footing, Euchella scratched a handful of shale from the bank and tossed it onto the ledge. Then, as he moved across the stream and looked down, he could see thread-like lines of stone hanging from the lip of the ledge. This was a peculiarity that he had never seen in the mountains around Soco Creek.

Beyond the stream was a slot in the side of the bluff where a large boulder had spalled out. The hole left behind was wide enough for him to crawl into, but Euchella hesitated. It was black in there and he had no way of knowing if something possessing better eyes than his own—and claws—already occupied the space. Just as he was about to back away from the hole, a puff of air touched his face, air smelling of the damp inside of the earth. It was a cave, he realized, not just a cavity between the rock shelves.

Euchella stood up and climbed down to the base. He found a clump of broom sage and cut a handful and folded it over a dry stick and bound it by weaving loose strands around the shank. At the pine trees that he had notched earlier, he smeared droplets of rosin into the torch until it was saturated. Then he sprinkled a few grains of gunpowder into a handful of dry grass. Striking together two flints that he had carried since his winter back in the Snowbird Mountains, he ignited the powder and grass.

When the torch burned steadily, he climbed quickly back up to the ledge and shuffled over to the opening in the rock. Holding the flame ahead of him, Euchella inched his way into the darkness. The farther he crawled into the cave, the more room there was to move. There were no signs of owls or bats, but something had swept along the ground, leaving scuff marks in the dirt. If it were animal or man, he could not tell, except there were no footprints of any sort. About twenty feet into the cave, there was enough room to rise, stooped over. Slowly, he swung the torch around.

Over time uncountable, the little stream had hollowed out an opening about the size of a sleeping lodge in the gray stone. Euchella could see where it now seeped out of the mountain and ran along one wall of the cavern. Strange pointed shapes hung from the ceiling. Others rose to meet them from the floor, like dripping wax that had hardened. All together they cast teeth-like shadows in the light of his torch. A chill swept through him as though he had blundered into the sacred ground of a long-ago god, or perhaps a cavern of witches. The torch trembled in his hand. What had made this place? He touched one of the points that hung from the ceiling. It was stone, hard and cold, with a surface that was smoothly marbled. No hand or blade of man could make a thing like this. Surely this was a place of a *Muskogee* god. It would be good for him to leave before a sickness that lurked in the damp air invaded his body.

As he turned to go, the light fell on a red clay pot with an opening about the width of two hands together. Kneeling to examine it, Euchella could see intricate, detailed shapes cut into the sides of the pot, ornamental images and signs that were unknown to him. Certainly they were not Cherokee markings. He traced the figures with his fingers—feeling the intricacy of the glyphs—hoping that doing so would somehow explain their meaning. It was said that the *Muskogee* made very fine cooking pots and that the Cherokees in Georgia often traded for them. Dust filled the bottom of this one. If it was made or used by *Muskogees*, it had gone untouched for a long, long time.

The *Muskogees* had been gone from the region for almost a generation, and only their mounds back near Etowah remained. *Muskogee*. If the *Muskogees*—or those who came before them from the west—had used this cave, then it was neither sacred ground nor a den for witches. Beside the pot lay a few bones, rabbit as best he could tell. They had eaten in here. Sweeping back the dust at his feet, he found ashes. Yes, he nodded, the *Muskogee*. It would be safe to stay here. Besides, it was much cooler here than outside, and if he built a fire, no animal would dare enter.

Euchella spent three nights in the cave. He laid his bedroll next to the wall farthest from the stream, and using the torch, started a small fire, enough to sustain the light, and discovered that if he kept it low, then the smoke would disappear though fissures in the walls. The rest of the morning was spent carrying sticks up the side of the bluff and cooking the bare carcass of the rabbit. In the afternoon, he lay in the mouth of the cave, watching the river. A flatboat passed, men poling methodically against the current. They were talking, but were too far away for him to understand what they said. There was no sign of those whom he had freed, but these men going upstream would soon meet any coming down. He hoped that the slaves were wise enough to hide.

Chapter 9
Quallatown
June, 1839

Deep in her belly, Kanaka felt her baby give a mighty kick. It was the first time that she had felt it in a week. Her time was near, very near, but her face betrayed no pain to Will Thomas who sat across the cabin, waiting for a bowl of stew. Since he got word of Euchella's journey to the West, Will had been in what she called his "White" mood—White, because it was not a state of mind that was common to the Cherokees. He alternated between being openly hostile—he had kicked his horse in the head when it stumbled and brushed him against a tree—and distant. In these times, she avoided speaking to him, never knowing what would come back in return. The baby seemed to provoke a special distress. Will acted like a man whose life was coming unraveled, not one who was about to become a father again.

Smelling the stew cooking, her dog entered the open door, but spying Thomas, it lowered its head and edged toward the far side of the cabin as though a stranger of uncertain temper were visiting. Will did not seem to notice but Kanaka did. She picked up the raw neck of the chicken, the body of which had gone into the pot, and flung it out the door. The dog loped after it. Born with a wild suspicion that was easily alerted, dogs sensed things before people did. A hard look or an impatient step will send one crouching. This one was happy to have a reason to go outside.

Kanaka made no attempt to talk to Will about why Euchella had gone west because she did not know why. But she would find out. Today, she would walk to the camp of the Luftys and speak to his brother. Will, of course, had failed to ask the question when he was there. He was just angry . . . or something else that looked like anger.

When he was fed, Will left to ride to his trading post on Soco Creek. Kanaka swung the pot that hung on a hinged rod away from the fire so that the remaining stew would not boil dry and scorch. Then, she washed her hands and set off up the Oconaluftee. The camp was not far, but she could not move quickly with the extra weight of the child, causing her to swing her feet from side to side as she walked. In one way, she was glad to go slowly; the air was humid and walking slowly was more comfortable.

From the right, the river called to her as though it knew a secret about her. This feeling was not unique. Others of the tribe gazed at the river hypnotically with a combination of wonder and understanding, and it sang to them in a whispered voice, of a journey that never ended, of births and battles, and of things that had been and things to come. With an almost sexual pleasure, she paused and rested her hand on the baby with the hope that the feeling that was now in her heart would be conveyed to the child. Only the river brought this experience . . . not the rising sun and not the wind at the top of the mountain. It was the voice of her grandmother, her mother, her father, Drowning Bear, and all the others who had gone before. One day, it would be her voice, too, and the child would walk along the river and they could speak the words to each other that only a heart can hear.

When Kanaka finally reached the settlement of the Luftys, she looked for Wachacha and found him using an axe to notch a log behind one of the cabins that they were building. There was no need for her to announce her approach because no one would see a woman so advanced in pregnancy as threatening.

He stopped working. "You are not long now," he said in a kindly voice.

"Soon," she replied. "It goes well."

"And the father? He goes well, too?"

"Are you a shaman? Even my dog is afraid of him these days."

Wachacha tested the edge of his axe with his thumb. "When he left here the other day, he did not look happy. I think that he is not pleased with my brother."

"Why did your brother go west?"

Wachacha began to draw a sharpening stone over the blade slowly. As he did, he told her the story of the spider and the web and the revelation that Euchella had experienced beside the burial mound at *Kituwah.* She understood the meaning instinctively. "We must rebuild our web," he said simply. "Euchella went to the West to tell the others of this."

"But Will Thomas has said that the Cherokee must become . . . citizens." She found it difficult to say the words.

"The Cherokees were Cherokee before there were any 'citizens.'"

"Must we not change?" She was careful to keep any hint of argument from her voice.

"Why? All over this land, spiders are spiders, fish are fish, and birds are birds. They did not change just because other men with strange ways moved into the land. We must remember that we are the Principal People." He pointed to her extended belly. "Your child should know this, too."

Kanaka took this for a rebuke as her oldest child now lived in the house of her White grandmother, Temperance Thomas. "He—or she—will."

Wachacha did not apologize because he had said what he thought. What she felt about what he said was up to her. That was the way of the Principal

People. "At first, I tried to talk my brother out of going to the West. But then he told me why he had to go and I knew that it was the right thing to do. If he is caught, he may not be allowed to return. I do not know how it is there. There may be soldiers there that make him stay. We will know if he returns. But he left me the story of the spider and told me to build him a house and plant him a garden, so I believe that he will return."

Kanaka turned to go, having learned more than she thought that she might. Then she paused at the corner of the cabin. "And what of the citizen way?"

"It is one way. Many will go that way. Perhaps, most will. But not my brother. Not me. I cannot speak for the others. They are free to do as they wish."

As Kanaka made her way back down the river, she came to the bend where she had paused earlier. The thick trunk of a sycamore hung over the stream, and she could taste the water in a faint breeze that swirled above it. The voice of the river whispered again, and she felt a great peace as if the anticipation, horror, and panic of the last three years were lifted. She breathed in the damp air. The baby was still as though it heard the voice, too.

Within sight of her cabin, she felt it, a pain so strong and unexpected that it caused her to stumble on the path. For a first contraction, it was severe. The baby had suddenly become lively. She bit her lip and began to hurry. Reaching the dark interior of her cabin, she collected a bone knife and a small blanket of rabbit skins that she had sewed together just for this occasion. The afternoon light was soft as, unnoticed, she climbed the mountain behind the village. She stopped once to lean against the rough bark of an oak as the pain came again, harder than the first, hard enough to take her breath away. The hill was steep, and weakened as she was, the going was slow and she pulled herself up by low branches. When the brow of the hill was in sight, her face was damp with the effort of climbing. She rested again until another pain tore through her lower belly and she gasped. Move on, she grunted aloud.

At the top, the roundness of the mountain became a dome and she passed into a pine thicket where the bed of needles was so thick that she walked with only the sound of her own breathing. Not much farther now, just beyond the thicket was a small clearing. She could see where the sunlight made a circle on a deep bed of moss that grew between two oaks.

Months before, Kanaka had picked out this spot, preparing a small depression in the moss where she could place the blanket of soft skins that would receive the child. She had planned this moment carefully, telling no one. There was a birthing lodge in the village and she had used it for her first child, but because the baby she carried would be hers to raise, she felt set apart from the other women in the village. So, the choice of childbirth was hers. She would do it the way ancient Cherokee women had done it, going off like a wolf or a cat to find a quiet, safe nest. This had been on her mind since she first knew for certain that she was pregnant. Will would not approve and he would fume and rant, but it was not his choice to make.

As she pushed through the last of the pine thicket, she became aware that her legs and feet were damp with more than sweat. It would come soon now, the real work would come soon. Settling onto the moss, she padded the skins into the hole that she had made earlier, then she rested, waiting for what came next.

The wait was not long. A suffocating compression filled her abdomen and she placed the handle of the knife in her mouth and bit down. The pain spiraled higher, past being able to stand, and a great grunting sound filled the silent woods. Desperately, she rose to a squat over the hole and hiked up her skirt. The pain was going to kill her. She had to push the child out, ready or not. Steadying herself on a small maple, she pushed back against the crushing pain. Now there was a new pain, sharp, tearing. Fluid poured from her. She did not look down to see if it was blood or water. More. Again. The pain rose higher. Desperately, she pushed back against it, screaming against the knife handle, against the ripping of her flesh, against the crushing agony, until she felt the head of the baby emerge from her. A gasping breath. One more push. Kanaka pressed down as though her upper body was trying to shove away the lower part, grunting, shrieking, with all her energy. And then, by a miracle, the baby was out, lying in the skins, moving slightly, coughing, crying.

Kanaka lay back on the moss, panting. Her body felt trampled, torn, and very weak.

In the days that followed, a Naming Ceremony was held for the child. Kanaka asked an elderly friend of her mother, a woman who had obtained status as a Beloved Woman of the village and was revered for her weaving, to name the child. It must be a name that would be significant to the child later in its life. The ceremony, itself, was in the ancient tradition of the Cherokees, and was performed by the only surviving shaman. He waved the child over a fire in the middle of the village and intoned a blessing. Then on the fourth day of its life, the shaman purified the baby by dipping it into the Oconaluftee and commended it to the Creator of them all.

Kanaka stood slightly apart from the others, immersed in her own thoughts. This river, that seemed both young and old, had washed all the children of the village, except Will Thomas. And now it washed another, but would this one be the last? Will, who stood nearby and wore a faintly dour expression, was taking the village in a direction away from these traditions. So, perhaps the children of the future would have a Christian baptism. Kanaka sighed.

When the child was lifted from the water, it was handed, dripping and screaming, to the Beloved Woman who cradled it in a fresh blanket. As the child's cries subsided, she bent her head. "Your name shall be Tayanita because you will seek beauty all your days, and you will have the strength to carry on when others discourage you." With this, she handed Kanaka her new daughter.

Chapter 10
Ohio River
June, 1839

uchella lay on a hill overlooking the confluence of the two rivers, never imagining that there could be so much water in all the world. In a journey filled from one moment to the next with amazement, this was the most amazing thing that he had seen. The Tennessee, itself swelled by hundreds of miles of drainage, now emptied into the wide, sluggish flow from the northeast. This must be the Ohio that Jonas Jenkins had described. In the moonlight, the water seemed not to move. How could there be a river that did not flow? Perhaps it was just a trick of the moonlight.

There were many signs of White people here, far more than in the passes, sweeps, and bends of the Tennessee. Along the low shoreline, lights from settlements twinkled. This was not good. From now on, as long as he was on the river, he would travel at night and sleep in the day as best he could. If he were challenged on the water in daylight, there might be no way to escape without a killing.

Rising from his lookout, Euchella made his way back through the tangle of brush to where he had beached the canoe, then shoved off. The water here smelled even worse than the Tennessee, stale and muddy, and he would be glad to be off it. Far over on the other side, a dog barked. Yes, there were too many people here. He dug the paddle in and stroked determinedly along the near shore that was well marked by the occasional lamp from a farmhouse or fish camp. This was hard work, but as the hours passed he was able to cover many miles over the water.

As dawn gave color to the sky, he crossed the wide river and eased the canoe into the mouth of a small stream that cut a winding trench through a marsh. Grass and cattails grew well above his head, and there were small trails made through the growth by muskrats, raccoons, and opossums. There was little movement of the water here either, and the mud of the bank had a heavy, fetid odor. Euchella eased the canoe forward until he came to a clump of willow that promised solid ground. Slipping beneath low limbs, he shook them to make sure that there were no snakes lying in wait. When the canoe was secure, he set to cutting enough of the thick grass for a bed. That would be better than his bedroll which was now damp from seepage in the canoe. It would dry some before he had to push on. However, there would be no fire here as any smoke would be visible for miles around. He would have to sleep hungry, but at least he would sleep dry.

As he lay back and covered his face with the hat to block out the sunlight, Euchella was exhausted. Very soon he fell into a deep, dreamless sleep on the padding and slept until the afternoon when something blunt poked him in the ribs. Removing the hat, he came face-to-muzzle with a rifle. It was so close that he could smell the residue of burnt powder. Holding the rifle was a small man who might be as much at home slithering through the grasses as a muskrat. Although very young, there was a fierceness about him of the sort that is common to men who have few options and are willing to do whatever is necessary to survive. His eyes and hands were steady. Easing to a sitting position, Euchella considered what to do, but with the rifle now pointed directly at his chest, remaining still was the only choice.

Under his own hat, the face of the small man tightened as though he expected the other to do—or at least say—something, but when Euchella remained quiet, he was perplexed. "Ain't seen you before," he said abruptly. Euchella did not reply, and this only increased the other's confusion. He scanned Euchella's body carefully, but never breaking eye contact for more than an instant. "What you doin' here?"

"Sleeping," was all the Cherokee said.

"I knowed you were sleeping. I want to know what you are doin' here," he said sharply, with a nod of the rifle.

"Traveling."

"I looked over your canoe. You ain't no trapper. If you'd been a trapper, I might 'a shot you where you lay. This is my marsh and everybody in these parts knows that. I don't hold with no poachin'."

"I'm going west."

"What tribe you be?"

"Cherokee."

"I knowed it. You are lucky," said the small man, lowering the rifle for some reason. "Why west? I thought all you people went that way last year."

"Not all. A few were left behind."

The wiry little man kept on hand on his rifle as he now squatted at a safe distance. "Why are you tryin' to catch up? What I hear is that the other bunch didn't exactly go willingly."

Euchella studied the trapper. Because he was young, his body sat comfortably in a position that an older man could not maintain for long. But he could think of no words to make this man understand why he was following the rest of the tribe. "I bring them news of those left behind."

The trapper looked at him skeptically. "That must be some powerful news. You'll be traveling 'bout a thousand miles before you are done."

Euchella shrugged. "A little goes by each day. I have come this far since the first sprouts of corn began to show."

Standing up abruptly, the trapper seemed to have made up his mind that the Indian meant no harm. "You best be careful. People around here don't much like Injuns. Best I can do is feed you and send you on your way." With no further word, he set off through the marsh, leading Euchella along a trail of mostly solid ground, dipping under limbs without breaking stride. They walked parallel to the marsh creek until they came to a rise where a lean-to stood. Although crudely built with an open front, the place had the look of permanence. Skins of many animals—beaver, raccoon, bobcat, and muskrat—were tacked around the outside of the shelter, drying. In front, a fire smoldered beneath a large iron pot. Euchella could smell the scent of beans cooking with wild onions and the meat of whatever animal the trapper had last skinned. When he spooned out bowls for each of them, they sat back from the fire and ate in silence, the Indian way, with fingers.

Euchella was hungry. It had been two days since he had eaten meat, and that had been far down on the Tennessee River when he stopped long enough to put an arrow through a squirrel and cook it on the spot. To his body, this stew was splendid, and he did not change his mind when the trapper told him that it included opossum and a large water snake. He wiped the bowl appreciatively.

"Were you here when my people were brought through?" Euchella wondered aloud.

"Was last fall, getting' on towards winter. That was the bunch that I saw . . . on flat boats, they was."

"Where did they make land?"

"Up the Mississip, up by Cape Gerardo, a few days paddle from here."

The two men talked the afternoon to an end, Euchella describing the old land of the Cherokee Nation, and how he and the other Lufty Cherokees had moved around to avoid capture by the army. But he left out the part about Tsali. In turn, the trapper—whose name was Willy—told him that his people had come from Arkansas. "I live here now. Don't nobody bother me, but that's because nobody wants this place. It's a swamp and the river sometimes floods to right were we are sittin'. I get by on trappin', but there's barely enough for me. I couldn't keep a woman, not that one of them from around here would have me. Last winter—just after your people came through—it got cold. Worst I ever saw. I had to rig a cover for the front of my lean-to. Was too cold to get out much. It caught me unprepared. I can stand anything if I'm prepared for it. But I wasn't ready for this. Even had to eat my dog. That was the worst of it."

Euchella understood. "When the soldiers were chasing us, we lived on squirrels mostly. A squirrel that is roasted over a fire is like eating an old moccasin."

"Tastes about the same," Willy said with a grin.

As the day drew to a close, Euchella had a last question: "I'm a stranger, yet you have not treated me as one. Why is that?"

"It was your clothes. I knowed them to be Cherokee. My grandmother was Cherokee, brought to Arkansas by my grandfather. She taught me of some Cherokee ways before she died," he said with a sad nod. "She said that the Cherokees were going to be in trouble. Looks like she was right."

Euchella agreed. "It still does not look good for my people. There are those who think that we must become like the Whites."

"But you don't think so?"

He shook his head. "Then we will no longer be the Principal People."

Willy scratched himself through his buckskins. "Then you may become a trapper like me."

Euchella smiled. "If I do, I won't do it here."

The small man laughed, but soon his smile faded and he grew serious again. "I am going to give you some advice, and from what you've said you may not like it. But around here, people are jumpy about Injuns. Was just a few years ago, they were still fightin' 'em and the thought remains that the only good Injun is a dead Injun. So—if I were you, I'd cut my hair. That long hair of yours will get you spotted as an Injun a quarter of a mile away. I, myself, did it after a couple of farmers took a shot at me," he said, lifting his hat to reveal a shaved head. "My hair's as black as yours, but I ain't been shot at since."

Euchella knew that his host was telling the truth. Still, he was offended by the idea that he should become something that he was not, so he just nodded.

As the light dimmed over the marsh, Willy led Euchella back to the stand of willows where his canoe lay. "You've got another two-three days before you reach the Mississip, then another day before you get to Cape Gerardo. It will be on the west bank, just after a big turn in the river. From there, you've got a long walk—all the way through what they call the Ozark Mountains and beyond. But I reckon you will be able to pick up sign. They say a lot of people died on that march."

"A White man told me that I could follow the graves."

"'Bout right. Story that I hear was that it was rough." The small man was silent for a moment before he spoke again. "You figurin' on comin' back?"

"That is my thought."

"You are welcome to drop in. The pot is always cookin' somethin'. But take this for now," he said, handing over some dried strips of meat.

Euchella shoved off and waved goodbye. He admired this little man who had so far managed to live by himself while surrounded by people with a larger and often hostile purpose. In time, either because he exhausted what there was to trap or because he would no longer be tolerated by the farmers, Willy would have to move on. When that time came, Euchella guessed that Willy would head the same direction that he was paddling now.

Two days later, Willy's words proved to be true. So much water lay in front of Euchella that he could barely see the other side. A thin haze covered an expanse that seemed to go on endlessly. This was the great Mississippi. It was the dull green color of lichens that grew on the granite rocks along the Oconaluftee. He pulled to the near shore and found dry ground between two large maple trees that were well anchored by spreading roots. Upstream, a crow announced his presence. He sat on a log and chewed slowly at the dried meat. Willy had not told him what the meat was, but it had the taste of something that had been in the stew, opossum perhaps.

Concealed behind a low growth of brush, Euchella gazed at the river. As the sun rose, he could make out several farmhouses on the other side. The water moved slowly before him, sometimes turning in eddies along the bank. Here and there, a fish broke the surface with a splash. Turning around, he discovered more water behind him; where he sat was a narrow island. That would give cover while he slept. He pulled the canoe up on shore and turned it over to dry for the day. One more night and then it could rest for a long time, perhaps forever if he were not able to return.

As he lay back on his bedroll, Euchella thought of his brother and the other Luftys. They would have their cabins built by now, and if there were any seed to be had, gardens would be planted. If they were wise, they would build a fish trap as Tsali had done on the Nantahala. They could almost live off fish alone. Thinking of Tsali reminded him of why he began the journey in the first place. What would he find when he finally arrived at the place where the Principal People were taken? Would they be crowded into the same kind of stockades as they had been held before they were moved? How many were left alive? Where would he find the people whom he knew from the mountain clans? Would they be guarded by the army? Sleep took him before he settled any of this in his mind.

Euchella awoke at twilight, groggy, reluctant to get going on the river again. Had there been cover enough for a fire, he would have lingered for a day or two, resealing the canoe and hunting the riverbank. But there were no pines or spruce on the island to notch for sap and this place was mostly a swamp that was choked with bull rushes. It might be a poor place for hunting, too, half land, half water, not unlike the swampy place where he had shot Tsali. It was just as well that he traveled at night and slept in the day. Witches and fevers were less likely to invade his still body during the day, and this place had the look of witchery about it.

As darkness settled, he righted the canoe and set off across the river on the last part of his journey on the water. Pockets of mist drifted by as he paddled toward the opposite shore, aiming for lamplights that glowed faintly in the distance. The going was easy as a light breeze pushed small riffles against the canoe and blew away a cluster of horseflies that followed him from shore. In an hour or more, he would be on the other side. Although he was several weeks walk from the new home of the tribe, this was the beginning of the territory where they lived. The giant river was the dividing line, separating the tribe that they used to be from the tribe that they were now.

Near the midpoint in his crossing, Euchella became aware of a low, menacing sound over the water. He felt it more than heard it, like the sweep of the wings of a great bird. Stopping the paddle, he listened. There was something there, but it was a long way off. It seemed to come from down the river. Swiveling around, he could see nothing but the lights along the shore, so he pushed on. But the feeling that he was not alone on the river would not go away, and for the first time since he had left the Oconaluftee, Euchella felt an irrational fear of something that he could not explain. Surely the river was large enough to breed things that he could not imagine, serpents, crawling things. There were stories of giant lizards from Southern Georgia. Perhaps they came out only at night to feed on unsuspecting travelers. Perhaps there were witches in the river of which he had no knowledge.

The breeze turned and came from the south, bringing a hissing sound that alternated with a deep thump. He looked about, but could see nothing in the darkness except pinpoints of lamps. The sound grew slightly stronger. He looked again, and this time one of the lights seemed to move. He stared at it for several minutes until it came nearer. The thumping sent a deep tremble through the water and the hiss was like a nightmare. He felt the pulsing compressions in his rib cage as though each were trying to press the breath from him. Panic rising, he dug into the water, paddling the canoe faster toward the far shore.

High above the river, lights like glowing eyes appeared on the front of the thing and smoke spewed from two black stacks above them. This snorting, hissing beast was as big and white as the plantation homes that he passed in Tennessee, and water broke in waves as it moved. What sort of monster of the river could this be? Neither Cherokees nor *Muskogees* had any stories or pictures for anything like this. Then it was on him. Too late to escape, Euchella held his paddle ready to attack as the beast loomed closer, water churning. But it seemed to pay him no attention and instead continued on a course up the center of the river.

Euchella sat unmoving, fifty yards away as it passed, glowing and pounding. The water beneath him rose and rocked the canoe, then settled and became smooth again. He could only stare as the thing pushed by, but what he saw he could not believe. People were riding on the back of the beast, outlined by the lights as they stood at a rail near the edge. Clearly now, he could see them. There was a man with a straw hat, and beside him a woman wearing a gown, pointed toward Euchella. They appeared as surprised to see him as he was to see them. The man waved his hat and in response, Euchella numbly put up his hand in return.

For a long time, he watched the machine recede in the distance upriver, pounding and hissing as it went. Whatever it was it was a thing of the White man . . . a giant canoe of some sort, or flatboat, inside which a fire burned to make it move as it carried a whole village along the water. No Indian could have imagined such a thing. This truly had become a White man's land.

Chapter 11
Soco Creek
June, 1839

iven steady work, this was not a farm that should fail. Slopes were gentle and the soil was deep and dark, full of silt left behind by the river that ran not far away. There was ample cleared acreage for corn, cabbages, beans, onions, and squash. Below a wooded knoll stood a cabin with a good fireplace and a roof that had been freshly shingled three years before. Beyond the fields, two streams served as boundaries for the property, providing more than enough water. And with a mule to help him with chores, an industrious man could raise a family here.

But not Able Jones. He had come here a year ago for the free land, and this place was what he claimed. It had looked easy enough at the time. This land was good land, but needed tending, and needed to be adapted to the White man's ways of tilling soil. Never having any land of his own before, Able did not know how. He could do what he was told, but he was incapable of planning, and thus had waited too late to get in any crops that he could harvest. He, his wife, and one child got through the winter on what he could shoot and what handouts his neighbors were willing to spare. At the trading post, Will Thomas extended a little credit to Able, but when he spent it on things such as a brass lamp for his wife instead of a new a harness for his mule, the credit stopped. Able was not a bad man or exactly a lazy one, but he had no talent for timing or making prudent decisions, so that made him a foolish one. And like wormwood in a ship, foolish men have a way of not only bringing themselves down, but others around them, too, so people nearby—White and Cherokee—never accepted him as one of their own.

Able Jones was not completely hopeless, however. He had learned the two most important things that a newcomer to the old Cherokee Nation needed to know: Will Thomas had money and Will Thomas was buying land. So, Able and his family would leave this place better off than when they arrived. He could pay off his small debt at the trading post and go back to live with his wife's relatives in South Carolina with a little money in his pockets. He would not go back successful, but he would not go back entirely broke, either. If only he had chosen a farm where there was more bottomland and fewer rocks. Those rocks could rip apart a harness or plow faster than a man could keep it repaired. He still did not understand how the Indians who had lived here before had farmed around the rocks. Ah, well, there was nothing to do but deal with the round little man who now approached on horseback.

Will Thomas knew this day was coming the first time he spotted Able mounting the steps of his trading post. There was an uncertain look about him, and he walked like a flatlander as though he might lose his balance on the gentlest hillside and tumble down. People had tried to help Able, some with seed and some with advice, but he was so ignorant that he did not even know what questions to ask to keep a farm running. Thomas had given Able a year and a half before he realized that mountain farming required more from a man than low-land farming where the soil was half sand and the seasons were more forgiving. But Thomas had guessed wrong by six months.

Well, today, would be the end of it. Able might hem and haw about the price per acre, but Will had the advantage of knowing the look of men who wanted out. And Able wanted out, wanted Will to save him from his own foolishness. And Will would oblige unless Able suddenly tried to act like a man who knew what he was doing and got stubborn about the price. If he got stubborn, then Will would beat him down to next to nothing. But, of course, he would tell him none of this in advance.

"Afternoon, Able," Will said as he swung down from his horse.

The farmer nodded. Like so much of the rest of his life, he did not know how to get started with what he needed to do. "You gonna make me a price for my farm, Mr. Will?" he blurted out.

"That I am." Will shuffled a little. Able made him uncomfortable. He hated to see a man be pathetic, unable to get out of his own way. "How much you have here, Able? Forty acres?" The question was pointless, as Thomas knew by heart the plat of all parcels in this region. But he hoped to get Able talking. Uncleared land was going for 6 cents per acre; farmland with a house—even a rough cabin like Able's—fetched 20 cents per acre.

"Forty. From the creek down there to the top of the hill," he said, pointing to the tree-covered knoll that, in a couple of hours, would hide the setting sun.

"It's a pretty good farm, Able." The statement hung between them like an accusation.

"Too many rocks," the farmer said sourly.

"The Cherokees worked around the rocks."

"Well, I don't know about that. Can't get a plow in it without bustin' somethin'."

"How much are you hopin' to clear on it?"

This was where these conversations always ended up. Someone had to take a position, and Able had almost grown accustomed to taking the wrong one, almost. This time, he had decided to ask high, figuring that he could always come down a little. But what he failed to think through was that Thomas was the only man buying and as such was making the market. Basically, he could sell to Thomas or not sell at all. Able did not have another option, other than abandoning the farm. As soon as his figure was out of his mouth, he knew that once again he had made a mistake. Thomas' face became tight and his eyes hard.

"That's way more than I was prepared to go."

"Well, what did you have in mind?"

Thomas quoted him a figure for uncleared land.

"But that's like givin' it away."

Thomas rocked back on his heels. This had the effect of making Able think that he was reconsidering his offer, but that comfort did not last long. "It was free land to you, other than what you paid to register the deed. How much more could it be worth?"

It was ugly logic and Able felt the shame of a usurper. "You draw up the papers and I will sign 'em," he said, barely controlling his temper. The only consolation was that this exchange had happened so quickly that his wife was still in the house and had not witnessed his humiliation. At least he could tell her that he got more.

The merchant clutched at the reins of his horse and mounted. "Come by the store in a day or two. They will be ready."

As he rode away from the farm, Will visualized how this plot would fit into the growing jigsaw of territory that one day would make up a new Cherokee Nation. There were still more holes than connected pieces, but the core of property around Quallatown was beginning to look secure. Able's place was outside the core, part of an outer buffer ring that would make the core even more secure if Will could connect the pieces.

By the time he returned to the trading post, there was a surprise in store for him. His daughter—

Demarius Angeline—stood waving from the stone porch. She was dressed in dainty clothes as befitting a rich White girl, which she was and was not, with a ribbon tied in her hair. Behind her stood his mother. That was the real surprise. Temperance was not opposed to matters of commerce, but since Demarius had come to live in her house, she rarely strayed from the large white home that Thomas had build for them on Stecoah Creek. Her stated reason was that it was because Demarius demanded so much of her attention. Will suspected that it was also because doing so enabled her to ignore the Cherokee half of the granddaughter that could not be denied much longer. No doubt about it, the child was growing up to resemble her mother. She would be tall and slender, probably taller than Will, and more and more showed the high-cheeked face of Kanaka. In a couple of years, if she were dressed in the colorful skirt and blouse of a Cherokee woman, she would be a young copy of her mother. And this was what Temperance seemed determined to avoid.

Temperance had no problem with Will trading with the Cherokees or even being their spokesman. But she never understood his need to *become* one of them. The business of him having a Cherokee name was silly. With a stern expression, she had quietly rebuked him for his attempts to assimilate with the clan in Quallatown. After all, he was different from them, he spoke a different language, wore different clothes, held different ambitions. Even his skin, which reddened severely in the sun, was proof of his difference.

Will was good with words, but it had been a singular frustration of his that he could not explain to her the sense of feeling at home that he experienced with Drowning Bear. Drowning Bear had been much more than a mentor, more like a grandfather who could teach freely without the burden of parenthood. That was the Cherokee way. In it, Will had prospered. But Temperance wanted nothing to do with it and could not understand why he did.

"She wants to make sure that you come home for dinner on time," Temperance explained now.

"I just have to draw up a deed," Will replied. "I'll bring the paperwork with me."

Temperance was well aware of his ambitions for the reservation. "Whose property this time?" That he was buying land for the Cherokees, but putting the deeds in his own name, did not sit well with her.

"Able Jones." He did not have to explain further. Jones' ineptitude was an accepted fact in the community, as was his much-speculated failure.

"We will say a prayer for his family at dinner," Temperance remarked stiffly.

Later, across the dining table, Will watched his daughter. She sat up straight on a high-backed chair and was well mannered. When she ate, she used the proper utensils and did so without speaking, having learned the childhood secret of asking for things on the table with her eyes. It had been thus for several years, the will of Temperance molding the granddaughter as though she were her own child. Pleasant as it was at the moment, something troubled Will about this. It was as though they lived on an island, an ocean away from any other people. At this dinner table, surrounded by cabinets of fine china, glass pitchers, candleholders, and platters of hammered metal, they could live the life in which Demarius was White. She could dress White, eat White, sleep White, and learn White stories of princes and kingdoms and the baby Jesus. Only she wasn't White. She was twelve, and in a very few years would be seen as a woman. But no White man raised to expect what she expected from life would want her because she was clearly Indian. There would be no drawing rooms, no social teas in her future. From his own experience, Will knew that life beat the childhood out of a person by degrees, and he dreaded the big and painful steps that he knew awaited Demarius.

He pushed back from the table and took his papers to a bench on the front porch, trying to immerse himself in the details of the land transaction. But it was too simple to be a satisfactory distraction. In a few minutes, Demarius joined him, and he put the papers aside. They sat for a long time, listening to the evening sounds of crickets and screech owls. Overhead, bats swept the sky in darting patterns. As the light faded and fireflies began to rise from the grass, Demarius stirred.

"You looked sad at dinner, Papa," she said in a voice that belied her age.

He nodded. He had never had to lie to her before, but he was sure that he could not explain what he had been thinking, so he plunged into other thoughts that were almost as murky. Out of earshot of Temperance, he said, "Your mother had her new baby."

"Can I see it?" Demarius asked, brightening.

"Of course."

"Will it live here with us?"

"I don't think so."

"Why is that?"

"Because I think your mother means to keep this one with her."

Thin hands clasped in her lap, Demarius thought about this. "Did she not want to keep me?" she asked in a serious tone.

"No. No. It was your grandmother who decided that you should come and live here."

This caused more thought. "What is the baby's name?"

"Tayanita."

"That is Cherokee."

"Yes."

"Will you take me to see it tomorrow?"

"I can do that. You saddle your pony in the morning and ride to the store. I have to take these papers there. We can leave from there."

The next day, as expected, Able Jones showed up just after first light for his money. Will laid out the transfer deed on the counter and Able pretended to read it even though both of them knew that Able could not read. When he was done, Will handed him a quill and pointed to the line where Able should make his mark. Jonas Jenkins, who was standing outside, was called in to witness the signature. "That makes it legal," Will said with a note of formality.

"How much do I get?" Able asked impatiently.

Will drew out another paper with an accounting of the farmer's debt. "Here are the figures."

"Well, just give me the money." When Will counted out the coins, the farmer grabbed them and walked as fast as he could from the store.

"Looks like you've lost a customer," Jonas chuckled.

"Knew this day was coming the first time I laid eyes on him. He was a walking disaster."

Just as Able marched away red faced, Demarius arrived on her spotted pony. Through a window of the trading post, the two men watched her. She rode with a naturalness that Will would never experience, light in the saddle and an easy hand on the reins. Very likely she was the only girl within fifty miles who had her own pony. Most families in the mountains lived like the Jones. This was not an easy place for White men to survive, and Able was a sad example.

"Papa, why is that man so mad?" Demarius asked as she slid down from the pony and tied it to a post on the porch.

"Things have not gone well for him and he is looking for someone else to blame. It's a common thing."

"Even with grown people?"

"Especially grown people," Jonas put in with a laugh that bore a peculiar fowl-like squawk.

Demarius considered this as her father brought his horse around to the front of the trading post. Together, they rode towards Quallatown in silence. If it seemed odd to her that she was taking this short trip to become acquainted with her own sister, she did not speak of it. She was comfortable beside him, indulged, wrapped in a paternal cocoon that was rare in those days. For her, her father did not make things into something that they were not, the way her grandmother sometimes did. And for reasons that she could not explain—even to herself—she knew that she was the only one to whom he did not embellish the truth.

At Quallatown, they were greeted with waves from people who paused for a moment from tending their gardens or carrying water. Will was their chief, their protector. But Demarius was an oddity, a Cherokee child who was also White. The two of them rode straight to the cabin of Kanaka that sat at the edge of the village, next to the forest, and hitched their horses to the limbs of a maple tree. As they dismounted, Demarius pulled a blanket from her saddlebag. They found Kanaka seated just inside the door, nursing a small brown face.

Demarius approached silently and laid the blanket on her mother's knee. "It is from my bed for the bed of my sister," she whispered.

Chapter 12
Meramec Springs
Mid-June, 1839

uchella awoke to the rank smell of earth and moss where he lay, on a flat ledge that was tucked into the side of a low hill. Mixed in the air was a hint of smoke that drifted from the west, on a breeze that was too light to rustle leaves. Far off to the northwest, a dog barked. Euchella lay beneath an overhanging layer of stone that was the dull yellow color of the mud that men back home prized for fire clay. He had never seen stone this color. When touched, a layer rubbed off in his hands. It was too soft for arrows or spear points, though where it broke, the shards were sharp with points that stuck easily into bare skin. The soil on the hillsides was thin and filled with this sharp gravel, giving a gritty quality to the wind. After days of walking, his moccasins were frayed along the soles.

When he had first arrived here from the big river—the one that the trapper, Willy, called the Mississip—these hills made him think of those around the middle towns of Tennessee and Georgia, rolling and not steep. But once he began walking, they proved to be quite different. Instead of soft pines and poplars, they were covered with tough oaks and hickories that ripped, unforgiving, at his clothes. As he sniffed the air, even the smoke here smelled different—cleaner—from the hardwood that was burning. Walking was not as slow as he feared because the forest was not as tangled with laurel and rhododendron and honeysuckle as it was in the Smokies. He had yet to come to a thicket that he could not get through, and he could cover ten or even fifteen miles on a good day. There were places where he had to cut through strands of briars that sawed at the skin of his knees, above his leggings, but most of the time he was able to stride freely across the hills. What farms he encountered were in the valleys along the rivers, and were easy to avoid. The sound of the barking dog and the smoke came from one such place.

What had stopped Euchella here, under the low-hanging ledge where he now sat was the condition of his feet and the river that he could hear rushing past below. He had no good idea where he was because he had drifted north of the wagon track. Jonas Jenkins had been right again when he said that the path marked by the Cherokees from last year would be wide and easy to find. Someone—Jonas, probably—had said that 645 wagons had been used to carry the people, and although he could not count past his fingers, Euchella guessed that was a big number. Certainly the wheel tracks that they left were still raw in the earth. And there were bits of cloth, cups, spoons, and hastily made graves lying along the way. It had been too cold last winter to bury anyone deep in the ground, so the best they could do was to pile rocks over the bodies. At least they remembered to lay them facing the rising sun. But eventually Euchella came to a river that ran too deep and too swift to be easily forded. Wagons had made it—tracks led down to the edge of the water—but a man on foot would be swept away. So he turned north to find a crossing. Then, a day later when he was on the other side, he turned south again in a lazy path, expecting to pick up the trail of the others. And that led him here, to this place of yet another unexplainable mystery.

Surely this must be sacred—or bewitched— ground. Although there were no signs cut into the stone walls or totems or relics or communal fires, there was the cold, blue river that sprang all at once, gushing and roiling from a wide hole in the ground. Euchella had been drawn to the stream because it was unusually cold and reminded him of the Oconaluftee and the Nantahala back in the Smokies. Early in the morning, fog lay over the rushing water, and dark, beautiful fish darted among the rocks that protruded above the surface. He had followed it because it flowed mostly from the southwest, where he would eventually rejoin the wagon trail. But the river had stopped abruptly, in the crook of a hill, erupting from a vertical shaft in the earth, in billows that were the color of the sky.

The sight both amazed and disturbed him. He knew many places in the Smokies where the trickle of springs bubbled up out of gray or brown mud; he had shot Tsali at just such a place. These were holy places to the Principal People, revered as sources of spirit and life itself, places of truth where the meaning of dreams were revealed and where confusing notions were made clear. But nowhere was there a river that flowed— whole—out of the ground as this one did. Surely this place was full of mischief. Realizing this, he hurried to build a fire beside the water to drive off any witches and give him some protection. But the fire would not light. Witches must have been everywhere in the damp, cold air that rose above the water. He stared into the roiling depths to see if he could spot one, but then reminded himself that witches could not be seen except in his dreams.

That night, he dared to camp nearby, under the overhang of the hill that faced the river, tempting a witch to visit. And at least one cooperated, bringing a vision that stayed in his mind for weeks. He dreamed of thousands of people marching—some alive, some dead—off to the edge of the horizon where no one had ever gone. The dead followed the living because they did not know where else to go. There was no place familiar for them to rest, so they followed their husbands and mothers and sons and daughters, followed them in their shadows, as if they were still alive, a step or two behind. Only the living did not know that they were there. Sometimes the spirits fell behind and could not catch up to the living again, and they wailed with the cries of screech owls, lost in this land that did not feel like home.

When he awoke, Euchella rolled over and sat up. He breathed deeply, anxious to see if the witch had left anything permanent inside him, but the only thing that he felt was hunger. He needed to hunt something. The jerky that Willy had given him had run out. He was thirsty, too, but would not drink from this river because doing so would mean carrying the witches of the water inside him. But if any were still around this morning, he would fool them. Sitting on the ledge, he began to hack at his long hair, scattering it in piles around the rock. When he was finished, he felt naked, less of a man and oddly weak, but the witches would find his hair and think that he was still here. Beside the stream, he looked down at his reflection. Willy was right. With the hat in place, he did look a little more like a White man.

In the days that followed, the green hills grew smaller and smaller as Euchella walked toward the setting sun. The forest of oak and pine broke open into patches of low brush and grass that grew to his waist. Travel was easier and sometimes he was able to cover twenty miles in a day. Once he found the trail of the wagon ruts again, the trail headed always southwest. He subsisted on the turkeys that were everywhere, in flocks of a dozen or two dozen, wandering through the woods and brush. By sitting still in the cover of brush, he waited until a few would invariably drift within the range of his bow. Grudgingly, he admitted that eating was good here. At night, he stuffed the turkeys with wild onions and cooked them over a fire, along with mushrooms that he knew to be safe. There were deer here, too. Soon he would have a new pair of moccasins.

As the days turned into a week, he began to comprehend that the great river divided the world as he knew it. On the eastern side was the familiar half, the side of high mountains and waterfalls and burial mounds and songs and traditions and festivals of the Principal People. It was the side where a boy would come of age with a significant killing . . . a deer, or if he were lucky, a bear. It was the side that made sense to a warrior, where a man could trust what he saw. On the western side lay the land of strangeness, witchery, and peculiarities such as sharp stones that would stick into his flesh but were no good for arrows. It was the side where it was said that grass and dust covered most of the land and squirrels lived in the ground. And although he saw no other river come straight out of the ground, this remained a place of inhospitable mysteries. In between the two lands, there was the great river, patrolled by the monstrous, belching canoes on which White people rode.

Euchella pushed on, determined, but apprehensive about what he would eventually see when he found the Principal People.

Chapter 13
Near Arkansas/Oklahoma Territory Border
June 20, 1839

I n the three and one-half years that he had lived in the Indian Nation of the Oklahoma Territory, Major Ridge—*Kahnungdatlageh*—never grew accustomed to the heat. North Georgia had been bad enough, and when, as a young man, he had warred alongside Andy Jackson against the Seminoles in Florida, the heat had been oppressive. How the Seminoles lived there, he could not imagine. But the heat of Oklahoma was relentless. And in these shallow hills, there was almost no place to hide from it. Only nearby Flint Creek could provide some momentary relief, but the Major had grown too old and prized his dignity too much for swimming. Even in the summer, he insisted on wearing the formal broadcloth and wool clothes of a White gentleman, and to dunk himself in a river—however cool and clear and appealing—was unacceptable. His only concession to the sun was a broad brimmed straw hat. It bothered the Major not at all that he looked like no one else in these hills—not farmer, not cowboy, and particularly not any of the many Indians who now lived within the patchwork nation of tribes. After all, he had earned the right to dress any way that he liked, but sadly what he really liked was what he had left behind in Georgia. His life there had been everything that he wanted; his farm was a plantation, complete with extensive fields, orchards, animals, and enough slaves to tend them. As his carriage jolted along on the dusty path toward Fayetteville, the Major tried not to think about Georgia. They had lost too much there to risk remembering it now.

For the first three years, the Major, his son, John, and his nephews, Elias Boudinot and Stan

Waite, had set about recreating what they could of their Georgia life in Oklahoma. With the slaves that they brought with them, they built a community of modest homes from the tangle of oaks and pines that grew in the region. By those who did not live there, it was sometimes dubbed Treaty Town because it was composed entirely of the people who had come west with them in 1835, after they signed the Treaty of New Echota in Georgia. To the earlier community of Cherokees that had been in Oklahoma for a generation, they were strangers, and were left alone, except for the stares that the Major and his wife, Suzanna, drew when they rode out in his fine carriage. And for three years, the members of the Treaty Party had been ignored, and the Major took no interest in Cherokee affairs, except for matters that directly concerned his family.

That feeling of comfortable isolation vanished with the arrival of the first group of émigrés from the east, late last year. They came exhausted, disoriented, starved, beaten—and bitter. Many had died along the way. More died after their arrival. The winter was terrible and the weak froze or succumbed to pneumonia. They were settled into camps where they could be neither warm nor dry. When a cemetery was created on a rise, just east of the camp, it grew rapidly, sometimes by three or four additions each week.

At first Major Ridge thought to help them. In Treaty Town, they had plenty. After much work with the hard, flinty soil, their gardens were well established now. Part of their corn and beans could be shared. But when he and John drove a wagon loaded with supplies to the camp and unloaded it, the men and women sat wrapped in their blankets, staring at them. A few children approached the sacks until they realized that the adults were not moving, then they retreated. He and John drove away, leaving the sacks behind. They never learned what the people there did with the grain, and they never spoke of it between themselves again.

As months passed, the new arrivals seemed to be waiting for something. Almost as if they were rudderless, they huddled together and tried to stay warm. Fires of scavenged wood burned in front of their crude tents. These people did not seek out Major Ridge or any of the others from Treaty Town, and whenever Ridge and Suzanna rode out in their carriage, the newcomers would turn their backs to them. At first, Suzanna was offended and hurt by this, then frightened to realize that the others treated them as though they were dead.

Then one day, there was considerable animation in the camp. People rose from the ground, let their blankets fall, and stood looking to the east. In the distance, a wagon train appeared, small at first, like the one that they had ridden on earlier. This was the last one that would come, and it rolled slowly, almost painfully as though those on board did not want to see what they were about to see. In the lead wagon sat a solitary figure. To the unknowing, it would appeared that this man was White, and in fact, by law he was. But to these Cherokees in Oklahoma, he was pure Indian. He was their Chief. John Ross had finally arrived from the old Cherokee Nation to the new one.

Ridge and the others of the Treaty Party were instantly on guard. Years ago in the East, Ridge and Ross had been the closest friends, friendly rivals for the position of Chief, then confidants and collaborators. Together, they had written the bylaws that governed the nation over the last ten years. In many ways, Ridge was Ross' spokesman, as ironically Ross could barely speak the Cherokee language. They had eaten, hunted, smoked, and planned war together. They had devised strategies to confound a president and stay the execution of the Removal Act for a decade. Over campfires, they had wondered aloud what would become of their tribe and their history and their traditions. And then they had split. They split over the inevitability of removal to the West. Ridge had heard from his son about the president's resolve not to intervene in the raids that White Georgians made on Cherokee farms and villages. He had seen the result of the raids, the broken fences, lost animals, men shot from ambush. Ross believed that it could be stopped, but Ridge knew that there would be no end to it. Not where there was gold involved, and gold had been discovered in the North Georgia part of the nation ten years ago. No, Ridge knew that nothing could keep the raiders out.

There is no hate that is as bitter as that which is born out of love. When Ridge eventually gave into the inevitable political tide and advocated for the best deal possible with the government, he and Ross never spoke again. He could not be absolutely sure, but he was convinced that it was Ross who had sent the assassin that day when Ridge signed the Treaty of New Echota, in 1835.

As he now rode along the road to Fayetteville, Arkansas, Ridge wondered what was it about Ross that had so enraged him about that treaty? A fool could see that they were going to be forced to move; why not take the best deal available? There was $5 million waiting for the Cherokees at the end of it, when everything was settled. Perhaps he was just piqued that Ridge had acted in his place in signing the treaty. Anyhow, he would never know. Ross was here now, living out of a house that was barely more than a lean-to with four sides. But it was Ross whom the people revered.

The Major respected that, and made no effort to contact Ross. It would do no good anyway; the man had pride enough for ten men and would not be reconciled to what he publicly described as Ridge's "betrayal"—even though he had eventually given in and moved west himself, even though, as a White man, he did not have to. Ross made no effort to contact him. Things were silent from the other side of the Cherokee encampment. That was just fine. At least there was no violence between them.

Suzanna worried about his safety, and that of her son, John. She did not like that the Major was now going to Fayetteville alone. He would be traveling for two days, out of touch, but he reassured her that he would carry his rifle. People knew that he carried it. It would be enough. The possibility of doing some business in cotton with the traders in Fayetteville was too tempting to miss. Besides, he was not so old that he could not watch out for himself. There was a little of the warrior that he used to be still in him.

The Major would have preferred that they be allowed to live in Arkansas. If it was not much cooler than Oklahoma, it was greener and made him think of the part of Georgia that the Creeks had occupied before they, too, were moved west. He was homesick. But Arkansas was not Oklahoma; their deal had been for Oklahoma, so Oklahoma it was. He would live out his days there.

The road to Fayetteville was mostly flat and easy on the big gray horse that drew his phaeton. Suzanna had prevailed on him to take this carriage instead of the lighter shay which he preferred. But she was right. This one had four wheels and there was room for a water cask on the back. At dusk, he would stop and make camp. How odd it would appear for a gentleman in a carriage to pitch a camp and sleep on the ground. He could find a bed in Fayetteville, but because he left Treaty Town at midday, he would not make it that far unless he pushed the horse, and there was no point in that. It had been a long time since he had slept on the ground—on the journey from the East three years before—but it was not a bad thing for a Cherokee to do, gentleman or not.

If it went well, the business in Fayetteville would give John a future. They had slaves enough to work cotton; he could grow rich again. All over the South men were growing cotton, to feed the mills of New England. He would show them that the Cherokees could do it, too. After all, parts of Oklahoma looked like one big, cleared field to the Major. If they could find a place where the soil could be turned, there could be no end to the cotton that they could grow there. The soil was the key. In these parts, most of it was hard, red, and dry—and filled with small bits of something almost as sharp as flint. When he returned, he would send men out to look for soil that could be plowed.

At the end of the day, the Major found a broad oak, standing alone beside the road. He pulled the horse over and unhitched it, allowing it to graze, then gave it water from a barrel on the back of the carriage. Using fallen limbs, he made a small fire and boiled a pot of coffee, then spread a blanket on the ground and leaned back against the tree. From a loaf of bread, he tore pieces from the soft center, rolled them between his fingers, and ate the doughy balls. Things were going to be good again, good for John, good for the others who had come with them three years ago—good for all the Cherokees if they wanted to participate in his plans. It was not Georgia, but it was something . . . a new life, a beginning, something that they could grow. When he drifted off to sleep, the Major dreamed of apple trees and slaves who stooped to work in fields. But into this scene edged a wolf that frightened the slaves, and they ran in fear. The Major tried to chase the wolf away, but it would only go so far as the trees

126

at the edge of the fields, out of sight, but still there. Knowing this, the slaves would not go into the fields again.

When he awoke the next morning, he did not know whether to be buoyed or apprehensive. Dreams were not dependable out here, and this one made little sense to him. Perhaps, he would consult an old man who was a shaman when he returned.

Chapter 14
Near Border of Oklahoma Territory
June 21, 1839

From his hiding place in the trees, Euchella watched the circle of men in a clearing as they argued quietly, but forcefully, among themselves. There were two less of them than he had fingers, seated around a fire. All seemed to have rifles leaning on a log behind them, but in the twilight he could not be sure. From their gestures, most of the group was arguing with one man who was seated in a way that obscured his face. One after another they pointed at this quiet figure, barking a few words, then fell silent, as was their custom. The quiet one only occasionally objected to what was being put to him. He seemed patient. Although Euchella was too far away to hear them clearly, these men spoke in Cherokee.

At the sound of it, his heart rose. Had he found the Principal People at last, after nearly two months on the river and walking across the scrubby hills? Euchella crept closer to hear better. Caught up in their debate as they were, there was little danger of them discovering him. Besides, he was downwind of their fire; if they had dogs, they would not get his scent. When he could hear clearly, their voices were familiar, but what they said was chilling.

". . . he should not have been allowed to live this long."

". . . a fourth of all our number are dead because of him and his son."

". . . and the son will be dealt with, too."

"We came here like women, not warriors. It is time that we act like warriors again."

". . . it is by his own words that he must die. Was it not *Kahnungdatlageh* who said that any Cherokee who sold Cherokee land must die?"

Except for the occasional popping of the fire and the chirp of crickets, there was silence in the camp. No one moved. Everyone knew that it was time for the one who objected to speak. After a thoughtful pause, he did. "I have known this man longer than any of you. I remember the days when he was a warrior, as brave as any of us. He has killed more White people in the name of the Cherokee Nation than any other. I have seen it."

Euchella stared, unbelieving. The man speaking was Junaluska.

"But he is a traitor! He sold our land."

Junaluska nodded. "I cannot deny that. But it would have been taken from us anyhow. They wanted the land. They wanted the gold. They always get what they want. We were not strong enough to stop them."

One man, whose back was to Euchella, leaned forward spat into the fire. "We should have died there. This place is not worth dying for."

Junaluska agreed. "This is not our old nation, and it will never be. But killing this man will not change that."

"It is the blood code."

"Even John Ross says that we must not live by the blood code any longer."

"John Ross lost his wife on the journey here, but I lost two sons. Who will avenge them if not me?"

When Junaluska did not answer, another spoke up. "I will do it."

". . . and I."

". . . . and I.

The others in the circle nodded in agreement. The man whom they called *Kahnungdatlageh*—Major

Ridge—had been condemned to death . . . for crimes, real and imagined, against the Cherokee Nation.

Euchella rose from his hiding place, visible now to the men at the fire, and approached them slowly, rifle and bow slung over his shoulder. One raised a rifle, but Junaluska grabbed the barrel and held it low. "I know this man. He is a Lufty. He is Euchella."

The man who had spat into the fire looked him up and down with the old eyes of an elder. "Why do you come to us like a snake in the grass? Why do you not come to us like a Cherokee and announce your intent?"

"Because this is not Cherokee country. From a distance, I did not know who you were. I did not know what I would find."

The old man seemed to understand. "This is true. What do you want?"

"To sit. I have not seen another Cherokee since I left our home in the East. I have seen nothing but strange lands and strange sights and strange people."

It was then that the others realized what he meant. "You did not come with the people and the wagons?"

"No. My people hid out on Balsam and other places until the soldiers stopped looking for us. After they left, we stayed up there—through the winter. It was not until spring that we came down from the mountain. I have been walking for many days."

The elder who seemed to be the leader of the group asked what all were thinking. "Why did you come if you did not have to?"

Euchella settled himself beside Junaluska as the others made room around the fire. "I had a vision."

The brooding faces considered this. Forced to accede to a will larger than their own, the Cherokees needed to understand the devastation that had occurred to them over the past year. Much had been made of dreams and visions in the last few years, and dreams were the only means the people had to understand their fate. Indeed, Junaluska had experienced a dream that foretold their betrayal, by *Kahnungdatlageh* and his son, John Ridge. As much as he was respected as a warrior and a chief of the Snowbird family, it was Junaluska's visions that had earned him esteem throughout the tribe. And it was for this reason that the other seven men sought him out to go with them on the killing party for *Kahnungdatlageh*, to bear witness to his death.

A young man spoke up. "Are you not the one who killed Tsali?"

Euchella nodded. "I am. I shot him at Big Bear Springs. He asked me to take care of his grandson, then he died well."

"Then, do you not think that *Kahnungdatlageh* deserves to die also?"

When he answered, Euchella looked at Junaluska. "Yes I do." But Junaluska showed no reaction. He was truly a patient man.

"Then will you join us in ridding the tribe of this snake?"

Euchella dipped his head. "No. It is my hope that Tsali is the last man I ever kill."

This brought another pause, then one of the others, a man with a deep scar on his face, said, "Will you stand against us?"

"I will not."

"Then it is settled."

For the remainder of the night, until they fell asleep, the men questioned Euchella about conditions and relatives who were left behind in the East. He told them of the death of Drowning Bear, and of Will Thomas and the thing that he called a reservation. The others listened intently.

"You mean, there will be Cherokee land where White men cannot go?" asked the youngest.

"No. Will Thomas, himself, is White. But it is said to be a place where White men cannot own the land, that it will be kept for the Cherokees alone."

"That is what we have here," put in a large man on the other side of Junaluska.

"Except that we are put in a place with the mongrel Creeks and the others that I don't know."

"How did you get here?" wondered the young man.

Euchella described the canoe that he and his brother made. "It goes well on the big river of Tennessee and the smaller ones. My brother learned of it from the northern tribes. I could paddle it close to the bank and travel unseen, under the brush." Then he told them of the men on flatboats and the slaves that they carried, and how he had set three of them free. Finally, he described the great boat that thundered, and then of following the wagon trail and sleeping near a river that sprang from the ground. This was the idea that startled the men the most. The marvels of the White man they could accept, but even in the dim light of the fire, he could see disbelief in their eyes as he described the river. "It is true. I took it to be a place of witches and cut my hair and left it there so that they would think that I was still there and not follow me."

"I would like to see such a place," said a small man who had not spoken before.

"Walk northeast . . . a week or ten days. When you get to the land of rolling mountains, find a river that is colder than the rest, then follow it upstream. You will come to a crooked hill, and the river comes out of a hole in the ground there that is wider than a lodge." The others nodded as one.

In turn, Euchella asked them how they lived in Oklahoma, if they were confined in stockades the way that they had been before they were transported west. What he learned surprised him. Most lived in tents. A few lived in the lodges that had been built before their arrival. And while some soldiers were around, they were not guarded. It was obvious to all that the great distance and the giant rivers were barrier enough to keep them from returning.

"What does Will Thomas do?" Junaluska asked suddenly.

Euchella took a deep breath. "How can I say what I do not understand? He buys land. He brings in White men of religion. The people drink less whiskey, but they forget the old ways. He has a Cherokee child that he raises as a White, and another that has probably been born by now. The people in Quallatown have made him their chief, and he proclaims himself to be chief of what he calls 'the Eastern Band' of the Cherokee. He talks of great things, but I know that there is something in his heart that he does not say. He says that he is Cherokee and the people believe him, but how can that be?"

No one answered because they were not expected to answer. A few knew Thomas from trading with him. What they did not know was why the mention of Thomas so irritated this tall stranger.

Later, as the others slept, Euchella gazed up at the deepest sky that he had ever seen. The very depth of it seemed to pull at his body, as though he was being lifted off the earth and flung out into the great darkness. Only by closing his eyes could he feel his own weight holding him onto the ground. When he opened them again, a shooting star scored a line across the sky from the east, trailing sparkling bits of celestial matter. It went so fast that he did not have time to sit up before it fell to the ground, somewhere beyond his vision. What did it mean, he wondered? When everyone awakened in the morning, he would try to remember to ask Junaluska about it.

Chapter 15
Near Border of Oklahoma Territory
June 22, 1839

U p to the time that he rode with Andrew Jackson at Horseshoe Bend, the Major had been known proudly as *Kahnungdatlageh*. But for a generation, he preferred to be called Major Ridge, the rank that Jackson had given him in Alabama. As he rode upright in his carriage, the morning sun was already on his back. The rolling green hills of Arkansas were falling behind, the flatter expanse of Oklahoma lay ahead. He had a long journey, but he would be back home just after dark.

The Major had reason to ride a little higher this morning. The cotton broker in Fayetteville had been happy to tell him that he did not care where his cotton came from, as long as he had a dependable supply to send up north to the mills there. They would send it down the Arkansas River, to the Mississippi and on to New Orleans. From there, it would go by sailing ship around Florida to New England. For Ridge, that meant that there was much to be done. His people would have to break new fields and learn more about this ugly little plant that was so prized for the white tufts that burst from it in late summer. They would need seed and some idea about watering, but it was said to tolerate dry climates. These details he could leave to John. The Major would concentrate on the brokers and learn the best moment to take the crop to market. At last, the people would be busy again. This was not the millwork of the Cherokee women that they had sold while in Georgia; this was the raw product. It would take much labor, but that's what they had in slaves.

The pieces were falling into place. The Major had first envisioned growing cotton here about a year after they arrived. All the Chickamaga clan who had come west with him needed something to keep them busy. Without purpose, they had grown sullen. Trapping was out of the question as there were too few animals and too many Indians from diverse tribes seeking them. Growing corn was a possibility, but there was no market for it, unless one converted it to whiskey, and even then you would need a way to transport it over long distances to sell it. And worst of all, John could never be talked into becoming a whiskey maker, not with that Christian wife of his.

Cotton would fit. No one was growing it here, and the market was not far away. A few big wagons were all that they needed to haul it to Fayetteville, and they could build them as they cleared the forest. Unlike whiskey, cotton had dignity. Cotton would not tempt men to steal it and get into fights. Cotton was clean. Grow it. Move it. Sell it. All he had to do was find out how to make it work.

From overhead, the sun baked the earth. The Major stopped and watered the horse from the barrel, then drank some himself. It was not cold, but he was thirsty enough so that it did not matter. As he stood looking east, a dust devil played along the road, picking up dirt, loose stalks of grass, bits of leaves. Before it reached the carriage, the swirling wind turned and moved out across the field, then died. It was an omen, he thought, something else to puzzle over. The Major climbed back into the carriage and chucked to the horse to continue. The farther west he traveled, the flatter the land became. Tenacious trees held to the rises that were divided by depressions and muddy streams. This was hardly good land for the Cherokees. None of the instincts that he had developed for planting, weeding, or harvesting applied here. But the Cherokees should make an effort to adapt. A festival from the old time would help. He would speak to John about it tomorrow. John would arrange it.

The horse picked up its ears as it trotted, then grew skittish in the harness. Something unsettled it. Instinctively his hand went down to the rifle and pulled it across his lap. One never knew out here. All manner of hunters and peddlers and men who needed to stay ahead of the law back east drifted through these parts. If he were being watched, he would let them see the rifle and that he was prepared to use it.

Without warning, an Indian leaped out of the high grass and stood in the road, a rifle raised high over his head. His clothes were those of an Over Hill Cherokee. The horse halted. From the carriage, Major Ridge could see a deep scar on his right cheek. Although his hair was the color of old metal, he was neither slowed nor stooped by age. For a moment, nothing was spoken as the two men stared at each other.

Then the stranger broke the silence. "You have caused the death of more of the Principal People than any man—White or Indian. The law of our people demands that this be made right."

The Major stood in the carriage and raised his own rifle. "I, myself, have killed no Cherokee who did not deserve to die. I have killed many Whites. I have killed many Creeks. But by my hand, I have killed no Cherokee who did not need killing."

From deep in the grass, another stood up. This one was very old. "Because of you, my sons are dead." Abruptly, five others joined these two, arrayed in a half circle in front of the carriage, one for each of the seven clans of the Principal People. Each held a rifle and on their faces was the look of purpose.

This was the moment that Ridge had imagined when he had touched quill to paper and signed the Treaty of New Echota three years before. This vision

137

had sometimes troubled his sleep, sometimes it intruded in the middle of a huge family meal, sometimes it crept up on him while he sat by the fire. These were Ross men, and if they were not, they thought they were. In any case, they all wanted to kill him.

Beyond the men with guns stood two more, unarmed. Ridge thought that he recognized the tall form of Junaluska, but the other man—equally tall—he did not know. Junaluska was a friend of John Ross, but if he had not come here to kill him, then he had tried to talk these men out of it, but had failed. Well, there was no time to think of that now. In the funnel of time, this was the last narrowing for him, only a moment to think about himself, about Georgia and the smell of the earth there, the feel of the trees in his orchard. There was no time to worry about Suzanna and John. In this instant, his next step became clear. He remained a warrior, no matter what, no matter how he dressed or lived, and whatever else they thought him to be, these men from Ross would know that *Kahnungdatlageh* was a warrior.

The sun seemed blindingly bright as *Kahnungdatlageh* brought his rifle to his shoulder and took aim to shoot the man with the scar.

Chapter 16
Oklahoma Territory
June 22, 1839

Junaluska led the horse that drew the carriage that bore the body of the Traitor of New Echota. The seven members of the killing party had wanted to leave him where they shot him and, perhaps, let his family find him like that days from now, picked over by buzzards. But Junaluska said that to do so was a disgrace. He and Euchella would return the body to the man's wife, traitor or not. After all, at one time he had been a great leader of the Principal People.

No one dared to express their anger toward *Kahnungdatlageh* by mutilating his corpse for fear of being contaminated by his spirits. Surely, in time, *Kahnungdatlageh* would be remembered as a child of Spear-Finger, the she-witch from antiquity. None of his executioners wanted to be tainted by bad vapors that must cling to him. They had done what they needed to do by putting seven holes in him. Now *Kahnungdatlageh* was truly dammed, and even centuries of lying in a grave facing east would not change that.

When the others shrugged and went their own way, Junaluska and Euchella began walking along the road toward the Indian Nation and that small niche called Treaty Town. Neither glanced over their shoulder at the body of *Kahnungdatlageh* that lay sprawled on the tucked leather cushions of the carriage. It was not their purpose to mourn him, only deliver him. The sun was still hot and the walk was long, but walking was better than risking contamination by riding in the carriage. By the time they reached Treaty Town, the body would smell. Because there was nothing to be done about it, they did not speak of the killing, but chose to speak of things that they recalled from their days in the old Cherokee Nation.

"Tsali was my friend," Junaluska said distantly, with no hint of recrimination for Euchella. "Before we were brought to this place, he came to me, seeking understanding of a dream, but, instead, explained a dream of mine."

"He was my friend, too. I hunted with his sons and the husband of his daughter. From him, I learned many things. Then I shot them all."

"They died well?"

"Yes. Like warriors."

"*Kahnungdatlageh* died like a warrior."

"Yes. But I did not know him."

"He was a brave man. He was the one who turned the battle at Horseshoe Bend." He spat for punctuation. "We would have been better off to fight with the Creeks than against them."

"They say that you killed a Creek warrior who was about to kill Jackson."

"May the Great Spirit wash away my error."

"Jackson is in Tennessee, now, and another man takes his place, and still they forced us to leave."

"They have their own law," said Junaluska, attempting to explain.

"But it makes no sense. Six years ago, John Ross told the people that the court of the White men had set aside their law, that we did not have to leave. Yet, here we are."

"We have all wondered about this," Junaluska replied with a sigh. "One part of the government says 'go.' Another part says, 'no, stay.' Who can understand this? It is better to count on what they do rather than what they say."

For a time they were content just to walk, with the rhythm of the horse's hooves between them. At

140

dusk, they paused in the shadow of an oak that was gnarled by generations of prairie wind and drank from the keg of water tied to the back of the carriage, giving some to the horse. Although they said nothing about it, both men were uneasy drinking the dead man's water, and each silently hoped that his spirits had not invaded the keg, but it was all the water that they had, and out here one did not know where you would find good water next. A wind rolled the grass as though it were a blanket being shaken, and pushed dust toward their eyes.

"Is there always dust?" asked the younger man.

"Except when there is rain. Rain will come soon." As this was said, a distant flash of lightning flickered on the horizon. "The rain may wash *Kahnungdatlageh.* Perhaps his blood will mark this path."

As the sky grew darker, the men ceased to talk. By the occasional flash of lightning, they could follow the road and when there was no lightning, they could feel the ruts made by wagon wheels. They were lucky in that the anvil of the storm passed to the south and they received only a brief, light sprinkle that was enough to dampen and settle the dust. The night became thick like a black cloud, and they walked carefully. Later, when the storm blew east, stars came out and they had no trouble seeing the way of the wagon path through the trees.

In the moments before midnight, Junaluska and Euchella reached a rise and halted. Before them, sloping away, lay a broad field, black now except for the dots of many fires that were far in the distance. As they walked on, the faint sound of wailing came to them.

Junaluska stopped. "Someone else is dead." Then he remembered. "The seven said that the son and his cousins would be dealt with, too."

When they were close enough to Treaty Town to make out the shapes of the cabins in the firelight, the wailing came as a series of prolonged cries. The two men stood in the darkness and watched for a time.

"More than one is dead," grunted Junaluska. "They will have posted guards. We better send the wagon in by itself or else they will think that we have killed *Kahnungdatlageh.*"

Euchella agreed. They whipped the rump of the animal, startling it so that it set off in a trot toward the village.

"Come to my camp. I will show you the way," said Junaluska. "You have much to tell us."

It was more than two hour's walk to the settlement of the Snowbird Clan.

Chapter 17
Oconaluftee River
Late June, 1839

achacha and the others of the Lufty Band heard the call from where they sat around a communal fire near the river. From the sound of the voice, a woman approached.
They rose in unison, not because they were apprehensive, but because it was unusual for a woman to walk alone at night. But as she came into the light, they could see that it was Kanaka and that she was not alone. She carried an infant wrapped in a light blanket.

As she moved closer, the men made room for her around the fire, then settled themselves once again. From across the circle, one man cut a rib of venison that grilled above the fire and handed it to her. She took it with a nod. As she ate from the bone, the infant stirred in her lap. The hard faces of the men, so recently accustomed to dodging soldiers and wintering outdoors, softened at the sound. When she was finished with the meat, she tossed the bone to her dog that had followed and now waited at the edge of the light. Then she settled back and fed the child.

"You are welcome here, but why have you come?" asked Wachacha.

"I would like to live among you," she replied without explanation.

The men were startled and showed it by whispering among themselves. Wachacha heard the name of Will Thomas mentioned. The entire region knew that Kanaka was Thomas' woman. That she would choose to live away from the village where he was proclaimed chief was puzzling, perhaps insulting. But each of the men around the fire was here because they followed Euchella and they knew that Euchella wanted no part of Thomas' village. "You are welcome to do that also," he said at last.

One of the men who whispered rose and put more wood on the fire. This was going to be a longer night than first expected. The new wood crackled as it caught.

"I could build my own lodge," Kanaka offered.

Another voice from across the fire weighed in. "Already we have an empty lodge, the one that we built for Euchella, for when he returns."

"Who knows when Euchella will return," said a third.

"We can build another for him then," confirmed Wachacha.

No woman had lived among them for two years, no baby for much longer than that. In the mountains, it seemed that they had been cold forever, and the cold and the perpetual fear had made them hard, made it easier to think about doing hard things such as killing and eating meat that they were too hungry to allow to cook thoroughly. Cold. Hunger. Fear. Wachacha realized that he had not thought much about being with a woman in all that time. They had lived as men at war, hunted, on edge. Food and sleep and escaping the perpetual wind at the tops of the mountains were all that they had time for.

The presence of the woman and the child would change that. But there was a delicate matter to consider. Wachacha wished that his brother were here. Euchella was more comfortable making decisions. But one thing was clear: That he could welcome Kanaka was not a problem; that was the custom of the Cherokees. However, neither he nor any of the other Luftys could help her leave Quallatown. That would be seen as enticement. He would have to make sure that the others understood this also. Whatever her reasons for wanting to live among

144

them—and away from Quallatown—she was still Will Thomas' woman and that had to be respected. If and how she got herself to their settlement was one thing, but the Luftys could not—must not—be the instrument of her departure. That would be a rift that was too large to be forgiven even at any Green Corn Festival in the future.

In the days that followed, the men gained a new appreciation for a woman's capacity for work. What Kanaka could not carry from her lodge in Quallatown, she dragged; what she could not drag, she disassembled and scooted piece by piece. She was like an ant relocating its nest, pulling, shoving, rolling whatever needed to be moved. And, as though she understood their position, she never once asked the Luftys for help. In her face was a look of determination. Everything would be moved, one piece at a time. Once, as she dragged her heavy cooking pot that was lashed to a travois, the men stopped their work and watched. With the child strapped to her back, she bent against the load and pulled without complaint.

"Maybe she heard about my brother's vision of the spider," observed Wachacha from the garden.

"She does the work of one," said a young man whose name was *Ayun'ini*, or Swimmer.

The final thing to be moved was a large bag that was stuffed with skins and cloth that she would sew into clothes for herself and the baby. She was exhausted from the work. As she stepped through the door of the lodge that had never been lived in, a new table stood in the middle of the room. A low fire burned in the fireplace and her own iron pot hung over it, bubbling with a soup made from the meat left from the night before. She rested the baby in its cradle and then discovered that a bucket of water had been drawn for her also. She drank deeply, then washed her face and dried it on her sleeve, now so exhausted that her body trembled. Finding a bowl, she dipped some soup from the kettle, spilling a little on the hearth. Kanaka could not tell if it was the best that she had ever tested or if she was just desperately hungry, but she ate as though she were starving.

When the baby was fed, she left it to sleep in the lodge and joined the men around the fire beside the river.

"Where is your companion?" wondered Swimmer.

Kanaka smiled inwardly. In their year of hiding, these men had missed not only the company of women, but also the inevitable softening that comes with having children underfoot. In earlier times before the people were gripped by the panic of removal, it was an attitude that men came to reluctantly, preferring the veneer of a warrior. But these men were eager to abandon whatever pretense of indifference they might have had. "She is with her dreams," Kanaka replied, as she sat among them, accepted as a sister.

A fire like this is the best thing. As the coals glowed and occasionally popped, what was on the mind of each person seemed to pass from one to another as though it were some curiosity found in the woods or dug from ground, examined wordlessly, then sent on. This night, their thoughts were of her, with both gratitude and apprehension. Like an onion, she brought a flavor to the broth of their settlement that was missing. There would be more laughter among them now, particularly with the baby there, crying, babbling, learning to walk. Having her here would also nudge the men to find other women and bring them here. Perhaps some women would even show up on their own, and the place would become a village, complete. They might even begin to remember the old songs and the old stories. Maybe even one day, there would be other children to whom they could pass these things. The harmony of a village was not achieved overnight, but they had made a good beginning.

But Kanaka also brought unique problems. By now, the villagers of Quallatown would have noted her leaving, and the lodge where she had lived would stand vacant, like the empty socket in a jaw from which a tooth was extracted. Her absence would make them uncomfortable; after all, she was part of the reason that Will Thomas came to their village, and now she was gone. And Will, himself, would discover her absence soon enough, and when he did, what would he do? Tayanita was his child, too. These thoughts went around the fire like circling smoke, from man to man.

They did not have long to wait to find out how Will Thomas felt about Kanaka's absence. At midmorning the next day, he rode into the settlement at a near gallop. The men who were working outside heard hooves pounding along the river before they saw him and stopped hoeing. Kanaka heard him, too. Nursing the infant inside the cabin that had become hers, she rose and stood in the door. Will reined the horse to a halt and looked about quickly. Kanaka saw him and clutched the child to her breast. Thomas spurred the horse in her direction and halted again as he came near, his face a fury.

As though this were defiled ground and he would not allow his feet to touch it, Will stayed in his saddle. "Was it your intention to shame me?" he hissed from above her.

Kanaka did not reply, but kept her face immoble.

"What . . . what could you want of me?"

"Nothing. I came here for myself, and for her," Kanaka said, inclining her head toward the infant.

"You dishonor me. You have made the people doubt me. You make them question everything that I have tried to do."

His accusations stung, yet Kanaka understood at an instinctive level that what he offered her was the very thing from which she must separate herself. It was not just him, alone—not his moments of temper and brooding or snoring when he drank whiskey or the odd things that he said that meant nothing to her—but the sting came from the truth that she needed to escape something that no longer held any appeal for her. There was a war going on inside his head, a battle of demons and martyrs, pulling him back and forth. Sometimes he went too far into his darkness and sometimes he went too far with the things that were meant to be good. If there was a middle to it all, then she might have thought that he lived in a harmony of his own making, but there was no middle, only the extremes, like two mountains with a bottomless valley between. And his passage back and forth exhausted her. He wore her down with his perpetual urgency. Here, by the river—as a sister to the Lufty men—she could breathe and not dread the moment when he would come through the door or the moment when he would leave. With all the back and forth with Will, she had begun to think like something that she did not want to be, a White woman. That would do her no good, nor her baby. More than ever, she needed to be Cherokee. In this place by the river, she had a chance to find her own harmony once more.

Chapter 18
Oklahoma Territory
Late June, 1839

The people who came west from the Snowbird village sat and waited in the hot morning sun, as still as lizards. Across their camp that lay in a once-grassy depression between two low hills, only children moved. The people had been promised that they would be fed until they could feed themselves, and the weekly delivery wagon was due today. No lodge had been built here yet, nor had any ground been broken for a garden. No well had been dug. Their dependence on the supply wagon was total and, it seemed to Euchalla, paralytic.

Under the watchfulness of the others, he stood up and walked to the top of the rise to the west of the camp. He had the curiosity of one who is unfamiliar with a place, but what he saw from the knoll was disheartening. There was no end to this land. Along a wet weather stream, birds sang from a line of willows that followed the runoff, but mostly a prairie of grass and trees and small hills stretched on endlessly. It was nearly the same looking back east, but with more rolling hills. Even the sky was larger here. This was a prison of limitlessness, its very size intimidating the people into staying put. Except for him, it had not been crossed by any Cherokee alone. No man would dare set out from here with a wife and children to return to their homeland, and so the nation that once had been the Principal People for thousands of years was severed from its roots.

He took a deep breath. This region was so different from their homelands in the East that it was hard to contemplate. After the recent rains, the grass was green and thick. But behind the rain would come heat, and the heat would be almost unbearable today, baking the life out of the people. Those who had the energy to do so would wander down to the willows to sleep in the shade and wait for the wagons; the older ones would stay mostly in the protection of their shelters. Night would come as a relief; daylight brought dread that made one want to find a cave and escape.

Like some ancient oak, the people had been transplanted to this place where even the soil was inhospitable. Where would they hunt for the wild garlic to flavor a stew of squirrel and rabbit? Where would they find obsidian for spears and arrows? Where would one find the confluence of rivers or a saddle between two mountains to visit with the spirits? Did the spirits even know of this place, and if there were spirits here, would they welcome the Cherokees? Where could they find sacred ground for a stomp dance? Where could they draw water that did not taste of mud? Could a people accustomed to the cries of circling hawks take root in a place where the most prevalent sound was the whistle of wind in the stubby oaks that clung to the land here?

He thought of these things. People adapt to the place where they are and the place changes them. The Chickamauga of the low hills in Georgia grew wide with their great harvests. By contrast, the Middle Town Cherokees were lean because their gardens were small and they had to hunt for their meat. Certainly Tsali's fish from his trap on the Nantahala had not made him fat. So what would this place with its endless grass and limitless sky make of the Principal People?

A noise behind him caused Euchella to turn. Junaluska labored up the rise. After the killing of Major Ridge and delivering his corpse to his family, they had found their way through the darkness to the Snowbird camp and were met by elders who waited for news beside a small fire. The men were as surprised as Junaluska had been to see Euchella, but little was said of it that night. They asked about *Kahnungdatlageh*, and Junaluska told them that he was dead, taking time to describe the killing as he knew that they needed to hear it, how well he died and that he was now in the hands of his own people. One of the others—whose name was *Ina'li*, or Black Fox— said that the son, John Ridge was dead, too, stabbed 43 times in front of his house. Elias Boudinot was dead as well. Only Stand Watie of that cursed family escaped and remained alive.

"They had to be killed," said Junaluska. "As long as John Ross lives as our chief, they could not live, but their deaths will not restore harmony to us. It will turn out to be just another killing."

Talking among themselves was not as easy for the men of the village as it used to be. Campfires had become places for brooding. People lived in their memories because their days were like a three-legged stool with one leg missing; they had memories and they had the promise of a supply wagon, but they had no future.

That first night, after the others went to sleep, Euchella found a place near Junaluska's family to sleep. Although he was exhausted, sleep was not easy. He rolled on the ground as images of the broad-chested Cherokee, who dressed in the clothes of a White man, pitched and jerked. Seven rifles cracked as one, slamming the body back against the seat of his carriage, and in death, *Kahnungdatlegeh* had the disjointed look of a doll that had been pounded on a rock by a child in a fit of temper. Then, somewhere in the dream, *Kahnungdatlageh* was replaced by Tsali, his body slumped on its side beside the trickle of water from Big Bear Springs. Their future—the future of them all, it seemed—had ended with Tsali.

Now, he and Junaluska stood on the knoll, looking west. Far off in the distance, campfires beyond counting sent smoke up into the still air. There were many people out there in what they called the Indian Nation—Choctaw, Creek, Chickasaw, a few Seminoles, and the others—many more than there ever had been in one region. But these were not a single people, even though the government wanted to see them as one. They were pushed together like the entire harvest from a garden—potatoes, corn, squash, beans—heaped into one pile on the ground.

Without a word, he and Junaluska made their way toward the meandering line of trees where they found shade and a slow trickle of water from the storm that passed the night before. The grass was soft and they settled into it gratefully. It was not long until they were joined by several of the elders who had been at the campfire the night before. Three important things had happened in their lives recently: John Ross arrived from the East, *Kahnungdatlageh* and his family paid for their betrayal, and this strange, sad man who shot Tsali appeared with some story to tell. In ones and twos, they assembled beneath the willows for the telling. Since the supply wagon had not arrived and there was little food to prepare, some of the women from the camp followed, too.

Junaluska began, because he knew these people. "Euchella came to us on the road to Arkansas, before the killing of *Kahnungdatlageh*. He said that he had seen many things, things that even we did not see in our journey to this place, and other things that we did see. He saw the river that divides the two worlds, and a mighty canoe that churns the water with a great wheel. Then he saw another river that is maybe two weeks walk from here that comes straight out of the ground. And along the way, he found a cave of the ancient *Muskogee*. But none of these things are why he has come here."

The old faces looked to Euchella.

"I come from the Oconoluftee. Many of my people were not taken in the roundup because it was said that we were no longer part of the Cherokee Nation. But some were hunted anyhow. The men who go with me hid out on Balsam and high above Soco where the soldiers and the militia did not want to go, so we avoided them. Some others from the nation tried to make it to the village of Quallatown where they thought that they would be safe. Most were caught. Tsali and his family were among them. They were caught on the Oconoluftee.

"When Tsali killed the soldiers, others hunted him, but could not find him. They caught his sons and son-in-law and put them in a stockade.

"Then a White man, the trader Will Thomas, came to our hideout near Balsam. At first, I though to kill him, but did not. He said that if my men and I would agree to shoot the men of Tsali's family—and Tsali when we found him—that we might continue to live in the old lands. He said that he could 'arrange it' with the army. Those were his words.

"My brother and I did all these things, but after we shot Tsali, we still did not trust that they would allow us to remain, so we went back to the mountains and stayed there until spring."

The old men in the gathering looked at one another, agreeing by their silence that they would not have believed Thomas or the soldiers either.

"When I came down from the mountains, the old chief, Yonaguska, had died. But then I saw two strange things. The people in Quallatown were living as though nothing had happened to the rest of the nation. They were preparing their gardens for planting. They drew water from the river and cooked

153

meals as if the soldiers had never come. Then they made the White man, Thomas, their chief. I saw this with my own eyes."

Looks were exchanged again, but this time there was a measure of disbelief.

"I remember Thomas," said a man with a narrow, leathery face. "I called him 'The Man with the Quick Eyes' because his eyes seemed to go everywhere at once. But he traded fair with me. He spoke our language. It is not common for a White man to speak our language."

Another agreed. "He is a White man who lived among the Cherokees and has a Cherokee name."

Euchella continued. "There is still talk of the people in Quallatown being moved here. The rest of the White settlers want them out, but Thomas has begun buying the land there, so the people continue to live there as though nothing has changed. They say that there will be a Green Corn Festival at the end of the summer."

In spite of themselves, those listening were struck with amazement mixed with bitterness that they could not conceal. They had been compelled to follow John Ross west, out of loyalty or at gunpoint. Some had watched family and friends die along the way, abandoning them in graves which they knew would not be respected as the years rolled on. Now they learned that a select few had been spared their ordeal. "We thought that those left behind would live in hiding," said Leather Face.

"Not in Quallatown. Elsewhere some hide, but not there. But it is not the way it used to be there."

The others caught this turn in the story. "They have a White chief. Although he has lived among the Principal People longer than he lived among the Whites, he speaks the way White men speak. His words make men do things that they would not think to do themselves. I know this because I shot Tsali."

Silence fell on the gathering, and for a long moment the only thing that could be heard was the fitful chirp of a sparrow in a willow overhead. Finally, Junaluska broke the silence. "Tell them what you saw that made you come here."

"Because of Tsali, I had no wish to live in a village where Will Thomas is chief. It is said that he protects the people of Quallatown from those who want all the Cherokees gone from our old lands. And this cannot be a bad thing. But he protects them by making them more White."

Again, looks were exchanged. The people of Snowbird did not know what to make of this news.

"One morning, at the hour when the sacred owl retires from hunting, I went to the old village of *Kituwah* by the Tuckasegee to listen to the spirits of the old ones there. I hoped to learn what a warrior could do now and how to live with what was left to us. I waited beside the mound of our ancestors. They seemed busy, and as they did not speak to me, I sat there some more as the sun rose.

"How long I remained beside the mound, I cannot say. The sun became very bright. But as it is with the hunter, when you are still, you see things the way an owl or hawk sees them. I began to watch a small spider build its web between two tall stalks of grass. It went about its work of repairing the web where it was torn in the night. First on one side, the spider spun new threads and fixed them to the grass. Then it went to the other side and did the same. It did not hurry, but just worked at what it knew to do.

"It came to me that if I waved my hand through the web and destroyed it, the spider would wait for a time to be sure that it was safe, then begin all over again. That is what we must do. We must become like the spider and begin again, no matter where we are or how many times we have to do it."

Faces on the elders relaxed and nodded. "It is a good story," said a woman whose hair was almost white and whose eyes were framed by concentric wrinkles.

"You have done well to bring this to us," said the man with the scar. "We will tell it again and again. It is a gift."

Chapter 19
Soco Creek
July, 1839

ill Thomas did not sleep well and had not for a long time. Dawn brought relief that night was over, but as gray light began to outline the dark profiles of spruce and balsam trees on the ridges, his body felt as though the pieces no longer fit well together. Coffee would help. Whiskey would be better. However, in keeping with the public image that he was fashioning for himself, he chose the former, while silently admitting that he would have preferred the latter. Whiskey would take the edge off the dream that he had been having, off and on, for the past month. In it was the face of John Ross, the Principal Chief who had gone west with the majority of the tribe. That was all he saw: the dour face of John Ross. Will did not much like Ross. Never had. He found him pompous and kingly, the kind of man with whom he would find it difficult to co-exist in the same room. In the times when they had met face to face—such as when Will acted as interpreter for the general who had come to the nation to assess the Cherokees' mood to move— Will found him to be pointlessly adversarial. But Ross was still chief of the largest portion of the Cherokees, and that faction would follow him anywhere. The very thought of Ross made Will's insides clinch as though a corset were yanked tight around his middle, and he wished that the memory of Ross would stay in the West where it belonged and out of his dreams.

Without Kanaka nearby, he was lonely. She was the only one who could distract him from these black moments of uncertainty. He missed the quiet way that she brought order to him. Of course, he could see her any time that he wanted to, and the baby, too, at the new settlement upriver where she had moved. But that would mean that he would have to endure the torment of being a visitor. Lately, he had torment enough.

At the dying wish of Yonaguska, the remnant of the tribe in Quallatown had made Thomas chief, but Ross was the legitimate chief of the whole nation. So what was Thomas but a pretender? Ross represented authenticity, and Will could not escape the feeling of being discovered as a fake, nor could he see how to make himself feel legitimate.

It had all been too easy, his becoming chief. There was the gathering of people in Quallatown following Yonaguska's death, some words flowed naturally and easily out of him—almost without his control—then their acceptance of him as chief. So why did he feel like such a fraud? Why did his dream of Ross seem more real than real life?

Doubts pursued him like horseflies, swirling, pestering, making him feel defensive. He would be in a flinty mood again today, snapping at people in the trading post when they asked inane questions that they could easily answer for themselves. But he should not be depressed. He had taken a big risk and things were breaking right. His vision of a reservation for the Eastern Band should bring satisfaction. After all, it was beginning to take shape. Scattered parcels of land that he bought were slowly forming a large, contiguous whole. Except for Euchella and that bunch of nitwits who followed him, there was approval from the people in Quallatown for what he was doing. And even some of the members of the government in Washington quietly wanted him to succeed. There was reason for optimism. The people were becoming industrious again. Farming was on the upswing. Pots were being fired. Women were weaving things to sell. The reports that he sent to Raleigh about Christian conversions and reduced drunkenness were true in substance, if not in absolute detail. So why the doubt? Why the perpetual fear that at any moment he would be unmasked?

A vague sense of exclusion dogged him as though there were some status that he longed to achieve that could only be conveyed by others who had already attained it. Would attaining this threshold put his everlasting anxiety to rest and dispel the notion that others held him in contempt? Could he never truly become one of them, but could only pretend to do so? Was this the specter of Ross or just all his own imagination?

Will stumbled into his boots and brushed his hands through a thick helmet of hair that hung almost to his shoulders. He smelled like a field hand. No, a field hand smelled of work sweat. Will smelled of nervous sweat. Even Kanaka's dog shied away from him lately. It knew the difference. He smelled like a man who was on the edge of a plunge into a dark place. Tonight when he came to bed again, he would bring a bottle of corn liquor with him, out of sight of his mother who would disapprove. He had to sleep, and he had to sleep without seeing the face of John Ross.

When Will walked to the creek that ran near the big frame house that he had built for his mother, he noticed that Demarius' horse was missing from its stall in the barn. It was early for her to be out, but she had been doing that lately. Like many other things that troubled him, Demarius was on his mind, too. Where had she gone? Subtle changes had come over her. They spoke less and less these days, or at least when he asked her a question, she answered with fewer words.

Will knelt beside the stream near the house and tossed cold water over his head and face. It took almost too much effort to try to wake up. His arms and hands seemed disjointed. The heavy sweet smell of honeysuckle that ordinarily brought such seductive pleasure now only made him more aware of his misery.

Later, when he arrived at the trading post, Will found Jonas Jenkins waiting for him. God only knew at what hour Jonas arose, with the roosters, perhaps. He seemed to haunt the trails and valleys at an hour when no sensible person wanted to be out of bed. Jonas' habits would make sense if he were coming home from an all-night drunk, but Jonas was not much of a drinker so that made his habits all the more peculiar. The only regular thing about Jonas was that he did not care that people thought that he was weird. Somehow, he made being weird normal. He was what he was and that was that. It was a little unnerving for Will to realize that Jonas was his only real friend. He did not know what to make of that, except that it made him less than normal, too, he supposed. On black days like this, Will found Jonas either unbearable or a welcome distraction. Today, he was a distraction.

True to form, Jonas never began a conversation with a preamble, but launched into it as though the person to whom he was speaking was pondering the same thing at the same moment. "Mr. Will, what will you do with all that land?"

"It's like a puzzle, Jonas. We put it together, one piece at a time. In a few years, there will be enough for several thousand people."

"But what *is* it?"

Will drank some of the rough, bitter coffee that he had made on the stove. Ordinarily, he would not light the stove this time of year as it made the trading post hot all day, but today, he needed the boost that it gave. "A safe place. They call it a *reservation*."

"And White people can't come on it?"

"No. They can come on it, they just can own it."

For a moment, Jonas retreated into his own thoughts. "Will they stand for it?"

Will raised his eyebrows. Again, Jonas showed that he was not the slow-witted fellow that most people took him to be. That there was wide support to remove the remaining Cherokees was no secret, but no one was as blunt about it as Jonas. "I can't say. But I am going to try to see that those who want them out never again have the power to make it happen."

After Jonas left to tend his garden, a post rider arrived at the trading post. He had three letters to be distributed in the community; one was addressed to the Hon. William H. Thomas. Will set the other two aside to wait for the recipients to appear at the trading post. Otherwise, he would deliver them himself after he closed up.

The letter for him was mysterious in that the envelope came from Washington, but it bore no return address. When he opened it, his sense of intrigue grew as there was no signature there either. He began to read:

Greetings from Mr. Jefferson's dismal swamp,

I hope this finds you well. You will know the source of this message from its content. For reasons of self-preservation, I dare not sign it.

There is great news and I thought that you should hear of it. Within six to eight months time, you are to be confirmed as the recognized agent of the Eastern Band of Cherokee Indians. This decision was made at the highest levels of my department.

The reason for the delay will be obvious in a moment. To make sure that there is no change in this decision, you must continue to send reports of progress that your

people are making in their path toward civilization.
There is some anxiety within the government that Whites
and Indians cannot coexist side by side, that "wild" and
"civilized" peoples are natural and implacable enemies.
The specter of Jackson lingers, and his final State of the
Union speech is still quoted, particularly the part where
he urged total removal. However, your reports paint a
very different picture altogether, particularly the
references to Christianizing the savages. Keep them
coming. It is imperative for your situation that you do so.

As I suggested, however, there is another faction and
they must be dealt with. Word will reach your ears of a
move within the department to test non-military means
of removing those Cherokees who remain in the East.
Someone will be appointed to visit your region to try to
convince them to leave. Money will be offered, and
heaven knows what else. For political reasons, we must
allow this to take place. Your people simply have to be
unanimous in their resolve to stay where they are and
refuse this offer, whatever it may be.

By this time next year, you will be confirmed as the
recognized authority and agent for the Eastern
Cherokees. Maintain your resolve and do not be
discouraged by contrary and avaricious forces.

Your good friend in Washington.

Will touched the letter with his fingertips as
though it were something alive that could bite. On
another day, it would have brought him rapture. But
today, with the memory of John Ross behind him, it
brought terror. His mind focused on phrases of doubt
. . . *Whites and Indians cannot coexist . . . have to be*
unanimous. He dropped the single sheet and it
fluttered down to the top of the stove. In a moment,

brown patches formed along the creases and he watched, fascinated, as they spread across the paper. A voice within him shouted for him to retrieve the letter, but his arms remained immobile as the paper curled and turned black, obscuring the words that brought him such fright.

Chapter 20
Oklahoma Territory
Late July, 1839

n the last magical moment before darkness, silvery twilight cast a luminescence on the huts of the Snowbird camp and the line of willow trees that meandered to the southwest.

Anything pale, such as the canvass on lean-tos and tents or white rocks, seem to glow with a light of its own. Junaluska had seen this phenomenon all his life, but he remained fascinated by it, passing as it did in the wink of a firefly.

This serene moment was in extreme contrast to the storm that had swept through in the afternoon, leaving grass on the hills laying flat and wet. It had been a great beast of a storm—black and rolling— unlike the warm summer thunderstorms back in his Snowbird Mountains. The people huddled down before it, and it came on them suddenly, relentlessly, and there was nowhere to hide in this land, no caves, no rock crevasses. Whips of lightning lashed the sky. When the wind came, it howled like a bear enraged, and was filled with bits of stinging things—sticks, sand, grass, and leaves. With no place to go, the people lay flat on the ground and trembled as the storm roared past. None of the others who waited out its passing had seen anything like it either.

When it was over, they rose bewildered, then began to examine the camp for damage. Some tents had collapsed, others were missing the whole canvass or sections of canvass. The ground was littered with pieces of clothing and the few metal pots that they used communally. In the center, the fire was out and some of the sticks that had been burning there now lay on the flattened grass.

It took hours to put the camp back together. Even so, they would sleep damp tonight. As night descended, the women had the fire going again, and the people gathered for a meal. Junaluska took this moment to slip away over the rise to the west and down the line of willows that grew along the gully. Water flowed there now. It would not last, but for the moment it looked like a real stream. Something pushed him to be alone, be away from talk, away from the concerns of staying alive. He was vaguely troubled by another dream. The night before was the second night that it had come to him and he wanted a place to sit where he could think and make something out of it before it came again. It was not frightening as had been the one about the owl and the squirrel's nest that he had experienced in the days before the traitors sold out New Echota. Old Tsali had explained that one, before he was shot. Now there was no one to explain dreams and few places to sit in this endless land to wait for an explanation to become clear. Where would he go?

Junaluska followed the trees, moving with a pace that suited his old legs. He drifted around fallen limbs that the people would burn tomorrow. When he came to a rise a long way from the camp, it was almost dark. Even in the faint light he could see a gap where a section of trees had been torn away by the storm. Oddly enough, they were not knocked down, but were sheared off halfway up the trunk. Splinters stood from the naked wood as though great teeth had bitten off the upper half. Crowns of the trees lay scattered on the far side, and there was a path scored through the grass as though some large herd had trampled it. This was a strange storm, born out of this strange land. How would the Principle People ever be at home here?

Marked as it was by the Great Spirit of this place, the prairie needed to restore itself. Junaluska sat cross-legged on the path of the storm to see if there were rhythms from it that he might feel and let his mind wander back to his dream. In all his life, there had never been a woman in his dreams, but there was one in this one. She was young and she was strong and she was slender—and vaguely familiar. In the dream, this woman, who could not have been more than eighteen or twenty, was shooting an arrow toward an approaching animal. The animal was not seen, and Junaluska could not tell from her expression if it were coming at her as a predator. Each time the dream came to him, she was standing on high ground, pulling back on her bowstring. Her face had the look of stone. But what did the dream foretell? A woman alone—hunter or defender?—it meant nothing to him. Cherokee women sometimes used the bow, he knew, but that was more in the time of his grandfather, when the land was mostly Cherokee and guns did not exist in the hands of the tribe.

Darkness was complete now. To the east, there was a faint glow of the fire from the camp of his people, but only starlight lit the hills. Even though the grass was still damp, he lay back in it to think some more. That was when he felt footsteps pulsating softly in his shoulders. They were made by a person walking Indian-like, on the balls of their feet. Someone approached, someone knew he was here. But he had told no one that he was leaving or where he was going, so it had to be someone from his own camp, someone who watched him leave. Euchella? No, the footsteps were irregular, stumbling. A warrior such as Euchella would walk with wide steps in places where he could not see clearly. Euchella would not stumble.

Junaluska rolled over to one elbow and put his ear to the ground and stopped breathing. The padding came closer. He got to his feet and circled in a crouch away from where he had been sitting and waited

nearby. A dark form came to the spot where he had been, then halted, probably surprised at not finding him there.

Like an old cat, Junaluska sprang out of the grass and with his large mass easily knocked the stalker to the ground. The intruder let out a muffled shriek as the air went out of them. It was the voice of a woman. Angered, Junaluska got up. "Who are you?"

The woman lay on the ground, stunned and panting.

"Why do you approach me with such bad manners? No Cherokee would approach another the way that you did without bad intent."

The woman rolled over. He still could not make out her face, only a vague form of her body lying there. "I did not want anyone in the camp to know that I talked to you."

He grunted, disappointed that his stalker was not another warrior. He had enjoyed a moment of battle, and a warrior, especially and old one, needs battle now and then. "What?" he asked impatiently.

"Your friend—the one from the East—he will return soon?"

"That is my understanding."

"I want to go with him. I want you to ask him to take me."

Junaluska took a deep breath and, although still annoyed, considered her request. "Why do you want to go back?"

"Because I cannot live here. Your friend knows the way and how to get there. I have heard that he has visions. I, too, have visions and they tell me that I must go back."

Junaluska sat down beside her. "Where was your village? You are not of my people."

She said that she came from a town on the
Hiwassee. That explained why she was in the camp of
the Snowbird people; they had been taken west
together from the same stockade near Chattanooga. If
he could see her, he might even recognize her. "My
family was the last of our village remaining when the
soldiers came. The others had been run off earlier in
battles with the Whites, or they had died of the fever
that came with the missionaries. There were raids all
the time. We were not enough to resist them."

Junaluska had heard of these raids. There had
been much killing, with little purpose. "Then your
village does not exist. Why do you wish to go to a
village that is no more?"

"I must go. It does not matter where. I am
wasted here. My dreams tell me this, that I have a
purpose beyond this place, in the old ways."

Junaluska was glad that she could not see his
face in the darkness because she would see how
surprised he was. "I, too, have had a dream, and in it
was a woman. Judging by your voice, she could be
your age. She was very determined in my dream."

"Will your friend take me?"

"I do not know. He had a very bad thing happen
to his wife. She starved when he went to the
mountains to restore in him what it is to be a warrior.
I am not sure that he wants anything to do with a
woman now."

"My husband died, too. He froze in the winter,
on the march after the boat, as many did."

Junaluska remembered the horror and the
burials. "Then we will ask him and see what he says."

The two of them made their way across the
cleared field, back to the Snowbird camp. Even in the
starlight, he could tell that he towered over her. She
was slightly built, too. No wonder he had knocked her

down easily. So much for his own moment of being a warrior.

As they neared the camp, the faint sound of a chant came to them. It was the voice of a hunter preparing himself spiritually for a long journey into the mountains to kill a bear. The song was one of ambition and apology, ambition for the hunter to assert his skill, apology to the bear for taking its life. But as there were no mountains and no bears in this place, the chant became a lament, and the sad irony of it gripped them as they approached.

"The old ways pull at us all," the woman said sadly.

On the crest of the rise by the camp, they could see the fire and the people gathered around it. Sparks flew into the air above the flames. In the flickering light, Junaluska could finally see the face of the woman. She had the high cheek bones and almond eyes that were common to many Cherokee women, but her face was narrow and her chin was pleasantly round. Her body, in spite of being slender, was strong.

Junaluska stopped walking and the woman turned toward him. "I will ask my friend to take you back. He must," the old chief said with a voice that sounded strange, even to himself.

"Why? Why are you so certain?"

He took a deep breath. There are things that can be explained, and other things that cannot be explained. Sometimes one just has to say what you were thinking and hope the person to whom you are saying it will understand. "You were the woman in my dream."

Chapter 21
Oklahoma Territory
Early August, 1839

uchella lay in the rabbit's nest of grass and limbs and leaves that he had erected for his own shelter in the Snowbird camp. It kept the sun off his face during the day, but not much else. It was similar to the nest that he had made a year and a half before in the mountains, to protect himself from the cold and snow when he had hid out from the soldiers. This one had not fared well during the storm that roared through earlier in the day, tearing at the camp like a dog that is possessed by summer madness. There were moments as he had lain beneath the limbs while the wind screamed overhead that he felt his body becoming light and being lifted upward. He curled his fingers in the grass beneath him to hold on. Later, he rebuilt the little shelter with new limbs and leaves, but if another storm came, it would be knocked down, too.

The heat from the land had abated enough to permit sleep, but Euchella could not sleep. Everything was still damp, and his mind was restless with thoughts of what he had seen and with what was to come. It was time for him to be going. The story that he had come here to tell these people was told, over and over, as people came from other camps throughout the grasslands to hear it. Even a clan of Choctaws had walked for two days from their settlement and braved the hostile glances of the Cherokees to hear what he had to say. They could make of it what they would. There was talk around the communal fire of a new Keetowah Society. Just tonight, one man was designated fire keeper to ensure that the sacred fire was never blown out again. That was good. There was a chance that the old ways would be kept and that the people would cling to some thread of what made them the *Ani'Yun'wiya'*. He had given them the vision. Beyond that there was nothing more that he could do here.

He thought of leaving. If he went soon he would not be caught by winter. He remembered the canoe that was hidden away in the crown of the fallen maple, near the big river that divided the world. If it was still there, the skins would need repair. But since he would need new moccasins by then, he could kill a deer on the way and solve both problems at the same time. Would any of the Whites who occasionally came to the camp try to prevent him from leaving? No one had questioned his excursions away from camp as he explored the rolling countryside, but then who could imagine someone walking their way out of here? That would be his advantage. He would leave at night, on a night like this when only stars were out, without a word to anyone except Junaluska. Perhaps he would head west for a while, then double back. By the time anyone realized that he was gone, he would be twenty miles east, too far away to track.

Euchella stared up through breaks in the leaves overhead. After the storm, the sky cleared except for small clouds that drifted by, making the stars alternately disappear then reappear. There was movement near his shelter, but he took little notice of it as people went out of the camp at all hours of the night to relieve themselves in the surrounding woods. Suddenly, there was a crash above him and a weight landed on him hard, covering his body. A searing pain tore through his left shoulder. Reflexively, he brought his knee up to repel the attacker, and caught the man in the groin. The other gasped and choked as the fight seemed to go out of him.

Disoriented, Euchella threw his attacker off and rolled out of the wreckage of the shelter, but when he stood up, his shoulder pained him so much that he staggered, dizzy. Three old men from the camp came up and circled him, drawn to the commotion. Each held a burning stick to light the scene. One pointed to Euchella, then reached out and pulled a large knife that was sticking from his shirt. Euchella felt his knees buckle and everything turned gray, then black as the pain vanished.

When he opened his eyes again, the sun had begun to paint the eastern sky. There was a growing feeling in his shoulder that his arm had been ripped from his body, and the agony of it spread even into his legs, and he realized that he was sweating profusely.

"He is awake." The voice was Junaluska's.

Slowly, Euchella became aware that there were others around him, then he became aware of the smell of burning flesh.

"He will be weak for some time." This was the voice of a woman, one that he did not recognize. It had a note of authority as though she had tended wounded men before and knew what to expect.

"How long?"

"A month. If he is well fed and the wound does not become infected. If it does . . . ." There was no need to finish.

Euchella watched the big head of Junaluska nod. He still could not see the woman and did not feel like turning his head to search for her.

"You will stay with him? I will go see what I can find to eat. I may be gone for a long time."

"What about the boy?"

"He will be no more trouble. Anyhow, he is tied up."

Euchella heard Junaluska leave and his place was taken by the woman whose face now appeared over him. She had a serious expression, with high cheek bones and almond eyes that turned up at the ends like those of a cat. Her nose was small and her jaw protruded slightly, giving her an angular look. In better times, she might have appeared softer, but no one in the camps was eating well. All had lost weight in the stockades before the migration, and meals had been irregular on the trail. Now, they had little fat to spare.

"Who . . . are you?" he rasped.

"I am Nanee."

Pain overcame him again and he drifted off. When he awoke, she was still there, and he realized that she had assumed responsibility for his care. For a moment, he wondered why. He had no family here, only a few people such as Junaluska knew him at all. Most people here thought of him as the bearer of news and the killer of Tsali.

"Who was that man who stabbed me?"

The woman leaned over his face so that he would not have to strain to see her. "His name is Wasseton, but he is barely more than a boy."

The name was familiar, but the throbbing through his body made thinking difficult. He did not seem to be bleeding, and the smell of scorched flesh told him that someone had cauterized his wound with a burning stick. With his right hand, he pointed toward his shoulder. "You?"

Nanee nodded. "It had to be stopped. You will heal now, but you will not be pretty."

Euchella could not respond to her humor, not even a flicker of a smile, but he was grateful for it.

It was two days before Junaluska returned. In that time, the woman, Nanee, fed him a thin broth that simmered in the communal pot in the center of the camp. It was not good, but it was hot and when he could eat no more, his body felt satisfied. Perhaps it was just relief that he was eating no more of it. Nanee was patient with him, and a little kinder than he thought necessary. When he had to rise twice each day to stagger into the woods and relieve himself, she steadied him, then moved away discretely until he finished. Very soon, he was glad for her presence. As he lay in the shelter where the people had placed him, she stayed by his side, covering the wound to ward off flies and occasionally fanning him with a sycamore branch.

He did not speak much, but asked her to talk about her family because it took his mind off the throbbing in his shoulder. She obliged by telling him about her home in Tennessee and the slow moving rivers there, the fields of corn, and the ballgames in the village. "The fields were good to us and the rivers gave us fish that would make the corn tall. We danced a lot then. I liked to watch the men dance." In a matter of fact voice, she explained how the village was reduced by a sickness that followed the missionaries. "My grandmother and grandfather died within the same month. It was the same for most of the families. We lost many people—mostly the young and the old— even before the raids by the Whites and our raids against them." When she got to the part about her husband, her voice became sad, but she continued, recounting how he had been a ball player for another village and that he had spotted her in the crowd of onlookers. "When the soldiers came for us last year, we stayed together in the stockade, but it was hot, and the food that they brought to us they would not have fed to their animals. Some people became sick and died before we left." Finally, she told him about the freezing after they got off the river, and how her husband had simply not waked up one morning. "We buried him facing the rising sun," she said distantly.

Euchella lay with his head on a loose roll of cloth and had closed his eyes so that he could picture her story. She bore her sadness the way a Cherokee woman was expected to bear it. Again, he wondered why she chose now to stay with him. It could be that she simply had nothing else to do, or because she had tended other wounded men and was experienced with tending them. But he suspected that there was a more personal reason, one that had to do with him. It was time to ask. "What do you want of me?"

She was silent for a moment, surprised by his insight. "When you go back to the East, I must go with you."

Euchella lifted his head. "Why?"

"Because I am called to go. I had a dream and it told me that I am wasted here, that I must go back and begin a family there."

Of course, dreams. He remembered the spider and the relentless way it rebuilt its web. "But your husband is dead."

"I will find another. That was part of the dream. There must be children, more children of the *Ani'-Yun'wiya'*."

He sat up completely and felt the blood surge in his shoulder. Holding his breath, he waited for the pain to pass. When he could speak again, he looked at her directly. "It would be risky. It was risky for me to come here alone. There are men out there . . . on the river, who care for nothing. I, myself, hid from them. I could not protect you."

"I know the risks. I have seen death and cruelty. But this is a thing that I must do and you are the only one who is willing to risk the journey."

He looked at her and saw that her determination was overpowering. Perhaps this, too, was part of the lesson of the spider. "In two weeks, we will go. But first, there must be a Green Corn Festival."

Nanee looked at him puzzled. "But we have no corn. No one has planted any yet."

For the first time since the attack, Euchella smiled. "Then I will ask Junaluska to get some when he returns."

Chapter 22
Northwest Arkansas
Early August, 1839

The seven men of the party that shot *Kahnungdatlageh* lay beside Junaluska in the weeds at the edge of the farm and waited for sunrise. Already the air was thick, but in spite of the humidity, it felt good to be warriors again, even if it was only a cornfield of a White farmer that they were raiding. Junaluska looked around and in the faint light he could see eagerness on the faces of the men, even the old one with the scar. In the time that they had been here, all the men had come to trust him and his leadership, although many were not of his village. However, they were the ones that he would seek out now when something needed to be done.

Far off near the farmhouse, a dog barked a warning. The men would have to move with stealth to avoid raising an alarm. There were other farms not far off, so they needed to get what they had come for and get out quickly. He looked again at each of them, then jerked his head forward. They began to crawl into the field, pulling empty feedsacks behind them. When they reached the ripe corn, they rose almost as one and began to twist the ears off the stalks. For a moment, the dog was quiet as if it sensed them, but because there was no wind or sound, it did not know where they were. However, when their sacks were half full, the dog set to barking in earnest. The men abandoned all pretense to silence and pulled corn as fast as they could bag it.

From the door of the farmhouse, there was the sound of a musket shot in their direction and a ball tore the tops off three stalks nearby. The Cherokee men ducked and picked up their own rifles and, in a tremendous roar, fired a volley in return. Eight shots were enough to make the farmer think that he was under attack and to keep him inside until they could escape back into Oklahoma Territory. Likely, he would barricade his door and not come out for the remainder of the day, or until the neighbors showed up with their own guns to help. Only the dog would be put out to determine if the raiding party had left.

Hoisting the now full sacks, the men shouldered their rifles and made their way out of the field. But instead of heading directly west toward the Indian Territory, they circled the farm, being sure to leave a trail that was easy to follow, alternately scattering in separate paths, then coming back together again to walk west as one. A good tracker would not be fooled by the ruse, but probably the farmer and his neighbors would never know how many were actually in the raiding party and be reluctant to follow.

It would be a long walk back to the territory because they had chosen to go deep into Arkansas to prevent any retaliation for the raid. The sacks would grow heavy, but for the first time in over a year, the men felt joy. The people would recreate the Green Corn Festival that had been neglected for three years in the East while they waited for the government to decide what it would do with them. Now that they were here, they could begin to be Cherokees again. This was the message brought by the man, Euchella. Be Cherokee again. The festival would be the first step.

It took two days to return and it was dark as they neared the camp. For the last few miles, the party followed a sound that they had not heard in a long time: a drum. Someone had fashioned a drum and the steady beat came to them like a heartbeat in the night. When they drew closer, they could see people dancing near the fire as to purify the ground for the ritual. For the first time since the wagons arrived here, this would be Cherokee land, sanctified in the old way. When the raiders stood on the hill overlooking the camp, people spotted them and ran to meet them.

Junaluska found Euchella sitting away from the fire. He was still weak, but healing. The woman Nanee stood beside him, clapping with the other women. She troubled Junaluska because her likeness to the woman in his dream was so strong that sometimes when he looked at her he wondered what was real and what was dream. Still, she was a healer, he reasoned, and kind. That Euchella was not dead was proof of that.

"I last ate corn with Tsali," said Euchella, "over in your country, the Snowbirds."

"We have come a long way from there. It is good to see the people making this place our own."

Women took the first sack of corn and piled it on top of the fire. Soon the scent of scorching shucks and steaming corn filled the air above the camp. The drummer continued beating the ageless rhythm and the men moved to the cadence, their feet pounding the ground with movements that they knew by instinct. Strangers from other settlements drifted in, attracted by the sound that carried for miles in the night air. Someone stood beside the fire with a stick to turn the corn so that the ears inside did not blacken. The eldest woman in the camp was given the first one to taste, and she tore at the steaming ear with the few teeth that she had left, then looked up at the people and grinned. A great shout went up and the other ears were pulled from the fire and passed around, to children this time. Another bag was dumped onto the fire.

Junaluska brought an ear for Euchella and another for Nanee, then went back to the fire to fetch one for himself. The three ate without speaking and watched as a dozen men continued the dance. Before long, one began to chant, then another picked it up tentatively as though he were uncertain that it was appropriate to sing the sacred songs in a place as alien as this. Then more joined in and everyone grew comfortable. They danced into the night, long after all the corn was eaten and the fire died back, then found someplace on the ground to lie down, exhausted, and sleep.

Euchella was the first to rise the next morning. He stood on shaky legs as Nanee opened her eyes and watched him from the spot where she had slept nearby. He seemed to survey the sleeping forms. "People of Snowbird," he shouted, "speak with me."

All around, the people jumped up.

"It is the time of the Green Corn Festival. Bring me the one who would kill me."

For a moment, no one moved, then two men from the back of the gathering disappeared over the hill. Nanee stood and touched his wounded shoulder, but he brushed her away. Presently the people parted and the would-be assassin was brought forward, bound. He was very young—looking even younger than he was because he was dusty and unkempt from sitting tied for days—and very frightened. This was the boy who had been with his grandfather, Tsali, at the killing of the soldiers on the Tuckasegee, the boy who had been freed by the army colonel at the trial of his relatives. He was not powerfully built, but he stared at Euchella with all the defiance that he could muster. Still, his face gave him away, with eyes and a mouth that were too soft for murder.

"Free him."

The ropes holding the boy's arms behind him were cut. Now he looked at Euchella with surprise.

"This boy is Cherokee. I am the one responsible for the death of this father and grandfather. What he did was an attempt to restore harmony." The people waited for him to continue. "It is our tradition at this time to put aside all grievances, except murder, from the past year. It is our way to cleanse each village of anger and go into the coming year as one people." He looked around at the crowd. "Before I shot him, his grandfather asked me to take care of the boy, and I said that I would. Now, I say let this boy be Cherokee again."

There were nods around the gathering. "It is right," said an elderly woman with braided hair. Others agreed.

Nanee looked at the boy apprehensively, as though now free he might attempt murder again, but the boy seemed bewildered. The rage had gone out of him. For the second time, since his father and grandfather had been executed, he was spared.

Chapter 23
Oklahoma Territory
Early August, 1839

Two days after the celebration of the Green Corn Festival, Euchella rose from the shelter that he shared with Nanee and stepped outside into the damp morning. It was time to leave. He was far from as strong as he was before the stabbing, but what gains to come in the next weeks would be small. He still could not raise his hand on the injured arm above his shoulder and was too weak to hold a bow. Nanee would have to do most of the hunting, but she could do it. If they did not leave Oklahoma now, winter would catch them somewhere in between. But what was it that continued to hold him here?

Nanee joined him outside and they stood watching the sun come up over the eastern forest. She took his hand as though she knew what he was thinking. "I have something to show you. It will make leaving this place easier." Euchella looked at her with wonder. Sometimes it seemed that she was a witch because she had a way of being everything he needed her to be. Even his wife could never do that.

He followed her as they made their way out of the camp and reached higher ground, turning northwest and past a stand of sumac that buffered the forest. They walked for a long time beneath the shadow of a small mountain. No words passed between them, but for the first time in his life, Euchella enjoyed walking behind a woman. Beneath the simple shift that she wore, her body moved as she ducked beneath low limbs and stepped over fallen logs. She was agile and light on her feet and moved like a fox. Though he did not know her in any way other than as his healer, he marveled at all the things that she could do and the matter-of-fact manner in which she did them. She could stalk and skin an animal as well as any man. When something needed to be done, she simply did it without fussing over whose chore it was. To Nanee, work was work and had no gender.

Until this moment, Euchella had thought of her as a companion and as someone who had once had her own life apart from his, not as a woman. He had not wanted a woman since that cold day two years ago when Tsali had come to the Snowbirds to tell him that his wife was dead. The hurt of that had taken a long time to pass, but it was passing now. This woman, Nanee, could heal wounds other than stabbings it seemed.

Again, as though she read his mind, she stopped in the dimness of the woods and turned to him. "I think that you like following me too much."

Euchella was embarrassed to be caught watching her. "It is a good sign," he said, ". . . that I am getting better."

Nanee made no reply, but there was a twinkle in her eye as she turned to walk again. The two continued until they broke out of a thicket on the edge of a small river. Nanee had to stop abruptly to keep from falling down the bank. "They call this the Flint River," she said in a whisper.

The water was a beautiful green, clear to the bottom where a ledge of gray rock lay. On the other side, a blue heron lifted one leg cautiously, alerted by their arrival. Turtles slipped off logs and dived for safety. Below where they stood, the stream pooled and was almost still, then moved on in cascades until it pooled again. It smelled like clean water. This was unlike any other stream that Euchella had found in these parts. About the size of Soco Creek, it sang softly on its way down the valley.

Nanee sat on the ground and Euchella followed her. They sat like hunters, unmoving, until the turtles reappeared and resumed their clumsy search for food. "You can go home now. The people can use this river to cleanse themselves and to practice our rituals. Babies will be brought here for naming. There will be counsels here and festivals. When a person is filled with doubt, they can come here to think on it and wait for a visit from the spirits. Women will come in the morning to draw water and wash their clothes. Like your story of the spider, things can be as they were, at least for the people of our camp."

She was right. This river would give the people the chance to be *Ani'-Yun'wiya'* again. "You do many things well." He did not know what more to say.

Nanee took his hand, less in affection than to get his attention. When she spoke, it was as though her voice came from the river. "When we leave, we must take the boy Wasseton with us."

Euchella considered this. The idea had been on his mind, too. For Nanee, her reasons to include the boy were obviously spiritual, part of her dream of returning to the tribe of the East. But for Euchella it was personal. He owed Tsali a debt. Returning his grandson to the home of his people would be a way to settle that. "Does he want to go?"

"Who among us would not?"

In the evening, Nanee invited the boy to their shelter and over a small fire where the body of a rabbit sizzled, she described their plan to go east. Earlier in the day, she had found mushrooms in a pine thicket that now cooked inside the carcass along with a handful of wild onions. The smell was seductive. Wasseton sat uneasily with them and accepted food reluctantly as though he expected to be punished for attacking Euchella. But Euchella gave no hint of resentment. There was no tension around his eyes to suggest that he was waiting for revenge. To him, the absolution of the Green Corn Festival was total.

"Will you join us?" asked Nanee as she cleaned the meat off a leg of the rabbit.

Wasseton glanced again at Euchella. "How would we go?"

"The same way that I came," answered Euchella. "We take the long walk to the big river. Then, if the canoe is still where I hid it, we reseal the seams, then go back on the other rivers." As an afterthought, he added, "If it is not, I will try to remember enough of what my brother showed me to build another one."

Wasseton nodded, remembering the long westerly journey, the cold that numbed the body, the infrequent meals, and the burials that were so frequent that they numbed the mind. "Spirits were lost all along the trail from the river," he said. "So many died, we lost count. It was like they were not even Cherokees. Sometimes all we could do was put them under rocks. My grandmother was lost, too. I am not even sure where she is. I think it was just after the boat."

"Perhaps you can find her," said Nanee.

The boy nodded. "Perhaps. If I can remember."

That night after Wasseton left, Nanee did not lay in her usual spot on the far side of the shelter, but instead lay next to Euchella. She smelled of the cookfire and of the earth. Her hand found the wound on his shoulder and examined it slowly with fingers as a blind person would. Pressing hard on it, she tested his sensitivity. When he did not so much as grunt, she was satisfied that he was healing well. Then she began to explore the rest of his body, carefully, curiously, marveling at how different a male is. He accepted her touch passively, indulging her curiosity, then responded to it. After a time, their breathing quickened and their bodies began to writhe together. To the rhythm of the slow song of the crickets outside, Nanee lifted herself on top of him and they consummated the desire that both had felt on their walk to the river in the morning.

Chapter 24
Missouri Ozarks
Middle August, 1839

ight days after they left the settlement in Oklahoma, Euchella knew that they were being followed. For the past three mornings, there was smoke from a campfire directly behind them. He could either see the plume rising or smell it. The distance varied, but it was never more than a couple of miles away. These were not other Cherokees shadowing them. Cherokees following them would not have risked building a fire and making their presence known. More likely, these were White men. He did not know what they wanted, but he could not see how it could be good. He also did not know why they kept their distance, but decided that whoever they were, they were biding their time to approach—or attack—at their own advantage. If they had horses, it could be that they were simply trying to establish the direction that the three were going, then race ahead in a circular path and lay a trap. For a moment, he regretted his decision to give the rifle that he had taken off the river men to Junaluska. That left them out matched, a fact that their pursuers would eventually discover.

Since leaving Oklahoma, Euchella, Nanee, and Wasseton had pushed deep into the Missouri Ozarks, edging along the trail cut for the emigrants coming west last year. The easy hills of Arkansas had turned into the low mountains of Missouri, and they were not far from the bewitched place where the river spews forth from the ground. Euchella regretted that the other two would not see it, but it lay too far off their course. Although the days were still hot, the nights had begun to cool, bringing the first hint of the change of the seasons. Until now, they covered over twenty miles each day when the walking was easy. Although not yet strong, Euchella had no trouble leading the way. Signs of the migration from last year still littered the trail, and the tracks left by wagon wheels remained deep. They found many graves, too, but none of them was the one for Wasseton's grandmother. They stepped reverently around each one. At night, Wasseton caught rabbits in a snare and they ate well, particularly when Nanee could work her magic on the meat with herbs that she gathered during the day as they walked.

Until now, there had been no challenge to them because they skirted settlements and farms along the trail without drawing notice. Nanee stood with Euchella on the brow of a hill and watched the smoke from the distant campfire. "What do you think?"

"I have been hunted before. We are being hunted now. They will come at us in their own time, I think, when they decide how strong we are. Perhaps that is why they wait."

"Can we fight?"

"Yes. But there may be a better way."

She grunted. He would tell them what he wanted to do in his own time. He was, after all, a warrior of great repute.

They walked eastward for most of the day, seeming to pay no attention to their pursuers. Where the cleared trail took a turn north, Euchella led them into the woodland, holding to their easterly direction. Near evening, when they reached a mountain that was partially wrapped by a small river on its north and east slopes, he took them along the north edge, then up to the spine of the ridge and down the eastern face to the river again. At that point, he halted, then had them retrace their path back to the north side of the mountain. There they jumped out onto near rocks in the stream, and without a splash lowered themselves into the water. The river was slow and shallow and the bottom was mostly gravel. In dense brush on the other side, they climbed out unseen.

Now they waited. An hour passed and twilight fell, deepening the shadows in the woods. Far away, a crow called. Euchella gripped Nanee's arm. "They come."

In the dim light, three figures descended the flank of the mountain, leading horses through the heavy brush. The one in the lead was Indian, but not of a tribe that they recognized. He was bare from the waist up and his head was shaved, leaving only a knot of hair in the back. Obviously the best tracker of the three, he kept his eyes on the ground as they walked. The other two were White, and appeared to be trappers, but their horses carried little in the way of provisions and no furs. A rifle hung on each saddle.

When the men moved past the spot where the three Cherokees had left the trail, Euchella whispered to Nanee. "Find something for horses to eat." Then he slipped into the river and crossed back to the other side.

It was dark when he caught up to the pursuers. They camped on a sandy flat across the river, no doubt confident of picking up the trail of the Cherokees in the morning. Euchella could see them seated around their fire, passing a jug of what he took to be whiskey. They ate little, pulling on hunks of dried meat, each more intent on getting his share of the jug. As he watched them into the night, the men grew progressively drunk. Over the burble of the river and occasional popping of the fire, he could not hear what they said. But he did not have to hear their words to know what they were talking about. Often touching themselves lewdly and laughing, their objective was Nanee. Somewhere back along the trail, they had seen the three Cherokees pass and had decided to follow and get the woman.

Euchella retraced his path, careful not to break a stick or set loose a rock, then crossed the river once more to where Nanee and Wasseton hid. When he emerged from the water, Nanee handed him an armful of wild parsley. "What will you do? Kill them?"

He could barely see her in the moonlight. "No. But maybe change places with them. Be ready to travel when I return." He tucked the parsley into his shirt and eased back into the river, allowing it to carry him downstream. He could have climbed back over the mountain again, but in the dark the going might have been too noisy if the men were still awake. Given time, the whiskey would ensure that they slept. He held his hands in front of him and bumped easily along the rocks that could not be seen at night. Another hour brought him close to the dying fire and camp of the pursuers. They slept now on the ground, exactly where they had been earlier. Whiskey is a powerful thing, he marveled. Slowly he rose from the water and waited until his clothes stopped dripping. The horses were tethered in a stand of willows about forty yards downstream from the campfire. Euchella approached them carefully. Two nickered nervously and stamped their feet. When he offered them the parsley, they became quiet and ate with a hunger that told him that they had not been fed except for what grass they could pick around the trees. They had not even been unsaddled for the night. These were not good men.

Euchella considered what to do. He could unsling the rifles and take them without making a sound. That would give Nanee, Wasseton, and him a major advantage, but he did not know what other weapons the sleeping men had on them, and he was not going to search them as they slept, drunk or not.

The other choice was to risk waking them by taking the horses, rifles and all. By riding, they would be at the big river in less than a week and be beyond the reach of these men. The only problem was that they would be branded as horse thieves if they were caught. No one would care that they took the horses to flee these men. And three Cherokees on horseback would attract attention.

Still, the risk was worth it. He untied the horses and led them one careful step at a time into the river. Aside from the splash from their hooves, they made no noise crossing. The mountain presented another problem. The trail that they had made earlier in the day was not wide enough to lead three horses abreast, so he tied one to nearby trees and led the other two over the hill. When he was opposite the place where Wasseton and Nanee hid, he whistled for them and they came across and joined him.

"Now we ride and they will walk," he whispered. "Stay with these two. I will go back for the other."

When Euchella returned with the third horse, they retraced the path that they had made through the woods, going back westward until they eventually crossed the emigrant's trail again. Here they mounted and rode cautiously eastward. None of them were comfortable on horseback, but in the silvery moonlight, they followed the wagon ruts in the direction that would take them to the big river that divides the earth. Once there, they would decide how to cross it.

Chapter 25
Lufty Settlement on the Oconaluftee River
Middle August, 1839

Sure that he was unseen where he sat in a thicket of rhododendron, Will Thomas watched Kanaka as she bent to hoe her small garden. This was the last time this year that the field would need it. As he watched, she pulled at the hoe with a practiced rhythm. It was not hard work if one did it regularly, paying attention to the small shifts of the seasons. After the potatoes were dug, weeds would be allowed to take over and cover the ground. Squash had been gathered and beans were drying in long strings that hung from rafters inside. Corn was ready for the festival to come. It had been a good harvest. With some fish and a good fall hunt by the men, the people would have enough to eat through the winter. There would be no repeat of the disastrous winter before the removal when Euchella had gone to the Snowbird Mountains to inspire the other men to act like warriors. In his absence, his wife and daughter starved. The shame of their deaths hung over the community as though their spirits lingered in the coves like early morning smoke.

Will's insides clinched. That should never have been allowed to happen. Old Yonaguska was still chief, but too feeble by then to tend much to the needs of the village. Will had been in Raleigh at the time, but the memory touched him even now, enough so that he rode out at least once each week to inspect the gardens to make sure that there would be enough for all to eat. In spite of the abundance that was now obvious everywhere, he could not rest. No matter how much food there was, it was never enough to make him rest easy.

Something was changing inside him, a slow sink into a mire where the bottom was murky. Unable to sit still, he was uncomfortable in his own skin. At night, he rolled back and forth in bed, worrying about the corn cribs and how many flanks of meat they would be able to hang in the smokehouses. Sleep became almost nonexistent. But it was not just the harvest or the memory of the two dead females in Euchella's family that troubled Will. He had become afraid to shut his eyes. In moments when he did, new and recurring nightmares crept up on him. Always nightmares now. In one, he saw a mongrel dog that someone had tried to kill with an axe. The axe had split the animal's muzzle down the center, deep into its skull, so that it was divided, tongue and all. From the looks of the animal, it could not eat this way and was starving. Will took this to be some symbol of the Cherokees, themselves, divided now as they were, and starving as a result.

It was the other dream, however, that frightened him the most. In this one, his father—his real father, Richard Thomas—who had drowned in Raccoon Creek before Will was born, appeared. He was a vision with a stern, unforgiving face, demanding an accounting of the business at the trading post, and then mocking his son's status as chief. Will did not like this father. He was not the kindly man who his mother Temperance described. This was a hateful, punishing father, the sort who never gave credit to a son for measuring up. This man madde him feel insignificant.

Will wished that his Cherokee father, Yonaguska, was still alive. That one had been good to him. Yonaguska had showed him how to do things, such as set a rabbit snare, then allow him to figure out the fine details on his own. He never criticized, never scolded. If Will had questions, Yonaguska would answer them in a roundabout way that always seemed to provoke a son's curiosity. Now he felt the absence of Yonaguska everywhere, as he rode into the mountains or as he stared into the endless flow of the river beyond his mother's house. These days, instead of spending his evenings listening to the old chief recount tales of hunts, and ballgames, and festivals, he sat in front of the fireplace brooding. Nothing had prepared him for the loss of the old man. Without telling anyone about it, he looked for him all over, hoping to be surprised and have him appear on one of the trails that led through the mountains. Some days, when he caught sight of a graying, stooped figure, his heart quickened. But it was always someone else. Now, without Yonaguska, the air was not as sweet and the buttercups that bloomed at the edges of the fields were not as bright. And he was tired all the time.

Temperance said that Will was still mourning the old man. That consolation meant nothing to him. Certainly it was no comfort, no help with the vague trembling fear that he felt most days. Words did not help. Whiskey helped, but it shamed him to think of it and how he sometimes acted when he drank. He cautioned the people in the village about drinking, but there were nights when he was like a watch spring that is wound so tight that it breaks, wrecking the delicate gears around it.

The worst thing, though, was the cat. He told no one about the cat in the barn, the one that he had killed with a hay rake. Because it had hissed at him. Will had taken to hiding his whiskey in the barn. There was no use confronting Temperance about it which would happen if he brought it into the house. On that night, the cat surprised him as he reached in the hay for his jug. In a red rage, he had pounded the animal until it stopped moving. He had been filled with righteousness at the moment as he beat the creature, but when it was over, he could not fathom why he had done it and was horrified that anyone would discover that he had.

This morning, watching Kanaka at work, he wondered what she would say if she knew about what he had done to the cat. He missed their time together, particularly now with Yonaguska gone. She might be able to make sense of the old man's death. Unlike him, she had a calm way of looking at things. But she was lost now, choosing to live here with the Luftys instead of in Quallatown.

A stick broke behind him. Will turned slowly to see Wachacha, staring at him. Neither man said anything, but Wachacha backed away. Whatever Will was up to was none of his business, it was a thing between Will and Kanaka. Even though she lived with the Luftys, this was not a thing for other men to touch.

Will was relieved that Wachacha had not given him away, but it was idiotic to stay where he was any longer. Easing backward out of the thicket, he crossed the ridge to where his horse was tied.

The child! In his drifting, he had forgotten to look for the child. She was one of the main reasons that he had come to spy on Kanaka. He had not seen the child since the naming ceremony when she was pulled wet and crying from the river, and that one brief moment when he had galloped up to confront kanaka. The image haunted him. Everything haunted him. Yonaguska. Euchella's wife and daughter. A father whom he had never seen. Even Tsali haunted him. Yes, Tsali, the old man, the friend of Junaluska, the man who had carried fish to sell at the trading post, the man whom he convinced Euchella to shoot. All of them. They came like horseflies, one, two at a time, flying into his sleep, biting him in places that could not be covered.

Ah, he was tired, tired of worrying about the people, tired of the deep, sharp anxiety of buying land with money that he did not have and really did not belong to him. It was making him crazy, but he could not stop what was happening.

Chapter 26
Mississippi River, near Cape Gerardo
Late August, 1839

lthough he had crossed it weeks before, nothing prepared Euchella for the sight of the great river again. The only sound it made was the lapping of ripples on the shore, but still it was mighty, even in the dark. A fetid odor of silt filled the air. As he, Nanee, and Wasseton stood at the edge staring at the few lights on the other side, they each thought the same thing: Their world was over there. Tomorrow they would search for the canoe and see if it was fit to carry them across. Tonight, however, there was other business to be done.

"I must get rid of the horses," Euchella said in a low voice. "They attract too much attention and we have no more need of them."

"You will not kill them?" Wasseton asked.

"No. I will leave them with someone, a farmer, perhaps."

With the other two settled unseen in a thicket of honeysuckle, Euchella set off down the river toward the lights of the town below. Along the way, he unsaddled the horses and threw the saddles, saddlebags, and rifles into the river. It troubled him some to get rid of good rifles like that, but it was better if they did not try to bring them along. He wanted nothing that would link them to the horses. And any shot that they fired would bring someone to investigate. What hunting they did they would now do the Cherokee way.

He walked carefully along the side of a hill, near the edge of the river, pulling the animals behind. Familiar with his scent after a week of riding, they followed willingly. Beyond a notch in the hill, the lights of Cape Gerardo glowed. This was not what he had hoped to find, but there seemed to be no farms between him and the town. He would have to find someplace there to leave the horses.

The dirt road that they had crossed earlier in the afternoon seemed to lead to the town and was empty. To mark the spot where he joined the road, he broke a limb down from a low bush. In the moonless night, he could barely see where he was going. The road was rutted by wagons and the runoff of rain, and he stumbled some, but reasoned that darkness was more protection than danger. On his head, he still wore the hat that hid his features, and in the almost total darkness, someone approaching might not take him for an Indian.

It was not long before this proved to be true. Out of the darkness stumbled a man walking in the opposite direction. When he saw Euchella, he halted, swayed backwards a bit, then caught himself before he fell. "Where . . . where you takin' them horses?"

"To town," Euchella grunted.

The man seemed to ponder this as though it were profound, but Euchella realized that he was just drunk. "Mighty fine . . . mighty fine animals," he finally got out, then touched his hand to his hat and staggered on.

Later, as Euchella approached the community, he heard music—White music—the kind that he knew comes from a large wooden box that stands on sturdy legs. As a young man, he had seen one of these odd things when he dared to peek inside the door of a settler's church and saw a woman pounding on it. It was the same sound that he heard now, and, curious, he decided to get as close to it as he could.

Inside the town, the source of the music was in a brightly lit building where men entered and left frequently, talking in loud voices. They appeared to be having fun, and some of them were as drunk as the man on the road. That was no good. Drunk or not, if the men noticed the horses, then he would be recognized in the light for what he was, so he took a side street and worked his way around behind the place. To his surprise, he came to exactly what he was looking for. A barn joined the place where the music was played, and a corral spread out beside the barn. In the corral, several horses stood still, nickering as he quietly slid back the latch at the gate. Pulling the three stolen animals inside, Euchella refastened the gate and began to remove the bridles.

With two freed, he reached for the third when he heard the click of a flintlock behind him. "Be still," a voice said.

Euchella froze. Footsteps circled him in the sand. Slowly a small, but powerfully built man came into view holding a rifle like the ones Euchella had just thrown in the river. He had the body of a hog and a round, whiskered face to go with it. His eyes were steady, betraying no doubt that he held the upper hand. Euchella decided that he would not have wanted to wrestle him, guessing him to be a blacksmith or a farrier. The man walked very slowly, out of reach, but close enough so that any shot from the rifle could not miss.

"What have we got here? Lord, almighty, it's an Indian. And a big 'un. Stealin' a horse." The man whistled. "I wouldn't want to be in your shoes tomorrow."

"I don't steal. I leave them," countered Euchella.

The man grunted and spat. "That, as they say, remains to be seen. But it is my guess that in the morning you are going to be a decoration on a big white oak tree down by the river."

Just then, a door from the back of the tavern opened and light flooded the corral. A woman stood in the doorway, dressed in a kind of finery that Euchella had never seen. He was used to seeing White women in plain dresses, but he had never seen one like this. It glittered like the gold that these people valued so much. And from her ears and around her neck and on her fingers she wore other things that gathered the light from inside and sparkled in the night. "What's the trouble, Chester?"

As the man cut his eyes toward the woman, his posture took on a hint of deference, something that Euchella had never seen a White man do. "Caught this Indian stealin' a horse," he explained. "He claims he's leavin' 'em, but . . ."

The woman raised her hand and silenced him. "How many horses are we supposed to have tonight?"

The man's eyes darted back and forth. "Five."

"And how many are there in the corral now?"

He took one hand off the rifle and counted. "Eight, I reckon."

"And how many bridles is the Indian holding?"

"I see two."

"So if he is holding two bridles and we have three extra horses, two of which are without bridles, I'd say the man is telling you the truth, Chester. You caught him taking their bridles off. Put your gun down."

She came down the stairs from the tavern slowly, dragging the fullness of her dress behind. Now it was her turn to circle Euchella, and as she did, he smelled an exotic scent coming from her, a scent like flowers. As she faced him again, a smile broke over a soft face that hid toughness underneath. "The more interesting question, Chester, is, 'Why is he doing it?'"

"Because I have no need of them," Euchella replied.

The woman smiled again. "An Indian . . . who comes to my corral to leave three horses . . . because he has no need of them. Let's see. My guess is that you 'took' them from someone else. And if you don't need them, you are probably headed east, across the river . . . with two others. Is that about right?"

Euchella made no reply.

"Let's assume that it is. Now, the question for me is did you kill the men from whom you took these horses?" She asked as if she did not expect an answer, but circled the horses again, inspecting them and talking to herself more than anyone else. "Probably not, otherwise you would just have let them go instead of trying to hide them with other stock. Let's see—no brands. So they came from out west somewhere . . . probably far out west is my guess. Could belong to anyone. Trappers. Hunters. Renegades. Maybe even other Indians, but maybe not with those bridles." She was silent for a moment, considering what was in front of her. "My guess is that you didn't kill the owners and you expect them to come looking for you to get them back. And if they come here—which they eventually will—they will claim them and I will have a real shooting on my hands. Which . . . tells me that I had better get rid of them quickly." She turned to the small man with the gun. "Chester, let him go." Then she faced Euchella again and pointed at him. "You have just had a lifetime of luck in one night. But you had better leave this country quickly."

As Euchella vaulted the railing, she called after him. "I hope you get to where you are going, wherever it is."

Making his way back up the dirt road, he reflected on the woman, and for a moment was tempted to feel grateful for her letting him go. Then the foolishness of his sentiment became clear. If the woman had him jailed, he would be hung for a horse thief, a matter that would be public knowledge throughout the region. He would be known as the one who brought the horses in. But, if he disappeared and she were able to sell the animals to three unsuspecting farmers, she would pocket the money and no one would be the wiser—particularly the three from whom he took the horses originally because they would not know either the seller or the buyers. In the darkness, Euchella smiled to himself. It was not just luck, he decided, but another lesson in White-man survival.

In the morning, they went to look for the canoe that he had left on his westbound trip, and found it not far from their camp, still tucked in the crown of the fallen maple tree. He had hidden it well; where it lay, it looked like part of the tree trunk, now covered with dead leaves. And it was untouched, except by a family of field mice that had built a nest in one end. There was a small hole there where the mice came and went, but except for that, the skins seemed to be in good condition. They were tight and dry for the most part, and when he thumped the sides with his fingers, they made a sound like a drum. Several strands of the gut that he had used as stitching were soft where the canoe had rested on the ground and would need to be replaced.

"I will find a deer," Euchella said. "We need meat and skins."

Nanee looked at him. "You cannot do this. With your shoulder, you cannot draw back the bowstring. Give it to me. I will shoot it."

Euchella remembered the man in the corral the night before, and realized that this was what it was like to be told what to do by a woman. He did not like it, but gave Nanee the bow because she was right. "Wasseton and I will run one toward you. Aim for the heart, between the shoulders."

Nanee's turned-up eyes danced at his discomfort. "You find it. I will kill it," she said.

202

And she did. When Euchella and Wasseton found two deer grazing in a meadow about a mile from their camp, they separated and stalked the animals carefully, driving them, bounding through brush, toward where Nanee hid behind a large hickory. Just as the smallest deer neared the tree, she let go of the bowstring. The arrow caught the animal in the opening between its shoulder joints. Momentum carried it past the tree where it fell, twitching. By the time the other two reached her, she was kneeling beside the deer, asking its forgiveness for killing it and thanking it for enabling them to continue their journey. Wasseton looked on with amazement and a touch of envy that he had not been allowed to kill it himself. Euchella looked on with unalloyed pride.

In the days that followed, Nanee proved to be as deft at skinning and preparing the meat as she was at killing. On the ground beside a shelter that they had constructed of vines, she worked a sharp rock over the inside, scraping it free of fat. At night, they simmered strips of meat over a low fire inside the shelter where it could not be seen. Nanee and Wasseton felt safe here and the tension of being on the run faded. They were too far from Oklahoma for anyone to search for them, and shortly they would be crossing the river to the side of the world that they knew. As Nanee dried the deerskin and prepared it to patch the hole in the canoe, Wasseton took time to search the region for his grandmother's grave, backtracking the path that the wagons had followed last year. He did not want to cross the river without explaining to her where he was going and why. But the summer's growth of weeds obscured anything that he recalled from the previous winter, and he came back to camp each night frustrated.

Unlike the other two, Euchella felt edgy. Most days, he wandered in long circular treks, settling in the brush beside nearby trails and hilltops, watching for anyone who might be watching the camp. Although they did not burn the fire during the day, a hunter with a good nose could smell the pungent trace of it that lingered in the forest. Anything that moved in any way that was out of the ordinary would eventually draw notice. It was the hunter in him that made Euchella watchful, and he was certain that there was good reason to be so. The three men whose horses they took would be smarting from the shame of having them taken—along with their rifles—while they drunkenly slept. Outsmarted, they would want revenge, and be more determined than ever to do what they set out to do in the first place. Would they attack an unsuspecting farmer along the way and take his horses to catch up to the three Cherokees? Euchella had no doubt that they would.

While he watched the approaches to their camp, he spent the idle time trimming straight limbs of cane to make arrows. It was strange to rely on Nanee to use the bow if they had to, but as his shoulder was still weak, she was the best choice. After all, he had seen her shoot, and she was fearless and accurate. Other than a knife, however, that left him with no weapon. He needed something that he could throw at the men if they showed up. This problem was eventually solved by a long shank of sassafras. Euchella cut a straight length that was taller than he was, then notched the thick end to hold a sliver of bone taken from the foreleg of the deer. Using some of the sinew that Nanee saved, he fastened the bone point into the spear. With his good arm, he could throw it hard enough to impale a man. Now at least he felt useful.

Work on the canoe patch went well. They managed to reseal all the seams and replace the rotted sinew with fresh string. When it was done, the meat smoked, and the three were rested to travel, Euchella decided that he was foolish for believing that their pursuers would catch up with them. Nothing suspicious showed up, there was no snapped limb or a cry of crows to tell him that they were being watched. Still, the foreboding would not go away. Only when they pushed off from shore would he feel at ease.

"We leave at dark," he announced over the evening fire. Then, by way of explanation, he said, "There will be no moon tonight."

Nanee glanced at Wasseton. He still had not located the grave of his grandmother; now he never would. Reluctantly he nodded his agreement.

"Then we go," Nanee affirmed. But before they loaded the canoe, she had a surprise for both men: new moccasins. "From the deer hide that was left over," she said simply.

There was little for them to take, other than a pouch of smoked venison and the cluster of arrows that Euchella had prepared during the last few days. When Nanee teased him about poking a hole in the canoe with his spear, he sailed it out into the dark water. As they prepared to shove off, Euchella held the stern, waiting for Wasseton to seat himself in the bow, then handed him one of the two new paddles that he had carved from pine. Nanee settled into the middle, facing the rear. Euchella would take the stern and test his shoulder with the paddle. The final thing that he did was to push his hat firmly down onto his head.

Underway, the canoe rode low with the extra weight, but still glided well. The sky was too dark to check for leaks; they would know how well the patch held soon enough.

When they were about thirty yards off shore, they heard the chilling sound of at least two flintlocks being cocked. Instinctively, all three ducked. The first shot took off Euchella's hat and it fell somewhere under their feet. The second split the air beside his right ear.

"The bow," Nanee hissed. In the dark, Wasseton handed it to her and she notched an arrow, launched it in a high arc, notched another, and launched it, too. In a moment, from the blackness along the shore, two screams were heard, about a half second apart. This was followed by a loud splash.

"How did you know where to aim?" Euchella whispered.

"I aimed for the muzzle flashes," she said calmly, notching another arrow in case they were fired on again.

Euchella retrieved his hat. "Let's get across," he said and began to paddle hurriedly to mask the amazement and fear in his voice.

Chapter 27
Mississippi River
Late August, 1839

n the eastern shore, the canoe eased into a dark stand of reeds and made a rustling sound as it scraped through. Euchella paddled alone now. Because his left shoulder hurt, he paddled mostly with his right arm, managing the direction of the canoe with deft touches. Somewhere inside the reeds there would be dry ground. In a moment, the bow touched mud and Wasseton stepped out and pulled the canoe forward. Nanee followed, helping him pull. As they shuffled through the water, the river bottom became shallow. Euchella got out, too, and led the way into the thick growth. He searched for a spot where a flood had receded, leaving the flotsam of dead reeds piled like a mattress. It would be dry and they could sleep, hidden from sight of the river or anyone who lived along the shore.

All three were tired, tired from paddling across the river, tired from not sleeping, tired from the panic of finally escaping their pursuers. But it felt good to have their feet on their side of the world again. When Euchella heard the crunch of dry twigs beneath him, he squatted down and felt the ground. This was what he was looking for. It had not rained in weeks. They would sleep comfortably now and talk about what to do next in the morning.

Nanee lay beside him and curled herself against the contours of his body. Euchella pulled her still closer, and she wriggled like a nesting puppy. In a moment, her breathing changed to the long, slow breathing of sleep. On the far side of the mound of reeds, Wasseton stirred, then he, too, slept.

Nanee had been right to bring the boy. She had been right about many things. He touched her face as she slept, exploring the sharp turn of her jaw, the folds of her ear. She had kept him alive after Wasseton attacked him. She had somehow managed to dull the cutting edge of the memory of his wife and daughter. She had made him feel purposeful again. The last thing that he remembered before the light woke him in the morning was the image of her face as he lay in the shelter after he had been stabbed. Even in pain, he could see the end of his ordeal in her expression. She would lead him out of it. It was how he would remember her always.

Wasseton awoke first, and Euchella found him standing at the edge of the dry reeds, looking west, watching the morning fog drift over the silt-stained river. "You will not see anything like it again."

"I was thinking about my grandmother. The worst of the cold weather hit just after we crossed last winter. She did not live to see much of the other side."

"We must find ourselves again," Euchella said.

Wasseton nodded. "What will become of the Cherokees?"

It was a question that Euchella had brooded on many times, before he found the spider beside the mound in *Kituwah*. "There are those who want us to cease to be. They would scatter our tribe all over the earth. And there are those who want us to become more like the Whites. They would mix the clans and have us worship their god, the one that is three men. Many of our people agree with this. But it is not for me." He was tempted to explain more about Will Thomas and the reservation that was being assembled in the East, but decided to let Wasseton find out about this for himself.

Nanee joined them at the edge of the water, chewing on a piece of the dried meat. "Men talk too much," she teased. "We have a long way to travel yet."

"We will not go far for awhile."

The other two looked at Euchella with unspoken questions.

"I want to find a man. He helped me on my journey west. He is two days from here."

Nanee grunted as she chewed. "You come with more people this time than you did before. Perhaps all of us will not be as welcome as you were."

A faint smile softened his face. "He is not a man like any other man," he said, pulling the canoe into the water. "He calls himself Willy."

Under the cover of cottony fog, they eased the canoe down river. Euchella kept them in the low current, well away from shore. Once in a while, a voice could be heard, from shore or once from another boat on the river, but for two hours they saw no one and made good progress. As the morning brightened and the fog thinned, Euchella guided the canoe back toward the shore where they slipped beneath a tangle of brush and eased along cautiously as he had learned to do on his outbound trip on the Tennessee River.

By the following evening, they were in the Ohio. They had made the turn at the confluence of the two rivers around noon of the second day, then, with the sun over their shoulder, they pulled against a slow current until Euchella found the familiar mouth of the little creek that led into the marsh. Sparrows flitted through the sparse bramble that grew here and there. Far off, a dog barked. Euchella lifted his paddle out of the water and allowed the canoe to glide into the clump of willows where he had beached it weeks earlier. "We will wait here. Make no sudden move," he said, getting out of the canoe and resting on a log.

They sat quietly for nearly an hour, until a rat-like face rose out of the tall grass. The muzzle of a rifle followed. The man stood motionless as though he could not decide what to do about the intruders on his territory. Mostly, he stared at Euchella's hat. Finally, a grin spread over his face. "You took a long time coming back," he shouted over the grass.

Euchella stood. "It was a long journey and there were many things to see."

"I have heard. I think I will have to see them for myself . . . very soon."

"Then we have much to talk about."

The three Cherokees wove their way up the path through the grass, following the wiry little man, and mounted the rise where his shelter stood. None, though, was prepared for what they discovered there. Standing beside a low cook fire was a man whose skin was almost the color of night. He, too, held a rifle, generally aimed in their direction. Barely older than Wasseton, he looked somehow familiar to Euchella.

"I found him in the river, trying' to pole a flatboat out in the middle," explained Willy. "He don't speak our language. He speaks some, but I don't know that he's sayin'. Don't even know his name."

Euchella approached him, wary recognition in both their eyes. "He was a captive. The men who held him were bad men."

Willy chuckled. "So that's how he came to be on that boat."

Euchella turned to Nanee. "He was a slave, but not the kind you would know. He was a slave that other men worked like beasts."

Nanee moved closer to the dark boy, curious. "What happened to the men who held him?"

"They thought to take my canoe," Euchella replied.

For the first time, Willy spoke directly to Nanee. "You notice that they did not get it," he said with a grin.

Over dinner that was more of the same stew that he had enjoyed on his westward trip, Euchella explained to Willy what he had found in Oklahoma, about the river that rises out of the ground, and about the killing of *Kahnungdatlatgeh*. Willy, in turn, described finding the young African and how the two of them had learned to communicate with their hands. They had become partners of a sort, hunting and trapping in the swamps along the two rivers. As before, the meat of whatever they caught went into the stew. "He knows that they will hang him if he goes out of here. What he don't know is that they will hang me, too, for hidin' him. That's why we gotta go west ourselves, away from this place."

The fire popped beneath the kettle. The African boy raised his eyes and looked at Euchella, then muttered something in his language, immediately realizing that no one could understand what he said. Then as an alternative, he bowed deeply in the direction of the tall Cherokee.

"I think he just said 'thank you,'" Willy explained.

Euchella removed his hat—the one that now had a hole in it—and handed it across the fire to the boy. "Explain to him that where you are going, he will need this more than I will. He will need to not appear to be what he is."

The boy was puzzled, but Willy took the hat and placed it on his head. For a moment, the boy touched the wide brim, then grinned almost as wide.

"There is one more thing that you can help us with," said the trapper. "Show me how to build a canoe like yours. We are going up river, up to where the great river divides into two, then take the fork that goes west. They say that there are mountains way out that way where a man can get lost. I figure that's where we need to be to keep a rope off our necks."

Chapter 28
Old Cherokee Nation
Mid-September, 1839

It took the three Cherokees a month and a half to paddle up the Tennessee River and reach the mouth of the Hiwassee. Along the way, they moved mostly in the evening and early in the morning, passing settlements at Savannah, Decatur, and Huntsville at night. When they traveled during daylight, they eased along beneath the canopy of trees and bramble that hugged the shore. Often, they encountered flatboats and keelboats moving on the river, carrying boxes and barrels, and occasionally cattle or horses. If a boat were going downstream, the three would remain still beneath the brush and wait for it to drift by; if they caught up to a keelboat being poled upstream, they shadowed it until the men on the boat stopped for the night, or they put one of the many slender islands between themselves and the other boat so they could pass unnoticed.

No sign of the other two slaves that Euchella had freed was found, nor did they ever see any of the boats that he cut loose that night four months before. A boat drifting on its own would attract the attention of other river men. It had been foolish to help the captives escape. They had no place to run. Willy's words came back to him. Likely, by setting them free, Euchella had gotten them killed. So that Nanee and Wasseton could understand his uneasiness about this, he steered the canoe to the bank one afternoon and signaled them to be quiet and follow him. From a tangle of weeds beside the river, they watched as twenty or more dark-skinned people bent to pick white tuffs from a field of plants that had turned brown over the summer. No one spoke; they just watched the work, and the man on horseback who watched the people work. Nanee was the first to back away; Wasseton followed.

In the days that followed, the air turned dry, then crisp as leaves of maple and oak and elm gradually lost the green of summer and took on the colors of sunset. Stands of poplar stood in great swaths of yellow across the flanks of the hills. Near where the Tennessee makes its big turn north, Euchella showed the other two the abandoned cave of the *Muskogees*. In the light of a torch, Wasseton and Nanee touched the walls of the cave as though doing so would reveal the stories of those who had once lived in here. He showed them the marks that he had made in the dirt, then the marks made by the ancient *Muskogees*. As it happened, they remained in the cave longer than planned. Three days of rain rolled up the river and turned the air cold. It was early for rain; Euchella expected the fall rains to come in November and he hoped to reach the Smokies before they arrived. When it stopped and the sky broke open again, they continued, their pace now quickened by the hint of cold weather that would arrive in several weeks.

Near the end of September, they eased past Chattanooga along the looping turns of the river. There were more lights now than Euchella remembered from his first passage. The river flowed faster here. In the moonlight, there were ripples in the center and around rocks, and they had to stroke harder to move the canoe. But on they went. Euchella's shoulder improved and he could swing a paddle without it throbbing. Still, it was not as strong as before. Once, when he tested it by drawing back the bow, the bowstring trembled. Nanee pretended not to notice. But in spite of his weakness, they ate well. Sitting in the front of the canoe, Wasseton became practiced at using an arrow to stab large carp that rolled and fed in the mud flats of the river. On his first few attempts, he lost the arrow when the fish, with a burst of strength, jerked it from his grip. Euchella solved this by tying a length of bowstring to the back of the arrow and tying the other end around the boy's wrist. From then on, they feasted. When they stopped for the night, whatever Wasseton caught was baked in their fire. Nanee searched for wild onions in the edge of fields and stuffed them inside the fish, then covered it in the fire until the skin was crisp and peeled away, revealing the white flesh. After dinner like this, they slept well, drifting off to the low calls of screech owls.

At the Hiwassee River—or as they knew it, the *Ayuhwa'si*—their course turned from northeast to southeast, and from here they could see the shoulders of the great mountains in the far distance. This was the *Sha-cona-ge*, the land of the blue mist. But the sight did not bring relief equally to all three of them. Nanee grew quiet, then progressively sad as they approached the location where the village of her youth and marriage once stood. She had risen every morning to the sight of these mountains, and knew from which notch in the ridgeline the sun would rise for each season. But when they eased past the actual site of her village, she almost did not recognize it. The only familiar thing that remained was a large white rock from which children used to stand and dive at the river's edge. Gone were the communal corncrib, the sleeping huts, the cabins. A thicket of sumac with scarlet leaves covered the common ground, right down to the narrow strip of sand that lay along the river.

"It was here," she said, mostly to herself. The village existed now only in her memory, the fields where she and other children played, the paths beaten by their feet through the forest, the spring where her mother and the other women of the village drew water, the sacred ceremonial ground—all vanished under the overgrowth. She bowed her head under the weight of the memory.

Late that evening, they pushed the canoe toward the first stars, with the glow of sunset over their shoulders. Reaching a wall of rock cliffs, they felt the current grow strong as the river narrowed, and it was clear that they would have to abandon the canoe soon. Beyond the cliffs, strata of jagged rocks lay diagonally across the flow, breaking the river into a succession of green pools. When they stopped again, Euchella cut a third paddle from a fallen poplar limb and gave it to Nanee. This would give them more power against the current. Still, the next day when they were within twenty miles of the confluence of the Valley River, they found themselves carrying the canoe over rapids and rocks as much as they were riding in it. Reluctantly, Euchella put it down one last time. Like a good bow or knife, it had served him well. Sensing his sentiment, Nanee touched his arm but said nothing. They rested the canoe, bottom up, between the limbs of two spruce trees, each laid a hand on it respectfully, then walked away, upriver.

The days remained bright as the three Cherokees reached the Valley River and turned east, and began making their way up the wide watershed. Just beyond the confluence, they came to the stockade that the soldiers had built two years before. Like Nanee's village, it was abandoned now. Thistle and polk grew inside and Virginia creeper inched up the walls. Not normally reflective, Nanee and Wasseton recalled the weeks when they had been locked up the previous year. Mostly, they remembered the fright and the terrible smells of dying people and rotting food, the drunkenness, and the flies that were everywhere, even up to November, when they were finally taken west. The log walls stood dark and threatening still, a reminder of the power that had swept away the whole nation a year ago.

"The boy was here in this one," said Nanee. "I was in another, near Chattanooga. Then they brought him and his grandmother from here to the one where my husband and I were held."

"I went inside another one up on the Little Tennessee River," said Euchella, "but only for a moment. My brother and I and the others with us stayed in the mountains where the soldiers would not go, so we never knew what it was to be trapped."

"It was like waiting for death," Wasseton put in. Surprised, the other two turned to stare at him. "It was like waiting for death, not knowing when it could come, but wishing that it would hurry. Everything we had known was taken from us overnight, and we did not know who we were. We did not know what to do. I was afraid for my grandmother all the time. I don't know how she lasted as long as she did. She was stronger that I believed possible, but, in a way, it was a relief when she died."

"Now we will see if we can begin again," Euchella said and began to walk once more.

In two days, they came to the end of this valley and started up the steep rise that would eventually lead them to the valley of the Nantahala and the land of the Middle Towns that lay on the opposite side. The higher they climbed, the steeper the going, until they finally reached a saddle between two ridges that ran nearly parallel, and they could see the way to the East. The valley in front of them now was steeper than the one that they had just climbed, the mountainsides dark and snakey with balsam trees and thickets of rhododendron and laurel. Wind blew steadily from behind, edging them forward. Moving down a ravine from one tree to the next, they were joined by a trickle of water that seeped from layers of rock jutting from both sides. As they went lower, the trickle became a stream, and moss and ferns grew profusely on the slopes. The air was thick with dampness. Lichens clung in heavy clumps on the bark of trees, and on the ground, mushrooms of many colors sprouted in the shadows.

"I always felt that this place was bewitched," admitted Euchella suddenly.

Wasseton laughed at the thought of the great warrior fearing anything. "I never saw one here. My father and grandfather took me on many hunts all over this country. We never found one witch." He laughed again.

It was a sign of the healing between them that the boy could mention his father and grandfather. No one had forgotten that Euchella had shot them. He may have done it at the urging of Will Thomas and the soldiers, but he had done it nonetheless. It was not now, and probably never would be, a thing that either of them could talk about, but Nanee and Wasseton sensed Euchella's regret for what he had done. Perhaps the forgiveness that they experienced in the makeshift Green Corn Festival in Oklahoma worked both ways. In any case, the three of them could go on now without the pretense that the killings had never happened.

The little stream that they followed downhill emptied into the Nantahala River at a point where it made a slow sweeping turn from north to east. As night approached, they camped here on the high side of a marsh where Nanee gathered watercress and mushrooms for their evening meal. She skewered the mushrooms on a sourwood stick and roasted them over the fire until they sizzled and turned black on the outside. Wasseton found a chestnut tree and picked a double handful of nuts off the ground. These, too, went into the fire until the shells cracked open. Then they ate without speaking.

This was familiar ground to the two men, the eastern-most edge of the old Cherokee Nation, the region where Wasseton had grown up with his father, grandfather, mother, and grandmother—all dead now. Euchella knew it, too, from the time he passed through to get to the Snowbird country where he hid out when his wife and daughter starved. Along the almost vertical walls of the gorge were caves that had been cut into layers of rock by centuries of slow, but steady flow. Sunlight touched the deepest parts only at noon and then only in the summer. It rained here more than any place Euchella knew. Certainly it seemed a place where witches and spirits were comfortable. It always made him uneasy to be here. He would not sleep well this night.

From her place beside him, Nanee said, "So, your village is gone, too."

Euchella nodded.

When Euchella awoke the next morning, Nanee was not there. The fire from the night before sent out a single tendril of smoke from the last hot coal that smoldered in the ashes. Wasseton lay asleep across from him. Rising to his elbow, he saw Nanee approaching from the river, her face wet. She had been washing. She had been doing this regularly of late. He should, too, he supposed, but this water was brutally cold, like the Oconoluftee, and the thought of throwing it all over himself gave him no pleasure.

It would take another day or two to travel down the Nantahala past Tsali's cabin, then they would come to the killing ground where Euchella and the other Luftys had shot Wasseton's father. He could still imagine the echoes of the rifles. Beyond that, it was perhaps another two days walk up the Tuckasegee to the Oconaluftee. And that would eventually take them to Quallatown and beyond, where they would finally find Wachacha and the other Luftys.

Euchella stretched with a laziness that he did not feel. He dreaded this part of the journey. Up to this point, there had been risks—like being caught on the great river with pursuers shooting at them, could have killed them. But he would soon have to lead them past the places where he had done things that he could not forget. What he had to face were his own memories. It was impossible to scrub the image of his old friend, Wasseton's father, *Chutequutlutlih*, from his mind, particularly the moment when he pulled the trigger and the body slammed back against the tree. For a moment, smoke from the flintlock had laid a curtain over what had been done, hiding the change that could not be reversed. These images he added to those of his wife and daughter who lay buried in the little cemetery above Soco. In two years after their deaths, almost everything that made him Cherokee had been taken from him. Of his past, only a brother and the other Luftys remained. Could he start over? Would his tiny vision at *Kituwah* be enough to follow?

As they left the camp, he could hear Nanee walking behind him, then Wasseton behind her. Warriors should not feel guilt, but he felt it now, as though it were a birthmark on his face that would not be scrubbed off. Forgiveness at the Green Corn Festival was one thing, but forgetting one's duplicity in the tribe's losses is another. By killing Tsali and *Chutequutlutlih* and the others, he had made Will Thomas' dream of a White Cherokee Nation possible. It was a token that tipped the balance; with the killings, the Cherokees could be seen by the Whites as being responsible to the state. The Cherokees could be . . . acceptable. Knowingly or not, Euchella had proved it.

The following day, when they reached the point on the river where the small stream from Tsali's cabin joined it. Euchella and Nanee waited on the opposite side as Wasseton crossed and climbed the slope of the cove. The boy was gone for almost an hour, and when they saw him returning, it was impossible not to know what he was feeling from the look of him. This had been where he had spent much of his childhood. He reported that no one had taken over Tsali's house, no doubt because the place was spectacularly unsuited to farming, perched as it was on the side of a ravine. Anyone with plans to plow would be discouraged, and surviving in this place would mean fishing as Tsali had done. If Wasseton carried any memento with him now, it was not obvious, save what his distant look said was in his head. Although still a boy, whatever he had seen would remain as the everlasting truth of his manhood. Perhaps, he had seen that the ghosts of his father and grandfather had found their way home after the execution. That would have been a kindness. More likely, though, he found a place that had been abandoned, then altered by a full growing season until it was barely recognizable from the way he remembered it.

Chapter 29
Soco Creek
Late October, 1839

ill Thomas was edgy. Not even occasional visits from his friend Jonas Jenkins with his easy going, loopy manner could distract him. The trembling beneath his breastbone—the same one that he used to experience as a child when he had done something sneaky—was permanent now. He even caught himself talking to himself, and would look around to be sure that no one had heard. Will's anxiety defied all logic. His greatest plans were in motion. Everything was on course for the reservation surrounding Quallatown. He was still able to acquire land as White farmers gave up on trying to till steep slopes and meager bottomland. It was true his own money was depleted from all the purchases, but his informant in Washington assured him that the first partial payment of reparations would be made to the Cherokees next year. After that, the greater problem was figuring out who owned what? There was considerable question as to whether or not the Cherokees—even those designated "citizen Cherokees" by the state—were allowed to own land. That would be cleared up, he supposed, once the upheaval of removal passed. Then who would own it? How would he ever get his own money untangled from all those deeds?

Perhaps his edginess was due in part to Kanaka, not money. No one in Quallatown said anything about her leaving and taking his child, not even Yonaguska's two surviving wives. But they looked at him—everyone did—and wondered about it, he could tell. They wondered what he had done or not done to make her leave. The two of them had known each other since Will came to the village years ago as a youth. They

222

had grown up together, then gradually attached themselves to each other. At that point, the people of the village assumed that they belonged together. As proof, the first child arrived. Then some years later, she was pregnant again. In between, there was the loss of Yonaguska and Will's assumption of the role as chief. That should have brought her pride. Instead, just a few months ago, without a word to anyone, she left the cabin that they shared, taking her newborn baby. Extraordinary. Women did not do this sort of thing unless they have a reason, and Kanaka was not known to be foolish. Perhaps it was a man and woman thing. That was known to happen. In any case, what she had done challenged him, even his right to be chief. He was sure that there were whispers about him to go with the sad looks. There had to be.

Will glanced in a mirror that hung on the wall of the trading post, near bolts of cloth. Women liked to drape fabric over their shoulders and imagine how a frock creation might look on them. Now, with no one around, he stared at his own image. A round face with a helmet of thick hair cut below the ears stared back. It was a quick, nervous face. That much was obvious, but he could see something in the face that others could not see . . . a small person hidden behind the eyes, past where the lines came down at the corners. Orphan. He always felt like an orphan. The thought came at him over and over again. But how could his mother, Temperance, understand that and not be offended? He missed old Yonaguska more than he could admit to anyone.

A log popped in the great stone fireplace, sending sparks out onto a flagstone hearth. Events rolled like waves, large ones pounding the shore, followed by small ones that made only a low hiss as they slid up the sand. Will was comfortable at the moment—or should be. The fire crackled with the season, and the sparks it sent out were harmless, the faint smell of smoke comforting. But one day, in an absent mood, he or Jonas might forget and load in a log of locust that would pop with great energy and shower hot coals onto the millinery. He would be outside or in the barn when it happened, and the trading post would catch fire in a way that was too big to extinguish. The image brought another snap of panic. He had seen that sort of fire before—the kind that has a great, howling will of its own, too great for the will of men to extinguish it. He was frightened by this kind of fire. The face in the mirror admitted it. There was never a time when he was out on his horse in the valley and smelled smoke that he did not glance quickly in the direction of the trading post to see if it were burning. This fear pestered him like a splinter that refused to be dug out. Kanaka could have helped with it, he sighed. She tended a fire as though it was a friend and never seemed threatened by it. But— Kanaka was not here.

The other thing that crowded in on him now was the possibility of returnees from Oklahoma and how they might scramble his plans. When he heard that Euchella left to visit the tribe in the West, he was at first offended at not being consulted, then relieved, assuming that he would never hear from him again. Euchella was noncompliant, like a dog that you had to keep your eyes on as you walked past, and Will was secretly pleased that he was gone. Oklahoma was far away . . . a world away. Oklahoma would see that Euchella stayed away. But now there was word that one man who was taken west actually walked the 1200 miles back to North Carolina, to his home near Snowbird. Will should not have underestimated the determination of these people. It was rumored that the Cherokee who returned found a White farmer living in his cabin, and the farmer, recognizing the rightful owner, panicked and tried to shoot him. The Indian disappeared into the woods, but now the farmer was paralyzed by constant fear of ambush. Word got around, and fear being contagious, other squatters began carrying their guns wherever they went. There were more reported sightings of stray Indians out in the old "nation" where they no longer belonged. How many more were lurking out there . . . ten, twenty, a hundred? Guns were discharged at imaginary threats, at the movement of a shadow, at a dog loping through the woods. One mule was shot accidentally in the ear. A rumble began to swell to get rid of all the Cherokees. And that meant the Cherokees in Quallatown, too. All because one determined man made it back. One could mean that there would be more. Maybe Euchella would make it back, too. Suddenly, Will hated Euchella in a way that he had never hated anyone—except Andrew Jackson.

Will needed to breathe. He locked the trading post and saddled his horse. Anyone who wanted anything could leave a note and he would deliver it later, if he felt like it. He had to escape the depression that was almost constant now. Inside the trading post, there was too much noise in his head for him to think. Chores and small tasks nagged and piled up undone. He had to sort out what was bothering him. He had to figure out how he could feel both surrounded and alone at the same time.

Riding west along the river, Will breathed easier, the autumn hillsides were an antidote to his sourness. The horse walked slowly, undirected except for an occasional nudge with a knee, picking its footing along the rocks and sand and driftwood. Bright leaves fell in a breeze and collected in a backwash in the river, behind a rock where they turned around and around on the surface, waiting to be swept down the main current. Kanaka used to speak of the river often. The river was a constant with her people. Yonaguska even gave it a word that meant "forever-ness." Such was their concept of time. The leaves floating on the clear water would find their way downstream . . . in their own time . . . or the winter would come and freeze them to the shore and the rocks. If the winter was hard, there would be an edge of ice along the shore. Children would come and step on it just to hear it crack. In spring, there would be a flood and the grass on the bank would lie flattened for a week. All the while, the river would move and the Cherokees would wait and listen to it sing. It had always been that way, since ancient times when the Great Buzzard formed the mountains by the down beats of its wings. It was supposed to be that way. The Cherokee stories said so. The stories brought the comfort of certainty. Until removal. Removal changed everything. Now it was as though the river had stopped, as though some great mudslide had diverted it upstream to run another course, leaving the Cherokees without their spiritual source. No stories or parables could explain it. The stories lost their power and the Great Buzzard had flown away. Removal separated the Cherokees from the river, and no songs or festivals could restore the certainty of the season, the certainty that everything would be right again.

That was it. As the horse plodded on, Will realized that he had brought it on himself to heal this great sore. The desire drove him, pushed him, and now judged him for things that were beyond his control. It kept him from sleeping, and made him irritable and a little violent. He swore too much. He drank too much. He dreamed of putting his arms around the entire village and fending off the wolves that circled outside, waiting to pick off strays. Against all reason and the will of two governments, he would make it whole again. Yonaguska would not disappear. His spirit would survive and the river would flow again as it had in the days of their youth before the warp and woof of their lives was ripped. Will would reverse this thing. He would work like a weasel, snatching what he could, when he could, ten acres here, thirty acres there. He would bring it all back, Yonaguska, too. If only he could get away with it.

Some miles downriver from the trading post, Will passed the ancient burial mound that rose unnaturally in a broad field by the river. The mound at *Kituwah.* The sight of it made him drift back. It was the mound that had spooked the army lieutenant—Smith—last year when he accompanied the soldiers who had first caught Tsali. That was just before this very horse slid on the riverbank and pinned Will underneath. His ankle remained sore from the accident, almost a year later. But the accident kept him alive. The lieutenant put him back on the horse and sent him home. Before the day was out, two of the three enlisted men in the detail would be dead, killed by Tsali and his sons and son-in-law. A third soldier was disfigured by a rifle butt to the face. Smith escaped. Will should have realized that the ambush was coming. Women and children were in the party and Smith was in a hurry to get the Indians to the stockade. He kept driving them harder. The little rebellion was bound to happen. But after it happened, Will found a way to take advantage of it. It was risky, but brilliant. All it took was convincing Euchella to find and shoot Tsali, and get the army to go along with the idea. It was a good plan. The remaining Cherokees would then be seen as citizens, responsive to the will of the greater nation. Afterward, the colonel in charge wrote the letter that became part of the foundation for enabling the Quallatown Cherokees to remain here. It had served Will's plans. But it had turned Euchella against him. He knew it. And now he hated Euchella for realizing what he had orchestrated.

A mile or so beyond the mound, the horse turned away from the river and followed a path that led up a knoll that was covered to the brow by dense pines. With no destination in mind, Will let the animal wander. It did not matter. What was important was the play at work inside his head. The horse paused at the edge of the thicket to pick tall grass. Will got down and took his rifle and strolled to the edge of the knoll. His mind returned to the moment. People had been spying on him, he was sure. Some who came into the trading post just wanted information. They wanted to take away the land that he was buying, take it for their own. Maybe they wanted to learn what he was doing so that they could report back to other men in Washington or Raleigh. In any case, he carried the rifle, the steel of the barrel was cold and familiar. If he saw any of them now, he was prepared.

Far below, wind swept up the river and made shiver patterns on the water. This was a good spot to sit in the sage and be Cherokee again. Will needed more time for the part of him that was Cherokee. Perhaps Yonaguska would speak to him here. Crows on the hillside kept an eye on him with their calls, but when he stayed motionless, they fell silent. Below, Will could see for over a mile along the river, from where Deep Creek flowed in, to upstream where it took a sweeping turn, to the southeast to skirt the mound. The air smelled of fall. Walnuts were coming down. Frost would be here soon, turning persimmons on the tree behind the trading post from bitter to sweet. And the small fox grapes would become good to eat. He and Jonas would kill a hog and smoke the meat, and Jonas' dogs would grow momentarily fat on the scraps. It was time for someone to rob a bee tree. There would be honey on the breakfast table for Temperance and

228

his daughter, Demarius Angeline. Bacon and honey and fresh cornbread.

Chapter 30
Tuckasegee River
Late October, 1839

The three returning Cherokees were finally warm. During the previous night, the first frost of the season had settled in patches on the north flanks of the mountains. On a knoll above the river, they slept in a nest of leaves to keep from freezing. Nanee pushed up close to Euchella for added warmth, but she worried about Wasseton who slept by himself. She wished that she had a sister so he could be warmer, too. They had built a fire, sheltered it with a wide ring of pine boughs to keep it from being visible up and down the valley, then settled themselves inside. But when the fire died, they shivered. To make things worse, there was little here to eat, not even mushrooms to pick on the hillside, only a handful of acorns beneath a great oak that covered much of the ridge where they camped. And without the canoe, the fish in the river were out of reach. So they went to sleep hungry, stomachs complaining. Even so, all three awaited the next day with excitement. It would be their last day on the trail before they reached Quallatown.

Morning broke sharp and clear. They smothered what remained of the fire with dirt, but did not bother to scatter the pine boughs. Anyone who found their camp could conclude whatever they wanted to conclude, but by the time it was discovered, the three would be settled in their new home. Since crossing the divide into the Nantahala region, Euchella had become less watchful. There were fewer settlers here, and knowing many of them, he had less fear of ambush. It seemed unlikely that they would encounter hostility from any of the farms that they would be passing.

It was less than an hour after they continued their journey along the river that the older two realized that the boy had halted behind them. They turned to find him gazing across to the north shore.

"It was there," Wasseton said in a voice that they could barely hear above the sound of the water. "That's where my grandfather and father killed the soldiers," he said, pointing to a cluster of large, flat rocks on the far bank that protruded into the river. "My grandfather knew that we could not go on, that my grandmother would die. We were wet. We were exhausted. They kept marching us. They thought that we would not attack them because we had no guns. Only the lieutenant got away. He ran before we could kill him, too."

Nanee asked, "I have heard that your grandfather went high into the mountains and hid, but that your father and uncles refused to go. Why did they not go with him?"

"They thought that they could dodge the soldiers and the militia. And they did. But they could not escape this one," he said, pointing to Euchella.

Only then did Nanee realize the magnitude of the compromise with which Euchella had to live. The code of the Principal People required that a warrior accept the consequences of his actions. But executing Tsali and the others lacked a warrior's purpose and was tainted by some doubt that Euchella had not revealed to her, doubt that he still carried inside. She wondered if it was related to the White man, Will Thomas, of whom she had heard much. Euchella could almost not bear to speak his name, and when he did, his face became cloudy as though the man had taken something from him that could not be repaid.

"That was almost a year ago," Euchella said, nodding. As they stared across at the killing ground, each remembered how much had happened in that year . . . the camps where the tribe was held and the heat that could not be escaped . . . the deaths of Wasseton's mother and grandmother and Nanee's husband on the march west . . . Euchella's own long journey to Oklahoma . . . the killing of *Kahnungdatlageh* . . . Wasseton's attack on Euchella . . . now the journey back.

When they resumed walking again, they came to a stretch of river where the water flowed in cascades, tumbling over and between rocks that lay across its span. Walking was like climbing huge steps. Their breath came out in small puffs. On an unbroken line of rocks, they crossed to the north side where silt from floods was damp beneath their feet and they moved almost silently except for the occasional drag of cane branches on their buckskins.

Close to midday, the three neared a sharp turn in the river where the water swept around a small island that was littered with pieces of dead wood that had collected against the trees during floods. The river was shallow and the bank was steep, so they walked with one foot on the rocks that lined the edge and the other on the bank. When they came to a small stream that could be crossed in a single jump, Nanee noticed that Euchella became edgy as though he expected to see something that she and Wasseton could not see. Instinctively, she knew that they were near the last killing ground. This must be where they shot old Tsali. This must be Big Bear Springs. Perhaps one or more of Tsali's souls lingered here; perhaps Euchella wanted to ask his forgiveness for shooting him.

Jumping the little stream, Euchella stopped beneath a locust tree where the ground was littered with black seedpods. All three were hungry, so he peeled one of the pods open and began to suck out the honey-like jell inside. For a half hour, they all sat in the warming sun, stripping the seedpods and tossing the husks into a clump of dry ragweed. Euchella was glad for the distraction. He could see that Nanee sensed his turmoil and had questions about this place, but she would not ask them in front of Wasseton. But there was more than Tsali on his mind. Wasseton had been right. The upheaval in their lives that began the previous year had come almost full cycle. What would they find of their old way of life when they finally found the Luftys again? He was jumpy about lingering here, but he was jumpy about what he would find on the Oconaluftee, too. Would Wachacha have built a cabin for him as he said that he would? Were the Luftys where he left them, or had they decided to join up with Will Thomas at Quallatown? If they had, what would he and Nanee do? All these things would be answered soon.

Abruptly, he jumped up from the strip of sand where they sat and began walking up the river again. The other two scrambled to their feet to catch up.

"How did you know that we had our fill?" Nanee needled him from behind.

Euchella stopped and turned for a moment to glare at her, but did not reply before he went on.

It took almost an hour for them to reach the mouth of Deep Creek, and Euchella was glad that the air was warmer because there was no way to cross it without getting wet. Where the clear water of the creek fanned out and flowed into the deep green water of the river, gravel lay just below the surface and it was safe to walk. Euchella stepped into it and began to move cautiously across.

When he was about ten feet into the creek, water flew up in front of him as though someone had softly lobbed a pebble in his direction. A moment later, the crack of a rifle sounded from somewhere on the far side of the river, then echoed back again. Euchella froze with his hand up to stop the other two. Nanee and Wasseton crouched behind a rock, waiting. The shot had come from a great distance, the slug landing with little energy. Still, someone had shot at him. Euchella scanned the opposite bank and then the hillsides. Nothing moved, not even a crow. Whoever had shot at him was still there.

He waited for a second shot, but it did not come. Whoever had fired the shot did not want to risk being spotted by firing again. Euchella straightened up, then without shifting his position, he signaled for the other two to cross behind him. Splashing quickly through the water, they made it to the far bank and hid behind two large sycamores. Euchella waited a bit longer, then started across again. Through the flat, clear flow in front of him, he could see something resting on the bottom that was not the brown or white or yellow color of the other rocks. He bent to pick it up and discovered that it was a rifle slug, the color of old pewter.

Reaching the other bank of the creek where Nanee and Wasseton crouched, he pointed to the far shoreline of the river and the knoll of the hill above, indicating for them to look for any movement. But after several minutes of silently watching, they shook their heads.

Euchella thought for a moment about what had happened, and who might have shot at them, and why. The why pointed toward the who. Whoever it was would not be Cherokee. A Cherokee would have welcomed them home. That left the settlers. Did they just shoot at any Cherokee around here now? That made no sense. It was someone with a reason, or someone who was not right in the head. Someone angry, or frightened—or both. No clear picture came to mind.

The three were cold from the water, so he began leading them, carefully this time, from tree to tree, up river. They walked for an hour this way, easing through cane breaks and the high tangle of weeds that grew along the edge, but saw or heard no one. When they came to the place where the river makes a great sweeping arc around the ancient village of *Kituwah,* the sun was behind them. By the time they were abreast of the old burial mound, their clothes were dry from crossing the creek.

Euchella paused, squatting as he had that morning in the spring when he had watched the spider at work—the vision that eventually pushed him to go west. A few cobwebs remained in the tall grass, but it was too cold now for spiders to be working. They were either dead or hibernating, tucked away against the winter to come. Tendrils of their summer nets remained, like small bits of cloth, swinging with each passing breeze.

"They will rebuild," said Nanee from over his shoulder.

Euchella nodded. "It was such a small thing," he said, "that made me take such a journey."

"You came all the way to the West just because you saw one of these?" Wasseton said, touching a remnant of cobweb.

He is still young, Euchella thought to himself. Then he did something that he rarely did. He explained. Explaining did not come easily, but this boy was worth it, and surely deserved it. "I felt the old ones speaking to me through it," he said. "Some days you never know what you are going to hear when you listen."

They began their walk once more.

"Who shot at us?" Wasseton wondered from behind.

"Probably a settler," replied Euchella. "A Cherokee would have waited until we passed close to them, to be sure that one of us was dead. But shooting from across the river makes no sense. It is so far away that it would not have hurt me if it had hit me. So why shoot?"

"A warning?" speculated Wasseton.

"Of what? We were too far away for it to do any good. I think maybe it was the work of one who is not right in the head. Nothing else makes sense."

It was nightfall by the time that the three passed the confluence of the Tuckasegee and Oconaluftee Rivers and followed the smaller, colder stream toward Quallatown. Dogs barked as they approached, but otherwise all movement in the village halted. People stood in the doorway of their cabins and watched as they walked through. Astonishment and much whispering took place among the people there, but no one approached them. All of them knew Euchella, and all knew that he had gone to the West. It was a much told story: one who went west who did not have to go. None expected to see him again. It was said that only one other had returned. Now there were three more. The woman who followed him was strange, but it was clear that she was Cherokee, and young. The boy following at the end was the most amazing of all. Those of the village who knew him to be the grandson of Tsali also knew that Euchella had shot Tsali. Now, they were here, together.

The three travelers could have stopped for something to eat. The smell of cooking was everywhere in the village, and any one of the people there would have fed them. There would be plenty of squirrel stew, cooked with potatoes and carrots for hours until the meat was tender. Although they were hungry, Euchella did not break stride, but continued his walk up the river. When they were beyond the village, it was completely dark, but darkness meant nothing to him; there was no danger of stumbling. He had walked this path so many times that his steps were instinctive, and he led the other two around roots and rocks and over logs that lay across the path.

Nearly another hour went by before they could see light again, this time from the large communal fire that burned beside the river where the Luftys camped. Euchella had set the stones there himself, more than six months before. He shouted a Cherokee greeting, then again. Another dog barked. He did not remember a dog; none of the men had a dog when he left. As they came out of the woods near the cluster of cabins, Wachacha and the other men stood up. A woman was with them, standing as though she belonged here. Women would be necessary, but Euchella recognized this one to be the woman of Will Thomas, Kanaka, from Quallatown. In the firelight, he could see that she had a child with her. What was she doing here?

The three travelers approached. "It is good to see you, my brother," Wachacha said, stepping forward to grasp Euchella by the arms. The others crowded around, curious. "I did not know if I ever would again."

"Did you build me a house?" Euchella asked, in mock seriousness.

"He did," interrupted the woman, "but I took it."

Wachacha smiled. "Kanaka came to live here. She brought her daughter. They are Lufty now."

Kanaka grinned in the direction of Nanee, obviously glad to find another woman in their midst.

"Who is this?" Wachacha wondered, looking at Nanee.

"She is Nanee. Her family was from a village on the Hiwassee. It is gone, as are the others, even those in the Snowbirds. She was in the West, as was Wasseton. She could not stay there. He, too, wanted to come back."

The small child began to squirm in Kanaka's arm. The woman looked at Nanee again, and a sly kind of recognition crossed her face, but she said nothing in front of the men. Instead, she left the gathering and went into her cabin nearby. She was gone for a long time.

Euchella, Nanee, and Wasseton settled around the fire and were handed pieces of rabbit that were left over from the evening meal. It had been cooking for a long time, and had the three not showed up, it would have gone to the dog. Hungry as they were, they tore at the meat, and although overcooked, it was good. Cakes of cornmeal were placed on hot flagstone to cook. It had been a good summer here along the Oconoluftee. For Euchella, it was good just to be home, to have Nanee with him. The others would like her, and he hoped that she wanted to stay, although he had not asked her. The only thing that troubled him at the moment was the other woman. "What is Kanaka doing here?" he asked between bites.

Wachacha sat back and rubbed grease into his hands. "She came here to raise her baby."

"That is Will Thomas' baby."

"True, but she is no longer with him, by her own choosing."

"Is she with someone else?"

"No. She came here after the child was born, after the naming ceremony."

"What about Thomas? Was he no trouble in this?"

Wachacha knew what his brother was asking. It was the same question that he had when Kanaka first came to live in their camp. He hesitated before answering. "Thomas has been no trouble, but it may be because Thomas has other problems. He is no longer the man you remember. He may be touched by a witch. He has days when he seems to have the sickness of the dogs."

As hungry as he was, Euchella stopped eating. "How do you know this?"

"I have seen it. He was here, in the woods behind Kanaka's house, watching the woman like an owl, not moving, just watching. I said nothing about it to her because he went away and has not come back. But they say that he rides out from his trading post and people hear him speaking to someone who is not there."

Euchella produced the rifle slug that he retrieved from the water at Deep Creek. "Does he have a rifle of this caliber?"

Wachacha turned the piece of lead over and over. "Perhaps. He has many. Where did you get this?"

"It was fired at us just as we were crossing Deep Creek . . . from all the way across the river and it fell near me. I found it in the sand."

"That makes no sense."

"That is what I mean."

The men fell silent as they considered the meaning of this news. Then one of the older men reminded the others that the settlers had grown edgy, having seen one Cherokee return from the West, to reclaim his land. "They might shoot at any of the Principal People they caught out walking." But that idea was dismissed because shooting at a man from four or five hundred yards was a waste of a bullet. No one had a satisfactory explanation, but all agreed that Will Thomas bore watching and that him being chief in Quallatown could mean problems for the Luftys in the future.

About the time the travelers had their fill, Kanaka returned from her cabin and sat across the fire from Euchella and Nanee. "When I came here in the summer, your brother was building a house for you, but because you were gone and he was not certain of your return, he allowed me to use it. Now, if you wish, I would like to share it with you until another cabin can be built. There is straw on the floor and room enough for all of us to sleep, even the boy. That way, I will not feel as though I have taken it from you."

Euchella felt awkward and said nothing immediately until Nanee elbowed him in the ribs. "That would be appreciated," he grunted, then cut a quick look at Nanee.

"We could be sisters," Nanee injected, paying no attention to him. The women exchanged looks that for the first time were noticed by the men. Some silent transaction was taking place woman-to-woman of which they could not be a part. "Then in the late spring, just around planting time, your baby would have a playmate."

Euchella stared at her as comprehension slowly set in . . . the daily washing and the fact that on the journey east, she was the only one who had gained weight. "Are you sure?"

Again, the two women shared a look as if to say that the male of the species could be very stupid indeed. "Yes, by planting time, you will be a father."

The other men laughed at Euchella's embarrassment. He could only grunt again. At least this answered the question about Nanee staying.

The fire was piled high with wood collected along the river, and the flame rose so high that even logs that were wet burst quickly into flame. Sparks shot far up into the darkness. A few people from as far away as Quallatown saw the light of the fire and made their way up the river, knowing that there would be much storytelling by the returnees and many questions answered about those who had been taken west. They were welcomed by the Luftys who made room around the fire.

On this night, all heard a story unlike any told by a Cherokee before or since. First, Euchella thanked his brother, Wachacha, for helping him build the canoe that carried him west and back again. Then he described the Tennessee River and how it cut through the hills in what had once been the old Cherokee Nation. He told about the two river men who he may have killed (Nanee's eyes widening as he had not told her of this detail), the Black slaves that he freed, then finding the cave of the *Muskogees*. An elderly woman from Quallatown asked if there had been witches there, but Euchella replied that he had felt none. Then he went on to describe the river that divides the earth, and the huge canoe that spews fire and on which White people ride. Many looks passed back and forth; how could a canoe breathe fire? Not knowing himself, Euchella went on. He described the river—the size of the Oconaluftee—that comes straight from the ground, and how he cut his hair to foil the witches that he was sure occupied the cave where he had slept. When he got to the part about finding Junaluska and the killing of *Kahnungdatlageh*, all grew quiet again. Many heads nodded, agreeing that *Kahnungdatlageh* deserved to die. Then, when he explained how the once-proud Snowbird people were camped in the new land, their faces grew sad. This was the fate that those who remained in the East had avoided. Tension returned, however, when he described how Wasseton had attacked him, stabbing him in the shoulder. They were all amazed that the two of them sat together now without hostility. "It was the Green Corn Festival," he explained, and they instantly understood the forgiveness that goes with it.

Nanee entered the story at this point. "I had asked Junaluska to see if Euchella would bring me back East. I dreamed that my future was here and felt that I could not stay in Oklahoma. That was just before Wasseton attacked Euchella."

"She healed my wound," Euchella told, "then along the way back, she shot two men who attacked us when I was still too weak to draw a bow—and shot them in the dark, aiming at their muzzle flash. It was a thing to see."

There was collective intake of breath around the fire. Across the way, Kanaka smiled, pleased that she had gained a formidable sister. Their children would grow well together with two strong mothers.

Details of the remainder of the trip included how they learned to spear fish with an arrow from the canoe and how Nanee's village was now overgrown with weeds and sumac. Each person in the wide circle nodded sympathetically in her direction. For the benefit of the people in Quallatown, Euchella omitted the matter of them being shot at as they crossed Deep Creek. The idea that Will Thomas might have anything to do with it would only arouse dissention, as these people were obliged to live with him.

As the fire died, so did the story. Weariness took over and people drifted away. Euchella and Nanee and Wasseton followed Kanaka into the house— his house that he had never seen—and settled on the straw that she had put out for their comfort. All slept well, untroubled by dreams. Perhaps most pleased of all was Kanaka who no longer felt alone.

Near dawn, Euchella rose and left the others sleeping, and set off back down the trail beside the river once more. It was all familiar. The feel of the rocks under his hands, the smell of the Oconoluftee as it hurried down the valley, the trees, the trace smells of early cooking from the cabins around Quallatown, and the damp earth beneath his feet. Like Nanee, he could not have lived in Oklahoma unless he had been forced to stay there. This was the small part of the world to which he belonged, that was as familiar—and indelible to him—as the lines in his palms. Perhaps, in time, those who remained in the West would be able to establish something of their Cherokee life there; in that way, the story of the spider that he carried to them would help, but he was certain that he could not do it himself.

Before Euchella reached the ancient village of *Kituwah*, the sun was beginning to give color to the sky. He was home at last, and now he knew that a new generation of the Luftys would be born. Settling himself beside the burial mound to watch the sun rise and feel the restoration of his spirit, he realized that by the time his child was born next year, the spider would return to this place and its work would begin all over again.

Epilogue
2004

n a cool morning in June, I went looking for Euchella on a hill in the Blue Wing Community, east of the present day town of Cherokee, NC, the place that had been known in his day as Quallatown. Rain from the night before left the leaves wet as my guides led the way up a steep slope that was shaded by an overhead canopy of oaks and poplar. When we reached the saddle that spans a gap between knobs of two mountains, mist rose from the valley below. Here and there, in the loose undergrowth of laurel and sassafras, shards of flagstone stand on edge. Each marks a shallow depression in the hillside, a dip as though the top few inches of soil had been scooped away. The earth covers bodies that were wrapped in cloth and buried simple, in the ancient custom. More recent marble stones stand on the hill, too, bearing inscriptions from the living who placed them in this serene place. Other graves are indicated incongruously with small metal nameplates, the kind left behind by funeral homes before permanent headstones are set. But most graves are marked only with plain lichen-covered stones or else are not marked at all. Only the depressions in the ground tell where the people lie. In any case, the graves all point to the east, to the restorative power of the rising sun.

It was typical of ancient Cherokees to bury their dead in a place like this. Locations where geological phenomena converge—particularly if they include a moving current—were spiritual gathering points for the *Ani'-Yun'wiya'*, as though in these anomalies could be found a window into the mind of the Creator. The confluence of rivers and a saddle that links two mountains were thought to bring great understanding.

Here on this mountain, a current of wind sweeps in from Tennessee, around the peaks, in an almost unending stream, and seems like a good place for meditation.

Wandering between the knolls, we searched for evidence that would indicate which grave belonged to Euchella. There are stones tucked beneath laurel, others standing in clearings of moss. But Euchella's name—in any of its phonetic spellings—appears on none of them. We would have to find subtler means of learning where he lay, and I began to wish that he might, in some way, help with the task.

I did not have long to wait. There is a touch of eternity about this ridge that confounds common conceptions of cemeteries. From the dip of the saddle, we aligned ourselves with the graves and faced east, feeling the warmth of the sun chase away our personal witches of uncertainty. Silence is almost total, and there is no intrusion of truck, television, or telephone. Into this vacuum, the mind supplies its own images, and I could imagine members of the tribe climbing the slope, shouldering the wrapped remains of someone who had done all the great and menial things that the living do—build a lodge, plow a garden, give birth, kill a deer, catch a fish—then cease to do. What lingers here is not a sense of finality, but one of forever-ness, as though the secret of life and death is not one of beginnings and endings, but of something ongoing and endless.

I did not anticipate enlightenment. Coming to pay respects to a man who had become an important, if enigmatic, figure to me, I had figuratively trailed him for four years, through vague references and the unturned stones of the history of his era. In my imagination, he had become a fleshed-out image . . . a man who was tall, powerful, determined to follow his own direction, resisting the drift toward the modern world, favoring instead the spirituality of the Cherokees that had evolved for eons. But did I get it right? Were there vital things about him that I missed? What more could I learn of him here? Should I apologize for adjusting the facts of his life to suit what was, at heart, my story?

The answers found on that saddle between the mountains were surprising. Begun in Western curiosity, my search took a turn for which I was unprepared. Clearly, a fragment of the old way of life lives on here, and one comprehends things through absorption, the way a frog drinks through its skin. Good and evil spirits become something felt physically, on one hand forbidding, on the other engaging. Tragedy lingers over some graves like a pending thunderstorm, and my guides admitted that there were cemeteries holding the remains of violent men where they refused to go. Over other graves lingers a quiet, benevolent presence. The White man in me wanted to dismiss this as superstition, but here such thoughts seemed more than reasonable.

I wanted to meet Euchella, talk with him across the one-hundred plus years that separated us, and to give a face to one who is now spirit. I did not care so much to know what he did as to know what he thought. What part of the Cherokee nature had he managed to sustain?

A voice that I could feel but not hear led me to move along the ridge to the east, and I shuffled noiselessly away from the others. Just below the knoll lay another piece of flagstone standing on edge, partly hidden in a spray of laurel. The stone is part of the everlasting earth, and it could have been the marker for anyone, but something drew me closer. The voice again. This one. Only this one, it said.

In the ground was the tell-tale concave depression as though the surface had been scooped away by a large spoon. Euchella would have been buried without a coffin. I studied the ground, my mind open to any message that might be forthcoming. But no more words came. I turned to go, feeling a little foolish. But just as I did, something caught my eye. There on one corner of the stone that marked the grave was a collection of threads, laden with dew in the morning light. It was a tiny web, attached between the stone and an overhanging laurel branch. A small spider worked its way back and forth between the stone and the limb, making fast the anchor points and waiting for its breakfast to wander into it, thus ensuring its continuity.

# # #

ISBN 1425176550

9 781425 176556